ACCIDENTALLY
IDENTICAL

LAYLA MCFADDEN

Dedications | xoxo

Brenda Carattini-Gonzales

You've helped me get out of my own head and out of my own way. I dedicate this book to you, because you made me believe in my skills and my abilities. When I needed you, no questions, you were there.

My Husband

Without you I wouldn't know what true love felt like. I love you with all my heart and soul. You inspire me. In every book I write, there's a piece of you and I.

My Betas

You ladies are the best!
A piece of you is in this novel. Thank you for your time, love, encouragement and believing in me.

TABLE OF CONTENTS | xoxo

TATUM EMERSON | ONE

xoxo

She pleaded with me to help. Her bloodied hand reached for me, the other clutched her stomach. She never speaks, but I can feel her every emotion. I wish I knew who she was. It was then her hand held out a locket. As she fell, the locket landed at my feet. I checked her for signs of life, but none were to be found. Tears streamed down my face as I grabbed the locket and opened it. Inside there appears to be a picture of me as a child on both sides, only I can't remember the second picture.

My phone alarm blares. I roll over and put in my passcode to shut it off. Every time! Why can't I finish the dream? There's an overwhelming sense of dread now, even with the sun shining into my room. Who is this woman? Why is she haunting my dreams? Maybe she's my mother. At least that's what I've always thought. That would be impossible though, since she's been gone for as long as I've been alive. I glance down at my phone to check the time, 2:45pm.

Shit! If I don't get going I'll be late, I think to myself.

I walk into the bathroom and flick on the light. I use the large shiny silver brimmed mirror to check my reflection. My slightly wavy dirty blonde platinum highlighted locks were a mess, and it looked as though I hadn't slept at all. My dark emerald green eyes stared back at me as I rubbed each eye to wake myself up. I grab my charcoal face soap and lather it up in my hand. I take the suds and massage my face to clean away any remnants of my not so pleasant sleep. I splash my face with cold water and then I reach into the shower, and turn the knob. I then, continue to grab everything I need to start my day. I quickly return to a steam filled room. I jump in, the scalding water erasing the memories of the dream.

I arrive at my job with just fifteen minutes to spare. I pull in and park in the parking garage. The Boston Public Library stays open until 9pm and I usually work the closing shifts. I don't work a lot during the week maybe one or two days if Diane needs me. I love my job, and I enjoy being around all the books. The library here is the second largest in the country. It helps pay for my college books as well, which is really amazing. Endicott College is expensive, but worth it. Most of my classes are online, so at least I don't have to drive the hour to the Beverly campus.

My boss, Diane, a seventy-two year old with a white chin length bob and her cute plastic black rimmed glasses that scream *librarian,* waves when she sees me.

"Tatum, we closed off the photography section today so it's going to be a slow day. We just need to finish with the book returns," she adjusts her spectacles as she points to the massive amount of books on the cart.

"Alright. Any chance I can start with M and move up?" I questioned.

"Go ahead, and don't forget to take a lunch around six, please," she smiles and continues her work.

Kate and Claire are running the front desk, which means I could explore while putting the returns away. I have questions that I need to answer.

I push my cart and head into the non-fiction section, setting out to find as much as possible about reading my dreams. I need to know everything there is to know.

Working through lunch was not going to make Diane happy, but my search was at least worthwhile. While looking up dream reading I found this:

Dreaming of a locket is a symbol of something that you want to hold close to your heart, either something with sentimental value or something that you want to keep secret. If you dream of putting something in a locket, this indicates a possession, a person, or even an idea which you want to keep safe and keep close to you.

Seeing someone or something that is actively bleeding suggests some sort of physical or even emotional pain. If that person is bleeding to death, it reflects a total devastation and the loss of will to stay alive.

It could only be my mother, but what is she trying to tell me?

Before I know it, the end of my shift was here. I grab my belongings and head for the main entrance. I double check the lights and type in my alarm code. Pushing the away button, I make my way out the door, locking it behind me.

On the way to the parking garage, the hair on the back of my neck begins to stand alert. I immediately feel as if someone is watching me. I grab my Nikon D3400 camera and start taking pictures with the flash on, hoping to blind whoever was there. I pick up my pace, and almost get my car unlocked when someone grabs me.

"We need to talk!" The shadow exclaims.

"Reed! You scared the shit out of me! Let go of me," I warn.

"I told you, I need to talk to you. This between us, it isn't done... not even close. Don't be a bitch Tatum!" He says smugly.

"We are done when I say we are! We are done, I can't stand cheaters! The only bitch here is you!!! Let me fucking go or else."

Before I give him a chance to respond I knee him in the groin.

"Leave me the hell alone!" I yell as I rush to unlock my car. I put my key in the ignition to start it and speed off.

On my way home, I think of today's events. What a day! Why do these things keep happening to me? First my dream and then Reed shows up out of nowhere. I can't believe he had the audacity to show up at my job. Why is it when men do stupid shit women are supposed to forget about it? 'Forgive and forget' is what they'll say. I'll forget alright, forget his ass.

I pull up to the apartment my best friend and I share. I park in the nearest spot on the road. I click the button to lock my car. When I get to the door I check the mailbox, it's empty. Aria must have already grabbed the mail. I unlock the door to find my best friend, Aria, on the couch sleeping. At least I wouldn't have to recall the events of today right now. We don't keep secrets, never have. I guess that's why we've been best friends forever. We are honest with each other and loyal to a fault.

I'll tell her tomorrow I think to myself. I'm off work tomorrow, so we can both catch up.

In my bedroom I strip off my work clothes and head for the bathroom. A bath sounds amazing after a day like today. I let the bathtub fill, and decide in that moment I need to add bubbles. I squirt body wash into the hot water and watch as the bubbles appear. I gently slide my body into the clawfoot tub and try to relax. I instantly nod off.

I see her. This time she's not bleeding, she's smiling at me. She's happy to see me. How did I end up back here? She grabs my hand and the locket appears. Are these pictures of me? I try to ask her, but my words don't make a sound. She shakes her head no. There are two, but not of you. Just as I'm about to ask another question...

"Hey bitch! Wake up! You know it's wicked stupid to fall asleep in there," Aria lectures.

"Holy Shit! You scared me! Why is everyone trying to give me a heart attack?" I snap.

Aria laughs, "Sorry I had to pee! I was worried and didn't want you to drown in all the bubbles. On second thought, sexy first responders? Unfortunate for you, HOT for me!"

"Not funny…" I scowl.

"I'll let you finish up. I'm headed to bed so goodnight! " She says while chuckling.

"Goodnight," I reply.

My thoughts immediately jump back to my dream. She HAD to be my mother. Who else would visit my dreams? I didn't know a lot about her because I was adopted when I was just a week old. All I know is that she loved me and she died giving me life. As I recall my dream, she did look so much like me. We share the same blonde locks, but she has blue eyes, opposite to my emerald ones. I had many questions, but no one to ask.

My biggest question of all was what did she mean by *"there are two, but not of you"?*

Talia Hendrix | Two

****

"Ms. Hendrix, I sentence you to 30 days of community service and you must pay restitutions in the amount of $1,400.98," Judge Holbrooke states.

"You have 60 days from this sentencing to make payment. The Lackawanna County Courthouse dismisses you," he says, ready to be done.

As I start toward the door, my father blocks the doorway.

"Talia, you are lucky that's all the judge gave you. Destruction of other people's property is no joke, not to mention the fact that you assaulted him," Charles says then heads for the door.

"I didn't assault him! I just kicked him in his nuts after he cheated! He deserved it!" I argue.

"You also took a baseball bat to his car. Did you forget already? Oh, and let's not forget that you keyed it as well!" Charles counters.

"No I didn't! I caught him with my *alleged* best friend! As if that wasn't enough I saw everything! So excuse me if I don't seem so remorseful, *Dad,*" I hiss.

"Let's finish this little chat at home. You're making a scene."

"Fuck you! It's not like you're my real dad anyway!" I spat back.

I walk out of the courthouse in a hurry. I didn't want to know what he planned on doing to me for embarrassing him the way I had. The bruises were still there from the last time I lashed out. He's beat my ass a time or two. I wish my mom were still alive. She would understand. I did not deserve this. I was stuck. I continued heading back to the house. Tonight was the night. I was packing my shit and leaving. I was done. I beat my "dad" home and packed one duffle. I don't know where I'm going, but something is telling me to leave.

Charles Hendrix always kept money hidden away. He had removed all the money from all banks, always used to go on about how you couldn't trust other people with your hard earned cash. He thought I didn't know where he kept it, but lucky for me, I do. He hides it in an old dictionary that's been hollowed out. I can only assume that he was taught from his military days to hide some for safe keeping. The dictionary is on the bookshelf next to a few of my favorites, all four volumes of *Calendar Girl by Audrey Carlan* and four of *International Guy by Audrey Carlan*. They are my ultimate favorites, I grabbed them along with the hollowed out dictionary. They are part of my prized possessions, I can't just leave them behind. Shit! I almost forgot all three of the *Fifty Shades* trilogy! I silently sent out a psychic apology to *E.L. James*. Damn that would be an unforgivable sin in itself.

I have an unspoken bond with books. I don't know why, but its always been that way.

I need to head out before he gets back, I thought to myself.

I take the money from the dictionary, $4,000. That should be plenty to get me away. I put all the books, including the dictionary in my duffle and zipped it back up. I throw the bag over my shoulder and head for the train station.

I was halfway there, but had to take a detour. I needed to find the nearest mailbox to mail my fine before I skipped town. Almost 1,500 down the drain, thanks Julian!! Asshole..

The rest of the trip was lacking adventure, which suits me just fine. I've had enough for today. I walk into the train station and sit on one of the many benches. I close my eyes and before I could stop myself I drift off to sleep.

A woman approached me, and offered her hand.. As soon as our hands touch, I see an image of another woman: it was me. Only it wasn't me. We looked identical, but she had a different aura to her. It was my twin sister. I had a twin. This woman: I've seen her before. I believe she is my mother, Delia. She showed me

7

where I needed to go to.

I shook myself awake and realize I had been asleep for almost an hour. I need to get on that train.

"Last call for the train to Boston, Massachusetts. Train leaves in approximately 10 minutes. Have your ticket ready for inspection," the automated voice instructs.

There were probably ten people in front of me. Hopefully I can get a ticket. If they're sold out I will have to wait here overnight and check the schedules for tomorrow. That would also give Charles enough time to find me.

"How can I help you, Miss?" The lady at the window asks.

"Yes, I'd like a one way ticket to Boston, Massachusetts, please," I request.

"Your total will be $149.65. Will that be cash or card?"

I hand her the cash, and wait for my ticket.

"Thank you! Have a safe trip, here you are!" She said, handing me my ticket.

I practically jog to the entrance. Handing the man my ticket, he checked it and let me through. I found my way to an empty seat, putting my bag above my head.

"Excuse me, Miss…." a voice says to me.

"Oh shit, I'm sorry, am I in the way?' I say while climbing into my seat.

"I just wanted to ask if this seat was taken. My name's Grant." He put his hand out, waiting for mine.

"I suppose no one else is sitting here. The name is Talia. Nice to meet you." I stood up and shook his hand, feeling instant goosebumps.

It was an instant connection. I look him up and down, taking him all in. His jeans hugged all the right places and his white t-shirt clung to his body enough, so that I could see that sexy six pack underneath. He was incredibly handsome. His hair was chestnut in color, long enough to run my hands through, and he had beautiful blue *fuck me* eyes that made it hard to stop staring.

He had a slight five o' clock shadow, but I could work with that. Call it intuition, but I felt this man was going to be a big part of my life. He just had to be.

"Talia, are you okay?" Grant asks.

"Y-yeah I'm great. Sorry. My mind is a little caught up. I have a lot going on," I look down, biting my lip.

"This is going to sound crazy, but you are wicked gorgeous," he says with his hand gently caressing my cheek.

"As attractive as you may be you need to remove your hand, please," I say firmly.

He pulls away with apologetic eyes. "I'm sorry. I shouldn't have done that."

I had to stop it before it even started. I didn't want to give him the wrong idea. Even though I could definitely enjoy this sexy man's touch, I knew once I started there would be no stopping. I can't risk getting in trouble for indecent exposure on a train.

"So what's in Boston?" I ask, changing the conversation.

"I'm going to visit my Uncle Mike. I'll be staying with him for a few weeks before I start classes for the next semester," he says with complete honesty.

"Has it been long since you've visited? I'm a Boston virgin, I've never been before," I divulge.

"I haven't seen him in almost a year, but we just found out he has early onset Alzheimer's. I'm spending a few weeks with him to help him out. He's moving in with his sister, who lives in Salem. I plan on helping him pack his things. What about you?"

"I don't know why. I just needed to get away, and Boston felt right. It felt like fate dragged me here, kicking and screaming."

9

XOXO

I tossed and turned all last night, and felt like complete crap this morning. I didn't have any weird dreams, which made it even more unusual. I was probably just stressed, maybe it was just a hallucination. I roll out of bed and head for the bathroom.

"Tatum, are we still going shopping at the mall?" Aria practically screeches from the other room.

"Yes, I need to shower. I'll see you in twenty," I respond, rolling my eyes.

I turn the shower on and jump in, lathering my blonde wavy locks as I give myself a scalp massage. I am starting to get a headache. I need to take off some of the pressure. I tilt my head back, and rinse the foam from my hair. Washing and rinsing my body quickly, I climb out, and reach for my warm fuzzy towel. I fit it around me and grab another for my head. Gently kneading my hair in the towel, I flip it upside down and add some mousse and leave-in to tame and help me scrunch my hair. I apply some of my favorite primer for my skin and start to work on my emerald eyes. I dab my eyeliner brush into water and smudge it into the deep brown shadow to put it on my lash line. Then I start to work on my brows, which luckily don't need much help. I put a little bit of the clear brow gel on them, grab my mascara and begin making the face every woman makes when they put on mascara. Yes, you know what face I'm talking about, and nobody can explain why we do it, we just do.

Once I was happy with what I saw in the mirror, I went to ransack my closet.

I grab my favorite lavender v-neck t-shirt; the one that hugs my body like a second skin without suffocating me. Then I went on a hunt for my favorite pair of jeans. They are holey jeans, but they are mine and I love them. Don't judge me, they don't even make pants without holes or rips anymore. I pick up my camera and place the strap over my shoulder. The strap that holds my camera is homemade. It has many pictures of books in various bright colors on it. Aria had it made for me. It shows my intimate relationship with books of all kinds.

I practically run down the stairs to find Aria.

"Aria??? Where are you?" I ask, ducking my head into the kitchen.

I give up easily, searching the cabinets for a snack before heading to her favorite local mall, Copley Place.

"Sorry, was on the phone with my ma. She told me to tell you hello," Aria says.

"It's okay. I'm ready if you are," I say with a chuckle as I tap on my non-existent watch.

We head out the door to get into my trusty Honda Accord, Ava. She's my favorite toy, other than the ones hidden in my drawer (if you catch my drift). I know; too much information, but I can't help myself! Just can't help it. I start up Ava and buckle up. As we continue on our way I turn on my radio, and speed down the highway.

Finding parking always takes longer than expected. Seeing as it's the weekend, I am not surprised.

I find a spot and I lock her up. Aria wants to go to *Victoria's Secret*, which is on the second floor of the mall. I'm glad we can do things like this together. We weren't always this close. There was a time when we were in completely different states. I'm not a Boston native, except in my heart. I lived in Ohio before I came here to live with Aria. We were long distance friends for the longest time, until I decided I needed a change of scenery for college. I got into Endicott College, and Aria actually goes there as well. She has family in Beverly, so whenever she wants to go to campus she usually stays with them. My intentions are to get my BA in Photography, but my ultimate love is reading. Aria is going for a degree in

Psychology but her real passion, is working with children that are on the Autism spectrum. It's amazing to watch her grow and learn. She's a very strong and intelligent person and I'm glad we found one another.

"Aria, I'm gonna go see if I can get an appointment at the nail place while you shop. I need a mani-pedi anyway. Meet me after you're finished, ok?"

"Yeah, that will be great. That way I can try things on without you nagging me," she says with a smirk.

I walk into Nails, Nails and Pedicures and head for the front desk. I ask the receptionist if there were any available appointments, and am told that the earliest one was tomorrow. Deciding not to worry about it, I begin to walk around the mall.

As I walk, with each step I realize how out of place I really was here. I've never felt like this before, and I'm not really sure what brought it on. It could be the stores that surround me: the two I could actually afford were Nails, Nails And Pedicures and *Victoria's Secret.* I snap a few photos of my surroundings, I can find the beauty even in the uncomfortableness of so many men in their high end fancy suits. Finding a bench, I sit down, and wait patiently for Aria to finish.

Unknowingly I pick a seat next to a very handsome stranger. I instantly feel my cheeks flush. Feeling his eyes burning a hole through me I turn, smile and pretend not to be completely flustered by his raw sex appeal. He definitely works out, even under his suit I could see his muscles.

"Well, hello there," he says, grinning right back at me. I don't respond right away, unsure of what to say.

"My name's Kendrick Sanders. Do you have a name, sweetheart?" he asks.

"Uhh, yes I do have a name. Sorry... I'm Tatum Emerson."

"Are you here by yourself?" He smiles, while gazing into my eyes.

"No, I'm not. I'm waiting on my friend. What's with all the questions?" I remark, returning the gaze.

Damnit! I shouldn't have done that. I look into those steely blue eyes and they set my soul on fire. I've never had this reaction to someone's gorgeous eyes before.

"Sorry, I just really want to get to know you. I know we just met, but you seem interesting," he smirks.

"So since you are so hell-bent on knowing about me, what brings YOU here?" I challenge.

"I was having lunch with my father at the seafood place down the way. I'm not a big fan of seafood, but my father insisted," Kendrick admits.

"I'm on the same page, I hate seafood," I grimace.

His phone buzzes and he grabs to check it, I'd assume it was to find out who it was.

"I'm sorry to cut this short. I really need to get going, but here's my number. Call me tonight and maybe we can get together soon," he smiles and, hands me his business card.

"I'd love to see you again and get a chance to take you out on a proper date, if you'll let me," he smiles.

He stood and before I could answer he did something unexpected. He lifts my unmanicured hand and gently pressed his lips against it so I could feel the heat from his breath. His lips were soft, sensual and wet. The sensation instantly gave me goosebumps. I want to feel his lips all over my body. I can honestly say I've never had that happen before, my panties were heating up and quickly. My body didn't care what my mind wanted. Deep down I knew I needed to feel his touch. How can I feel this way about a man I just met? I think I'm going crazy. Before he can leave I stand and push my body against his and press my lips to his in a passionate kiss.

I could tell he feels it, the electricity surging between us, the heat between my thighs as he wraps his strong arms around me like he had no intention of ever letting me go. I didn't want him to. I needed this man, and from the looks of it he needed me too.

"Tatum there you…are," Aria's eyes bulge out.

We break the kiss quickly, both embarrassed that we got caught like teenagers.

"Uhh..umm.. Sorry. Kendrick, this is my bestie Aria. I will call you tonight. I wanna see you again," I say, and I mean it.

"Nice meeting you, Aria. I'll talk to you later, Tatum," he says then blows a kiss at me.

I think if we had continued I'd have more than just wet panties to worry about. Holy shit! I need to make that man mine! I need to know him and that body! WHO the hell am I turning into….

"Tatum….. Soooooo who was that? I don't remember knowing anyone by the name of Kendrick, and I sure don't remember you telling your best friend you were dating, let alone almost fucking someone here *in public* at the mall," she says accusingly.

"Okay, I'll fess up. I just met him and he's super fuckable. He kissed my hand, I kissed his lips…. No big deal right?" I chuckle nervously.

"Tatum!!! You little slut, you don't even know him!" She teases.

"Yep, I'm a slut…. I know...Are you ready to go?" I whine.

"Does he have a brother?" Aria asks..

"I'll be sure to ask him when I get that date he promised me," I smile and bite the side of my finger.

On the drive back home she continues to give me shit about my sexy stranger. What are best friends for? Aria knows me all too well. I couldn't hide anything from her. Aria, on the other hand, has been there for me through so much that she is closer to me than most of my own family.

I think she was surprised mostly because I am not that spontaneous. I haven't dated since Reed, and that didn't turn out so well. Reed mostly tried to take advantage of me and my body. That was until I caught him with *her*. Aria was there for me, she threatened to kick his prep school ass. She has a way with words, I'll say that.

I really believe in my heart that my prince charming is out there, that sounds naïve I know, but I believe everyone has a soul mate. Maybe Kendrick will be a stepping stone to that.

I don't know this man but I could've fucked him today. I say that, but I'm not experienced in that area. He has me all kinds of messed up.

TALIA HENDRIX | FOUR

✗✗✗✗

The train ride was a long one, so I was thankful for the good company. Grant was sleeping with his head on my shoulder and I felt relaxed. I haven't felt that safe in awhile.

Living with my adoptive father wasn't easy. He tends to be abusive and I suppose it's partially my fault for being such a fuck up at such a young age. I suppose it all stemmed from losing my mother when I was so young. Charles became more violent and angry as time went on. Anything I do seems to trigger him. I get that he is missing my mom, but I didn't expect him to take it out on me. I was grieving too. I cry myself to sleep on many countless nights.

Amelia, my adoptive mother, was the most incredible woman I've ever known. She was so kind, compassionate and beautiful. Her death was an unexpected one that none of us saw coming. She didn't want us to fuss over her, so we had no clue. I should've noticed. She was always at work, she was a nurse constantly taking care of everyone else, never took care of herself. I should've known! I should've been there to take care of her. I was her only child. She had told me they weren't able to have kids of their own, so God blessed them with me. We didn't have much, but Amelia's love was enough for both of us until she was gone. It felt like my heart had been ripped from my chest. The pain never went away, not even now.

I suppose I dealt with it by going to parties, sleeping around and drinking at an early age. Of course this also included many trips to the police station. I was what they referred to as a 'frequent flyer'. They knew Charles' name and number by heart and knew who I was. Not only that, but they knew Amelia. The first two times at the police station I got a slap on the wrist. The more I fucked up, the more severe

16

it would become. Charles made sure that I felt the pain for many days and weeks to follow.

This last incident wasn't the greatest, I admit. I smashed in my ex-boyfriend's windshield. I'm not sorry about it because he cheated on me with someone I thought was my best friend. Turns out, she just wanted everything I had. Little did she know my life was far from the fairytale she thought. I would give her my abusive dad any day. Let her deal with the bruises and broken ribs he left me. I suppose anger became a friend of mine. If you do me wrong, watch your back, because I'll be coming for you when you least expect it.

Too much thinking of the past. I shrug it off and I decide, since I have a sexy sleeping man on my shoulder, I would get some shut eye as well. I lean over, put my head against his and close my eyes.

She appeared again, but this time she wasn't alone. There was a woman beside her. She had long curly salt and pepper hair and I'll never forget those eyes. The most beautiful shade of violet. Who is this? No answer. She wrapped her arms around me and I felt safe, just like I did with Grant. I have a twin, don't I, Mom? Yes darling, you do. How do I find her? Seek her out and you shall find.

I wake up to find Grant staring at me with those delicious baby blues. I instinctively licked my lips.

"Sorry, I didn't mean to wake you. You're cute when you talk in your sleep," he hums.

"I hope I didn't say anything too bad," I smile.

"What were you dreaming about?" Grant questions me.

I wondered how honest I could be with a stranger.

"My mom. She passed away after she gave birth to me," I say with sad eyes.

"We don't have to talk about it if you don't want to," he says, reassuring me.

"There's not much to tell. She died and I was too young to remember," I murmur.

17

"We are 20 minutes outside of Boston. Please remain in your seats," an automated voice instructs.

"I'm scared, but excited to start over. First thing I will have to do is find a place to crash," I confess.

"Would you be interested in crashing on the couch where I'm staying?" Grant offers sincerely.

"Are you sure that would be okay? What about your uncle? You don't really know me Grant. How can you make an offer like that? I appreciate it, but can't accept," I say regretfully.

I knew I needed a place, but he didn't know me and I sure didn't know enough about him to sleep in a stranger's house.

I did need a place though...

"It would be my *pleasure* to have you. I can't imagine you on your own in a new city. Please let me help a beautiful lady," Grant says with a grin.

"You want to have me, huh?" I tease.

"Yes of course, but that's not what I meant," he says wrinkling his brow.

"Okay, I'll stay with you, but only for the night," I say, trying to convince him. Maybe I was trying to convince myself.

"Good, then it's settled. You'll stay with me, safe and sound," he said smiling.

"When we get off this train, how will we get to your uncle's?" I question him.

I could feel the train coming to a halt. The scraping of the wheels on the railroad tracks was enough to make me nauseous.

"We have reached the destination: Boston, Massachusetts. Please gather your belongings and exit accordingly," the intercom blared.

I look over at Grant to see if he was ready. He was already standing up to grab both my bag and his.

"Babydoll, are you ready to head to my uncle's?" he says, trying to be cute.

"Oh it's "babydoll" now, huh? I thought my name was Talia, but I guess I'm wrong," I laugh.

He grabs my hand and guides me. At least he knew where he was going. I wasn't familiar with the big city of Boston. If Boston was like Grant I was already in love with it.

"Welcome to Boston Landing," the sign reads. I wondered how far we actually were from his Uncle Mike's house.

"Stay here for a second, I'm going to order a cab. Sit tight," he says with a wink.

He walks a few steps ahead of me, opens the app on his phone and orders a car to pick us up. Apparently it was that easy.

"Our driver will be here in 8 minutes, so we can stay out here and enjoy the sights," he says, feeling proud of himself.

"Good job! Bet that really took some effort, Grant," I chuckle.

Sarcasm seems to be a defense for me. I was trying to keep my distance, but for some reason I just wanted to be close to this man. I reach my arms out to embrace him. He wraps his strong arms around me, surrounding me with his protection.

"Thank you for everything," I whisper in his ear.

I could see the goosebumps my whisper had just generated. He is attracted to me, and it seems like I turn him on. I want to see how far I could use this to my advantage. I know what he wants from the bulge in his pants. If I could do that, I knew I would hold all the cards in my hand. He would soon be putty in the palm of my hand and I'd play with him until I either got bored or he was so in love with me it hurt. If he could take care of my needs maybe he was worth keeping around. I bet he's wonderful in bed. He better be, I don't like to be disappointed.

I felt him grab my hand, not realizing I had zoned out for a second. He led us to our driver's car. The driver hops out of his small environmentally friendly car, and loads our bags into the trunk. He gets back in the front seat and waits for us to join him.

"So our adventure begins," I say, smiling at Grant.

Grant opens the door for me and I slide in, waiting for him to slide next to me. Once we both are in the vehicle and buckled up our driver Ty heads to our destination. I watch out the window, taking in all that this city has to offer. I feel at peace, like I was meant to be here. I decide now is the perfect time to test and maybe tease Grant. Yes don't judge me, I'm an asshole.

I put my hand on Grant's thigh and give a little squeeze. He's caught off guard, but smiles at my advances. I continue gently rubbing his thigh, moving up ever so slightly. It's then I realize Grant is well endowed. I could feel him and he was enjoying every minute of it.

His sexy blue eyes are shut tight and he is biting his lip. He touches my hand and puts it right on his big bulge as I continue to gently stroke him through his pants. He puts his hand over mine to stop me and leans over to whisper in my ear.

"Talia, if you keep going I'm going to have to explain away the wet spot on my pants. Tonight, we can finish what we both obviously want and need," he says.

He leans over and kisses my forehead. Tonight some amazing fuckery will happen. I really wanna feel him deep inside me. I smile because Boston is already feeling like *Home.*

TATUM EMERSON | FIVE

xoxo

A couple days have gone by since my last dream of my mother. I've often wondered if it's just a crazy dream.

I decide before I give Kendrick a phone call that maybe I should find out some information on my sexy stranger.

With my internet search of Kendrick Sanders, I found some interesting information. The search results showed no social media, which was interesting in this day and age.

Kendrick Prescott Sanders, son of Prescott Sanders, is currently a partner at his father's company P.S. Trust & Invest. He is currently on the list of top 30 eligible bachelors of Boston, but has not been shy about bringing women to events. His net worth is currently close to $2.2 billion dollars. Here is the playboy at the most recent charitable events. This particular event raised a whopping $500,000 for St. Lawrence's Hospital.

Tonight we are going out on a first date and I'm nervous because I look nothing like this perfectly enhanced blonde bimbo in the picture with him. It's not that I'm insecure or anything, but I haven't seen him since our heated make-out session at the mall.

I stand in front of my full length mirror and examine myself in the new bra and panties I just purchased. If it comes to it tonight, I hope he likes them. I search through my closet for the perfect dress to wear tonight. I'm having trouble deciding and that surprises me because I'm a creature of habit. Usually it's my favorite black dress, but tonight feels different.

My eyes fall on the beautiful, full length, emerald green, backless dress with the tags still attached. This is the one that would make my eyes pop and if Kendrick felt the urge he could skim his hand against my bare skin. Just thinking about it makes me shiver.

I step into my dress and manage to zip it myself. *It's a miracle,* I thought to myself. That never happens. I have about an hour before he's supposed to be picking me up, so I opt to finish my hair. I section it off and grab my inch curling iron, starting to manipulate my curls. Once I'm completely finished curling them I run my fingers through the locks to separate my curls, giving it a little spritz of hairspray for some control.

All I had to do now to finish the look was add a little mascara to my lashes and I would be ready to go. I apply my blackest midnight mascara and then, using my eyelash curler, I crimp them into submission. I look into the mirror again and smile at my myself. I think my mother, Victoria, would be proud. She had bombarded me with what I always thought were useless beauty hacks. Turns out I got to use some of them. I should text a picture to her. She'd love that.

We were always close until my father died. I chose to move away with Aria for college. I wanted to cut the proverbial cord, and learn how to survive on my own. My parents were always overprotective, but my mom still wanted me to know how to look and act like a lady. For once I was glad she had taught me. Kendrick Sanders was another ballgame completely. He comes from money. He is a trust fund baby and meeting him that day had surprised me. He wasn't what I thought, that's for sure.

The doorbell rings, and quickly tears me away from my thoughts. I walk to the door, hearing my heels clicking along with me. I open the door and find Kendrick with a dozen red roses in his hand. The roses smell amazing, but whatever cologne he is wearing smells better. I smile and thank him, all while taking in his tailored black suit with the matching black tie. His hair is styled to perfection and he has the front pushed back. He looks absolutely delicious. He catches me staring.

"Everything okay, Tatum?" he says with a smirk.

"Just perfect. You really know how to woo a lady, don't you?" I lift my eyebrow accusingly.

"Only for the very special ones, like you. I just have to say you make that dress look beautiful. I mean you look beautiful in that dress," he says, stumbling with his words.

"You don't look like a guy who makes many mistakes in his life, so should I take that as a joke gone wrong?" I question, trying to keep the smile from showing.

It's very difficult not to smile. He obviously enjoys charming the pants off people or, in my case, the dress off me. I'm sure that him working with his father has taught him that.

"No, but you are so gorgeous it makes me lose my train of thought. The words just float away," he professes with a loving look in his eyes.

I smile from ear to ear and place a kiss on his lips.

I lean in and whisper "Don't worry, you drive me crazy too. The feeling is mutual."

"Let me put these flowers in a vase. Come on in, I will only be a few minutes."

I walk into the kitchen, fill my favorite glass vase with water and sprinkle some sugar to help the roses flourish. Old wives tale I suppose, but I always do it just in case. I slip the roses into a vase and a thorn pricks my finger.

"Dammit!" I hiss.

Kendrick peeks his head in the kitchen and asks. "Hey, everything alright in here?"

I suck on my freshly pricked finger to stop the bleeding.

"Will you go to the bathroom and grab me a bandaid out of the medicine cabinet please? It's the first door on your right."

He returns with the bandage, carefully handling my wound.

"Here, allow me. I'd love to have the chance to play doctor with you," he says while preparing it for my finger.

He places the bandaid ever so gently on my wounded finger and wraps it around, careful not to make it too tight.

He leans down and kisses the bandage.

"Now my job is complete. Are you ready to head out to dinner?" he asks.

"Let's go, I'm always up for an adventure."

When we get outside of the building it's still light out. You can see the sun on the horizon, getting ready to set on a brisk November evening. He walks me to his Mercedes-Benz S-Class Maybach, (yes I know my cars). Now this is a beautiful car. Definitely speaks to his upbringing. As we get closer, I realize his driver is standing outside waiting.

"Good evening Ma'am. My name is Marcello," he slightly bows as he opens the door for us.

"Thank you, Marcello. It's nice to meet you." I smile at him.

Marcello was clearly built. Everything about him screamed suave, badass bodyguard. He has to be about 6'1, because he towered over me at my height of 5'7. His short black hair was slicked back, just like you see in the movies. The name wasn't the only thing that gave away the fact that he was Italian; his flawless olive skin and that sexy Italian Bostonian accent definitely did as well. He's dressed head to toe in a classy coal colored suit with a gorgeous navy tie with its intricate pattern. As I look up and meet his eyes, I study his face from his chocolate brown eyes to the lightly trimmed scruff covering his face. Then my attention moves to Kendrick. My heart flutters. I've never been this close to two gorgeous men in my life. Hell, I've never been near a man who's important enough to have his own bodyguard. I feel my lips drying out, and I swipe my tongue over them hoping not to show my own nervousness.

"Marcello, I'm going to let this lovely lady pick our destination, then we can be off," Kendrick explains.

"I've never been to this place, but they have good reviews online," I say unsure of my choice.

"What is it called?" Kendrick asks.

"*Yvonne's*. I've heard it's beautiful inside. Pictures probably don't do it any justice." I say, while showing him photos on my phone.

"I can honestly say I've never been to this particular place. I hope the food is good."

"Me too. Marcello, do you know where it is?" I call to the front.

"Yes I do, Miss Tatum. Very good choice," Marcello praises.

"The restaurant is themed as a library, but has definite hints of being a speakeasy. They had to find ways around the law in forms of secret places like this very one. This place was once occupied by *Locke-Ober,* who was very influential in Boston for around 150 years. I apologize, I hope I'm not boring you two with too many facts," he marvels in the glorious city history.

I smile, "I love hearing the history. I'm not originally from Boston, so it's great to hear all of the antiquity."

"Thank you for entertaining this beauty, Marcello."

KENDRICK SANDERS | SIX

XOXO

When we got to her place I wasn't feeling nervous at all. She kissed me when we first met, so how was tonight going to be any different? Tonight was about one thing for me: getting my dick wet. I would woo the shit out of her, take her back to her place and bang her brains out until she screamed my name. It didn't matter what I had to do to get her in the sack, I'd do it.

I'm Kendrick Fucking Sanders, nobody tells me no. If she's what I want, she is what I'll have. Don't get me wrong or judge me, I'm not saying she's not gorgeous, smart and whatever else. I was out to get laid, that's all. If it lead to other things then that was a bonus. I really hope she's great in bed.

I had Marcello stop at the florist for me on the way, so I could pick out some flowers for my newest conquest. I opted for roses; red ones tend to get the ladies' panties wet. Women go crazy when men actually pay attention to them and care about what they think. I'll play prince charming tonight and never see her again anyway. I'll even go as far as letting her pick the place where we dine. She will actually think I care about what she likes.

I purchase a dozen red roses and head back out the door to the car. Marcello holds the door for me, then we head to Tatum's place. She lives about twenty minutes away from the florist. We park in front of her place. Marcello opens my door and I head up the pathway to her door. I confidently stride to the door and ring the bell.

She answers with a quickness that surprises me. I expected her to not be ready. That's another trait of every woman I've known: they take fucking forever to get ready. They put a pound of that makeup shit on their face so I don't recognize them in the morning.

She greets me sweetly as I hand her the dozen roses. She seems genuinely surprised. I wasn't expecting that reaction.

After some idle chit chat and shameless flirting, she leaves to go put the roses in a vase so we can leave. I'm starved, but not just for the food. That dress she has on made me wanna rip it off her body. It fits her like a glove.

I look around the apartment and I can't seem to figure out how women find anything. Everything is always all over the place. The couch looks comfy; maybe that's where I'll have her for dessert later. I was ready to take a seat on the couch to try it out when I heard her yelp from the kitchen.

I peek my head in the kitchen and ask her if everything was alright. Actually I was really trying to figure out why it was taking so long to put the damn flowers in water.

She tells me she's fine, but she needs a bandaid. I look to see what happened. She stuck herself with something and her finger is bleeding. I feel bad for maybe a second, then she asks me to go to the bathroom to get a bandage for her. Being the gentleman I am, of course I oblige.

She said it was the first door on the right, I have no idea how I'm going to find anything, but I'll try. I'm not a quitter. I head down the small hallway and take the first door on my right. I walk into the bathroom and head to the medicine cabinet checking my reflection in the mirror as I search. The things I do for pussy. I open it and am immediately overwhelmed by all the shit she has in there. Makeup, women shit, the only thing I recognize is the toothbrush and toothpaste. I grab what appears to be the box of bandaids and head back out to the kitchen.

I turn to her and say, "Here, allow me. I'd love to have the chance to play doctor with you." *I wasn't lying, not in the least bit. She could be my dirty little nurse*, I thought to myself.

Putting the bandaid on her finger, I lean in to kiss it and make it better.

"Now my job is complete. Are you ready to head out to dinner?" I ask her.

"Let's go, I'm always up for an adventure," she says smiling.

She wants the dick, so this is going to be easy. Just a few more hours and I'd see what's hiding under that emerald dress..

TALIA HENDRIX | SEVEN

✕✕✕✕

We are headed to Uncle Mike's house and I couldn't help but hope that I wasn't going to get Grant in any trouble for inviting me to stay. This may be more nerve wracking then I intended. On the ride I wonder if Charles had discovered that I had stole his savings. He would never be able to track me here, and even if he did, it's a big city. It would take him a long time to find out my exact location. I don't honestly believe Grant would let him hurt me, he seems like a protective guy.

"Talia, you okay?" Grant asks.

"Yeah I'm fine. I just hope that I'm not going to get you in any trouble for staying at your uncle's without him knowing me," I confess.

"It will be fine. My uncle won't say shit about it," he says confidently.

He pulls me close to him and we watch the sights of Boston fly past us. I lay my head on his shoulder and enjoy the scenery with him. I could stay like this. Never before have I felt this much warmth from one person. It intrigues me how a person can be this good to others. I think maybe it's time to take a chance on a stranger.

"Talia, I have a question for you…" he hesitates.

"Ask me anything. I'll answer you if I can," I agree. Why wouldn't he have questions? He would be completely crazy if he didn't.

"I saw the bruises on your arm. Did someone hurt you? Are you running away from them?" He asks, deadpanned.

Before I could answer, he cuts me off.

"If they did, I will protect you. They won't ever touch you again. I promise,

29

you can trust me," he blurts out.

"To be honest, I was hoping you wouldn't notice. I'm just not prepared to talk about it. Please believe me when I tell you that I will tell you when I'm ready to," I sigh.

"No pressure, babydoll. I'll be your listening ear when you're ready," he clarifies.

"Again with the nickname, huh? I guess I'll have to pick one for you….Maybe I'll name you spanky," I said, almost giggling.

Grant grins. "I could work with that one, but only if I get to do the spanking."

"Are you trying to play dominant with me right now?" I try not to grin.

The driver looks in his mirror with surprised eyes. I really have to remember to watch my mouth. I completely forgot that we were with a driver.

"Oooops! Sorry Tyler! I didn't mean it to be so *sexual*," I apologize to the driver.

I really did, though. I meant it as sexual as it could be. I was not afraid to be myself, and that included some of my kinkier tendencies. I can't help that I like being spanked and maybe even possibly giving some spankings out to others. I was into a lot of different things, but I wasn't about to let Grant know that….*yet*.

"We can finish this conversation later Talia. We are here," he smiled.

We get out of the car and the driver had our bags ready to go. I think he was ready to be rid of us. Grant had already paid him through the app, so he grabbed our bags and we headed to the door of his uncle's house. I'm not as nervous as I was earlier, for which I am grateful. Grant lays down our bags and knocks on the door. The door creaks open and a man peaks out the opening;

"Hey Graham! It's great to see you here. Who's this lovely lady with you? Come in, man. It's been forever!" Mike exclaims, opening the door wide.

We step in and I immediately remember…his Alzheimer's. He doesn't

30

remember him. That's awful. My heart sinks and I immediately feel distraught for Grant.

"No, Uncle Mike, it's me Grant. Do you remember?" He asks.

Mike hesitates, "Of course! I know my own nephew. How the hell are ya? I miss having you around here!"

"I'm great, Uncle Mike. This beautiful lady next to me is a friend of mine. Her name is Talia. I told her she could stay here with us while we pack everything. I hope that's okay?" Grant queries.

"Sure is, I love the company. Sue wants me to be out in Salem as soon as I can. I don't know why that woman is so damned determined," Mike grimaces.

Grant smiles, "Well you know Aunt Sue, she has to be in control of everyone and everything all the time."

"Who's Sue? Graham, is that the girl you brought with ya? She's sure beautiful," Mike said smiling in my direction.

"She sure is. She is very beautiful," he says smiling my way.

"We are going to head up to our room and get settled. Let me know if you need me, okay?" He says, ignoring what Mike couldn't remember.

We head up the stairs and I immediately feel tears falling. I wouldn't wish that on my worst enemy. Forgetting is the worst possible curse. Then again, so is remembering things over and over. I wipe my eyes in hopes that Grant wouldn't notice me tearing up. I don't know this man, but my heart hurts for him. I'm not the type to cry at these things. I don't know what is happening. Something must be wrong with me. Hormones, that's it! Nobody cries over all my pain and suffering, why should I waste my tears on someone else?

I'm about what's good for Talia and that's the only thing that matters. I'm only here because I have nowhere else to go. I can't catch feelings over some guy. He's making me soft. I have to put some distance between us and quickly.

"Grant, is it okay if I go outside and get some air?" I ask.

"Sure, just make sure you're back before dinner. I'm cooking lasagna, my specialty," he says, trying to impress me.

I nod and head out the door as fast as I can to get as far away as possible.

I take off running. The only time I can think clearly is when I run. I run past the bus stop that was right down the road and head west, not knowing what I would find. I run for about 10 minutes, until I end up in some sort of forest or park.

Grant Thomas | Eight

✗✗✗✗

Every time I see my uncle it's a struggle. He doesn't remember me and it takes more than I'd like to admit out of me. This time Talia is with me which gives me more than one reason to put a brave face on. I know, as a grown man, I shouldn't admit to these feelings, but I feel like I've been through enough to own it.

I'm really surprised that Talia didn't run screaming or freak out when my uncle didn't remember me. She stayed really calm the whole time, even when he called me Graham. She never once questioned it and when she gets back from getting air, I will explain it all to her. I'm not sure what it is with this woman, but she makes me want to bare my soul to her. I know it sounds cheesy, but maybe my soul recognizes its counterpart.

It wasn't enough that she was breathtaking. Her blonde wavy hair almost hit her breasts, but was not quite long enough to hide her nipples from me. Her smile, even though I hadn't seen it very much, could bring light to even the darkest room. Talia's stunning emerald eyes were enough to make my dick stir in my pants, fuck I swear she could see right through me. She has that perfect shape, definitely not a toothpick. She has one hell of an ass, her breasts are killer, I would have to say definitely C's. I wipe my mouth to get rid of the drool as I smirk to myself. How did I get this lucky?

It's already five o' clock, I've daydreamed enough. I guess I should probably start my famous lasagna. Luckily enough for me Aunt Sue had stocked the fridge just a day ago. She knew I was going to be doing all the cooking and she bought the ingredients I would need for this lovely dinner.

I put water in the pot to boil, then add the pasta until it's soft and not al dente.

I prepare the dish and began to make the sauce while the noodles cool. I add tomato sauce and juice together, then add the already cooked meat from the fridge. I mix those with Italian seasoning and just a pinch of salt. I grab the ricotta cheese from the fridge, along with mozzarella.

I slowly put the noodles in the bottom of the dish, spread a thin layer of ricotta cheese and then layer the sauce. Once the sauce layer is complete I sprinkle enough mozzarella to cover the sauce. I continue this pattern until the dish is completely full. Once finished building my lasagna the remainder of the mozzarella cheese is placed on top and the dish goes in the oven. Then I have to work on the garlic bread.

I hope she makes it back in time, I wouldn't want dinner getting cold. Better yet, I hope she comes back. Something seemed off when she left. Guys aren't supposed to worry about things like this.

Tatum Emerson | Nine

xoxo

"So what made tonight my choice?" I ask Kendrick.

"My mother has always taught me that women deserve respect and to have all their needs met. This tends to include food. There's something about you that tells me your different, and I want you to have everything your heart desires," he divulges.

"Your mother sounds like a smart woman!" I say, in almost a chuckle.

"She is a smart woman. She always said there's always a smart woman behind every successful man. She keeps him grounded, honest and successful. She didn't come from a wealthy background like my father. She worked hard for everything she's accomplished, and she taught me to be an honorable man. She even went as far, when I was a child, as to make me take dance lessons. She was convinced I would need them one day. When I got married or something similar," he explains.

"Every woman likes a man who knows how to move his body. You'll have to show me some of those moves sometime. Save me a dance, will you?" I smile.

"So what about you, Tatum? How did you become this sexy, sophisticated woman I'm seeing tonight?"

"I don't know if I would go as far as to say sophisticated, but I'll take sexy as a compliment. I grew up in a small town in Ohio with my parents. Nothing really special. I dearly love both of my parents. They adopted me when I was a week old. I don't really have much information on my birth mother other than she died giving me life. My parents worked non-stop to make sure I could have as many options as possible. They enrolled me in art classes and photography classes. I'm working on my BA in Photography now. I'm doing online courses, but I still have a year to go.

35

I'm also an avid reader. I've worked at the library since arriving in Boston, which will be 3 years in February."

I hate talking about myself, but this was the plan. To let this man in, let him know me and get to know him too.

"We have something in common already, I also am an avid reader. I have a full library at my home. Maybe I can show you sometime," he remarks.

"I would love that, Kendrick. I've always wanted a library of my own. You've seen *Beauty and the Beast*, right? I want a ginormous library like that! I'd never have enough time to read every book, but that's beside the point. I'm weird! I love the way books smell and feel. Some have shiny covers, others have velvety ones….I'm sorry. I'm rambling, aren't I?" I say with apologetic eyes.

"It's okay, don't be sorry. You're cute when you ramble. I enjoy listening to you talk. The way you explain things is very interesting. I understand, when you have a love for things you tend to want to speak out about them," he nods.

"It's refreshing to have a man appreciate me for my words as well as everything else," I encourage.

"Mister Sanders, Miss Tatum, we have arrived at our destination," Marcello states, getting out of the car.

He comes over and holds the door for us. I wasn't used to this level of attention. Hopefully Kendrick actually would drive himself sometimes. I can imagine how awkward it would be if things were to get hot and steamy in the car. That's not exactly something I want Marcello to see or hear.

We walk to the entrance, which is black with black and cream colored signage. Reddish orange writing spelled out *Yvonne's*. The outside makes me very excited to see the interior. We walk in and Kendrick requests a table for two. The room is like a mini library, with lots of books and pictures on the wall. One wall has several lights on top of the wallpaper and a photograph of a man. It is so beautiful. I have never seen anything like this before. This may have been way out of my price range, but it was my favorite place and I haven't even tasted the food!

Kendrick held my chair out for me and then sat down himself. The waitress gives us menus and takes our drink orders. Kendrick orders us two glasses of their best Chardonnay, I don't correct him even though I'm not a wine drinker. I do however speak up to the waitress;

"Miss, may I please get a Cherie Amour, and hold the second glass of Chardonnay; I'm not a wine drinker. Thank you."

"Sorry to change on you, but do you mind, instead of the wine, I'll take the 1975. It's her night, so if she doesn't like wine there won't be any here, either. Thanks, sweetheart," he says, smiling coyly at her.

His attention then turns back to me;

"I'm glad you spoke up, I like confident women. It sounds like you know what you like and what you want. That's very sexy in a woman," he winks at me.

"Flattery will get you nowhere, Mr. Sanders; or maybe it'll get you everywhere, but that's my choice," I say, flirting back.

"Have you decided what you want to eat yet? I think I'll have the Grilled Viper Chops or the Sujuk. Remember, you can have anything you want. Tonight is your night," Kendrick stares into my soul. I feel my breath hitch, then prepare to give him my order.

"I think I'm set on the Niman Ranch Long Bone Ribeye Steak, but I wanna hold off on the ranch."

The waitress appears with our drinks and sets them down on the table.

"Are you guys ready to order, or do you need a few minutes?" The waitress asks. Her name badge says Amy in bright gold letters.

"Yes we are ready. I will have the Grilled Viper Chops and the lady would like the Niman Ranch Long Bone Ribeye Steak, but please hold the ranch," Kendrick says, placing our orders.

"How would you like your ribeye cooked?" She queries.

"Medium well, please," I chime in.

I pick up my drink and take a generous sip. This drink tastes phenomenal and I can feel my taste buds exploding with pleasure. I could feel the sudden flush of the alcohol (I forgot to mention, I'm a lightweight). I lick my lips, taking in the taste of the remaining liquid and smile sweetly at Kendrick. He has no idea what he's in for later.

From across our table he reaches out his hand for mine, so he must feel it too. I have to get myself under control. It's our first date. I can't give him the wrong idea. I'd love to see him naked, but not tonight...

That doesn't mean everything is off the table, I think to myself.

"So far tonight I've learned a lot about you; you don't like wine, you're confident, sexy and very intriguing," he says, taking in every bit of me.

"I've learned that you like to have control over even the smallest of things, so it must be a big deal for you to let me choose," I say matter of factly.

He smiles, "Was I too obvious?"

Instead of a response I slip my heel off and gently push my foot between his legs under the table. The only thing *obvious* about this situation is that he is hard and I gently nudged him with my foot. The fact that I'm the reason for his current erection in a certain section...made me hot. His face gives away that he is enjoying every bit of attention I am giving him. I decide I am going in for the kill.

I look around us to see if anyone is watching us. There is no one in sight, so I *accidentally* elbow my silverware so they would fall to the ground.

"Oops, how clumsy of me. I better grab those," I tell him.

I then slide under the table without anyone seeing me. I proceeded to crawl under the table towards his legs. I gently use my hands to spread his legs apart, unzip his fly and let his cock spring free. I grasp him in my hand and proceeded to take him in my mouth. He jerks ever so slightly. I think he was in shock that I was this ballsy.

ACCIDENTALLY IDENTICAL

I continue pleasuring him, plunging him as deep as my throat will allow. I can hear him biting back his noises. I circle the head with my tongue and then take him completely in my mouth. His cock is bigger than I expected, but I take it all.

The more I know he is enjoying it the more wet I become and that's without even being touched. I can feel the tension building... before I know it, I am lapping up all his hot juices, swallowing them all. He is very surprised. I feel his body stiffen as I hear the waitress arriving with our food.

TALIA HENDRIX | TEN

✳✳✳✳

I follow one of the pathways off deeper into the trees. My only hope was I could escape the thoughts that plagued me. Grant is like every other man I know. always used them before they could use me. The only thing they wanted was to hurt me or to destroy my heart. Not to mention to use me for their own pleasure.

The trail splits into a smaller beaten path. Following that path, with the sound of the leaves crunching under my feet, I am paying attention to each beautiful tree and the leaves that have started to change. It looked incredible, like a sunset. This was my favorite time of year and it could be my first fall in a new state.

I loved that I was so close to the ocean, even if it was a bit too chilly to swim in it. My thoughts continued arguing with each other. One wanted me to let Grant in and the other wanted me to push as far as I could until I was on the ledge of nothingness.

I wondered how it would feel to finally meet my sister. I'm positive that she doesn't know I exist. That alone seems to haunt and hurt me. I yearn for family and all that comes with it. I hope her life was happier than mine. I secretly want her acceptance. I stop and lean on the rough bark of the tree. I needed a few minutes to catch my breath, I had been running so much that I was out of breath.

Suddenly I hear a branch snap behind me.

I survey every direction, wondering if someone had followed me. What did they want? Did they know who I was, or what my intentions were?

"HEY! Tatum, I didn't expect to see you here today. Aria said you were on a date. Did it end early or something?" The stranger questions me.

I don't know who this person thought I was, but I didn't have time to find out.

"Sorry! Gotta Go!" I yelled in the stranger's direction.

I took off running, trying to remember exactly which way I needed to go to get back to Grant. The sense of urgency was real. I needed to get out of there, and fast. I didn't want someone chasing me, and I surely wasn't in any condition to outrun anyone.

I retraced my steps, and soon found myself on Huron Avenue. I opened the door to Grant's friendly greeting.

"I'm glad you made it back, babydoll. Is everything alright? You look like you've just ran a marathon," he points out.

Little did he know, I had.

"I'm fine, I just didn't want to miss the opportunity to taste your cooking skills that you keep bragging about," I say smiling. *Glad to be out of harm's way,* I thought to myself. .

"To think I thought you just missed my pretty face," he laughs.

I need to be consoled, so I walk closer and hug him. Probably tighter than I should have, and with more passion than I wanted to admit.

I murmur, "I did miss you, actually."

"I'm glad you missed me, babydoll. I really missed you too."

"It's just difficult for me to express myself sometimes. When I tend to get overwhelmed, I have a habit of running away from whatever is causing me stress."

"That's understandable, but please don't feel like you can't talk to me. I'm here if you're having any problems. I will always be here. More importantly, please don't run from me."

"Always is a long time to promise. Are you sure that you can live up to that?" I raise an eyebrow at him.

"I don't tend to say things I don't mean. I'm *not* your normal everyday

41

douchebag," he says as he stares, almost looking offended.

"Sorry, it's not you. I tend to have problems trusting people. Especially with everything I have going on."

"Well, I'll tell you what. Let's go eat this dinner, because I'm starved. We can talk or I can listen and you can talk. Tell me your every worry and every care. I'll listen." He means every word.

"Deal. Is there any wine in the house? After what I'm going to tell you, we will both need some!" I laugh.

He wraps his arm around me and guides me to the kitchen. I smile genuinely for the first time in a long time.

Maybe this wasn't as awful as my brain wanted me to think.

My frozen heart was starting to crack, but in a good way.

We sit down to the beautifully prepared dinner. Lasagna happens to be one of my favorites! He had no idea, but this was the greatest thing to happen. He knew me and he didn't even know it yet.

"I want to propose a toast, to us," Grant smiles.

We raise our glasses and clink, while staring deeply into each others' eyes. I've heard this is the correct way to toast.

I take a sip of the Merlot that he had poured into coffee mugs. He tried so hard, and he would never realize how much it meant to me.

I cut a piece of the lasagna, put it in my mouth and began chewing. I take in the wonderful flavors, realizing that he did a great job. I could taste every ingredient that he lovingly included. I believe he must be part Italian, because this is probably the best lasagna I've ever had. I take another bite and the tomato zest particularly dances with my taste buds.

I relish in every bite I take. I feel completely whole and filled to the brink. I take another sip of my wine and watch him devour his creation. He doesn't seem to completely chew his food, but he makes a glorious sound as he tastes it.

I refill my mug and ask him if he would like more. He nods to me and I pour until it is full.

"Promise me you won't run screaming when you find out what I want to tell you?" I plead.

"I promise."

"My mother died giving birth to me, I've been having dreams of her. Recently one of the dreams lead me here to Boston, where I met you."

"I suppose your subconscious has a lot it wants you to know," he nods for me to continue.

"My adoptive parents raised me until this point. I didn't have a great childhood. Nothing to write home about. My mom died and my adoptive father became abusive," I grimace.

"That son of a bitch! Is that why you came to Boston? He will never touch you again, Talia. I promise!"

"It's okay, I didn't get to the worst part. I was in quite a bit of trouble before I left. My ex cheated on me with my best friend, and I use that term loosely. I smashed his car with a baseball bat. I promise I'm not as psycho as this looks," I say taking a gulp.

"Sounds like he got what he deserved and I'm sorry that someone would do that to you, babydoll."

"I had a court appearance and had to pay a fine. Charles, my adoptive father, would've probably beat the hell out of me if I hadn't left. I stole his money, took everything that meant anything to me in the world and left," I confess.

"You still ended up in my arms at the end of the day. I'd say it's looking up for us."

"I've just been in a lot of trouble, I'm scared he will find me..." I fretted.

43

"I'll keep you safe as long as you stay with me," he offers with honesty in his eyes.

"I'm sorry. I shouldn't have dragged you into my drama. I have family I'm supposed to find; my mother Delia needs me to find them. I know this sounds crazy, talking to the dead or whatever the hell you want to call it. She visits me when I sleep. I thought I was an orphan..turns out I may have some family after all."

"Babydoll, I know we haven't known each other for long, but I think I'm really taking a serious liking to you," he smiles.

"Ditto, Grant," I say feeling my cheeks blush.

"I'm glad we are on the same page. Do you know where this family member lives?" He questions.

"No, I have no way of knowing if she's real or if it's just in my dreams. I have no concrete way of finding her, other than the fact that we are related. I don't even know her name," I say, withholding some of the truth.

"I'm really sorry, Talia. If you need help, I will gladly volunteer."

"You already are helping me more than you know. Giving me a place to stay has taken some of the edge off," I sigh.

"Not to change the subject, but since you're being open and honest...Where did you go today when you left?" He queried.

"I went on a run and ended up in a park... Kingsley Park. Do you know it? Of course you do! Well I ran on one of the trails there. I love seeing the changing of the seasons. Someone approached me, I'm not sure who they were. They thought I was someone else, that's why I was so scared and out of breath when I returned. I ran the whole way."

"That's very strange. You're okay though, right? This stranger didn't hurt you?"

"No, it seemed that they were very familiar with me. I don't know how, though. I've never been to that park."

"Just stick with me, it'll be safer for you that way," he smirks.

"I mean you did promise always, right? That wasn't just a cheesy pickup line?" I tease.

"Never- not with such a beautiful woman," his eyes met mine.

"Thank you!" I smile.

His eyes are gorgeous, I bet they make girls do stupid things… *Not me,* I decide.

He interrupts my thoughts. "Do you want to go sightseeing tomorrow? I can take you into Salem. I can use Mike's car and show you all the sights."

"That's where the magic and witches are, right?" I ask curiously.

"Salem is more than that, but it was made famous by The *Salem Witch Trials,*" he states.

"I know that. Sorry I didn't mean to come off as ignorant. I'm actually really fascinated by all of that… so to answer your question, YES I want to go!" I almost shout.

"Glad to hear it, it's only a 35 minute drive. We can stop by *Salem Willows* too. I know you'll love it," he takes another sip of wine.

"Sounds great, I'd love that."

"Do you mind if we continue this conversation outside?" He asks.

I stand up instead of answering and let him lead me out the front door. I close the screen door gently so it won't be too loud. I smile to myself as I see the chairs on the porch. This is the epitome of family life. The kids would be in their beds and the parents sneak away outside to spend some alone time. I sat on the wicker loveseat next to Grant. He wraps his arm around my shoulder, pulling me closer.

"I brought a blanket just in case you get cold," he says, pointing to the blanket.

"That would be fabulous," I say feeling very serene.

"Anything for you, doll." He grabs the velvety blanket and pulls me close. There's something about feeling someone else's heartbeat next to you that just makes you feel safe and loved.

We look up in the sky and at that very moment we see a bright streak of light moving rapidly across the darkness. It's then that I make a wish, on a shooting star.

I snuggle closer to Grant under the blanket and watch the wonderful light show the sky was providing. I wonder if my sister is watching as well.

Tatum Emerson | Eleven

xoxo

Shit! How was I going to get back up to the table?

Kendrick gently touched my head, my signal that the coast was clear. He zipped up his fly and I peeked out to make sure no one was watching. I slid back up to the table, gulped down the rest of my drink and noticed she had brought me another one. This waitress was astonishing. I would make sure she received a big tip.

Kendrick had a happy, sated look on his face and I smile back at him. He is in shock. I really don't think he was used to letting the woman have control over him. Breaking our eye contact, I take a look at my plate. I have definitely worked up an appetite, so I begin cutting my steak and eating small pieces.

"So are you always so daring?" he questions.

"It's the booze. I'm a lightweight; it loosens me up and I do things that I have only dreamt of," I wink.

"Are you finished? We can take the rest to go if you'd like. I'd love to see what's under your dress, so I can at least return the favor," he says smoothly.

I squirm in my seat. I have some sexual frustration and he would be glad to relieve it for me. But do I let him? That was the big question in my head. Could I stop if we got started? I opted to not open my legs so quickly.

I have already sucked him off until he came and kissed him on the first day we met. I was beginning to give myself a reputation I wasn't fully capable of upholding.

"I think I'm just going to spend the night alone. I have to wake up early and start a paper for class. I would like a second date, however. Maybe next time you can drop your silverware." I smile at him.

I didn't really have a paper to do, but he didn't know that.

Kendrick signaled the waitress for the check and to get us some to go boxes. Once dinner was paid for he made another offer, but this one I wasn't prepared to refuse;

"Would you at least like dessert? We can stop for some ice cream? Sound good?"

"Uh is that even a real question? Of course I do!!" I practically squeal.

We head out to the car, where Marcello graciously opens the door. We slide in, fasten seatbelts and let him know where we would like to head to next.

"Marcello, we would like to go to the best ice-cream parlor in town. Do you have any suggestions?" Kendrick questions.

"Sir, there are two that come to mind. Would you like to select between the two?" Marcello responds.

"Tatum, the choice is yours, darling," he says, looking at me.

"What are my choices, Marcello?" I query, smiling.

"J.P Licks or Juicy Spot Cafe, both of which are ranked the best in Boston," he declares.

"Marcello, I know we've just met, but will you select which one you think I would like best?" I hum.

"Yes Miss Tatum, it would be an honor."

"Surprise me then, please." I smile sweetly.

Kendrick runs his piano playing fingers over my knuckles causing a smile to emerge on my face. I enjoy the personal attention, but decisions were not my strong suit.

I turn to look at him; "Thank you for this. I've had a wonderful time. Most men don't go to the trouble, and I just want you to know that I appreciate that."

"It's not a problem. It's my pleasure.."

We pull up in front of Marcello's choice for ice cream. His choice was J.P Licks. It has a cute black and white cow with a pink ice cream scoop on a sugar cone. We walk in the brick building into a wonderful cafe style ice cream parlor. Just from eyeing the menu I see ice cream, coffee, yogurt, muffins, and breakfast. This place has everything. I was suddenly overwhelmed with choices I didn't know if I could make.

I notice the front area is decorated in red barn wood, and there is also what appeared to be a green wall of grass. I had to laugh, I had never seen anything like it. The lights above us looked like partially inflated balloons. It also had a bar area, where patrons could eat their goodies and look out on the wonders of the city. I loved the quaint feeling to this place.

I can't believe that I've never been here before. I would have to be sure to thank Marcello.

I take a look out the window to see Marcello with the car parked across the street. *That's a good way to keep an eye on your vehicle,* I thought to myself.

There were a few people in front of us so we both waited patiently while scanning the menu. When it was finally our turn we walked up but with so many decisions I couldn't just decide on one thing.

"Hi! Welcome To J.P Lick's. What can I get you today?" she asks us with a smile.

I chime in, "I would like a Thin Mint and the El Diablo Hot Chocolate please."

"I would like two Frozen Hot Chocolates and an El Diablo Hot Chocolate, " Kendrick says with his winning smile.

"On second thought can I add two adult t-shirts as well? A medium in the pink and large in the black one, please?" He adds.

"Large, please. I like them a little baggy," I interrupt.

"Two large it is then!" He says, finding humor in me.

"So what are the t-shirts for?" I tilt my head to ask.

"I figured you needed a souvenir from your first time here."

"I appreciate that. Question: why did you order *two* frozen hot chocolates?" I smile at him.

"I ordered one for Marcello. He did an amazing job picking this place. Don't you think?"

I nodded, "He really did! That's sweet of you. Does he just drive you around, or is there more to his job description?"

"He's my driver, but his main job is security. He's more of a bodyguard than anything else. He's been with me since I started working in my father's investment company, P.S. Trust & Invest. We buy and invest money in companies that are failing, and we also help companies with their investments as well."

"If this works out well enough you can give me a personal tour of your office," I say with a wink.

"I feel the need to be completely honest with you. I'm not sure what it is, but I'm drawn to you like a moth to a flame…" he whispers.

"I'm not that special, Kendrick. Don't spill all your dirty little secrets yet. Let's get through a second or maybe a third date before you show me your skeletons…"

"So you already want to see me again? We've only been to dinner and ice cream," he says as he sips on his El Diablo.

I take a spoon full of my Thin Mint ice cream. Mmm. It really tasted like the cookie. I was going to have to come back and see if they have this in a pint or a gallon even.

"This is going to sound weird, but I love listening to you eat," he chuckles.

I couldn't help but smile, "Thank you? I think…."

"I just enjoy the sounds you make when you're tasting something delicious.." he adds.

I bit my lip, unsure of what to say next. From the corner of my eye I spotted Marcello.

"Sir, we need to head out. Something has happened and I need to get you both home now," he says with seriousness in his tone.

We both hurry, grab our things and leave with Marcello. He keeps eyeing the area, checking for some unknown threat that I never would have known existed.

He opens the door quickly and we both slid into our seats. He jumps in the driver's seat and high tails it out of there. When I look over my shoulder to see why we were running I see a black SUV following us, too close for comfort. Marcello drives in and out of traffic trying to lose whoever was tailing us. Kendrick pulls me close to him while angrily dialing a number on his cell.

"Someone is fucking tailing us. Please have security waiting when we get there. This is urgent; I have a guest in the vehicle. This is unacceptable! Is there anyway of finding out who this is?" He is practically yelling through the phone.

I'm starting to get scared. Things like this didn't happen to people like me. Marcello speeds up, once again passing and cutting people off. The black SUV rams into the back of our vehicle. My head jerks forward and I slip onto the floor in front of me. I should've probably worn my seatbelt. We left in such a hurry I didn't get a chance.

"Marcello! LOSE this fucking asshole! Get us back to the estate, NOW!" Kendrick demands.

We had to be going close to 90 mph now, weaving quickly through traffic. We turn off several times, finally losing the black SUV. We speed all the way to Kendrick's.

I look out the sunroof, mesmerized by all the stars and the next thing I know everything went blurry and I lose consciousness.

51

CHARLES HENDRIX | TWELVE

✗✗✗✗

FUCK! I lost them! She thinks she can steal from me and just get away like that? Little bitch! She doesn't know what's coming for her. I saw her get in the car with the suit... she's probably draining his money too. Filthy whore is probably fucking him for a payday.

She stole $4,000 from me, took her shit and took off. I never would have found her, but I got lucky. The first place I went to look was the train station. I showed her picture to the woman at the window and she recognized her. Sure she did. Who wouldn't remember that slutty blonde hair and those puke green eyes. She was very careful to cover her tracks, just not careful enough to disguise herself.

I stole her ex-boyfriend's SUV, hoping that would scare her enough to bring her out of hiding. That Julian is a fucking schmuck. He probably thinks Talia stole his SUV.

I had been parked on the street for about an hour, not even looking to find her. I was looking for a hotel in the area when I saw her going into the place with the cow on the logo. I watched, copied down the plate number and waited for my chance.

I don't know what Amelia ever saw in her.

She thought we couldn't get pregnant and I never got the chance to tell her the real reason behind that fact. I made sure I couldn't have any. Snip, snip and it was a done deal; no kids for this man.

I didn't have any desire to share my Amelia. She was mine...the best part of me. She's gone now and it's all Talia's fault.

ACCIDENTALLY IDENTICAL

I don't even remember how Amelia found out about Talia, but she did. If she weren't around I would've been able to save my love. She hid her sickness in order to protect that little bitch. She stole the last piece of her I had; Amelia's golden heart locket. The locket was gone with the money. She came home with Talia and the locket, so I assumed she had it made, but I asked no questions. She wanted a child that I couldn't give her, so I let our family adopt the orphan. Biggest mistake of my fucking life.

Amelia protected Talia every chance she got. Anytime she would get in to trouble, we'd bail her out; she'd make excuses for our daughter's behavior. I'll never forget the last words my wife said to me: "*Take care of Talia. Protect her; she's more important than you know. Tell her I love her. I love you Charles.*"

It was always about *her.*

The selfish slut stole the love of my life. I'll fucking kill her if I get the chance, but not before I make her little boyfriend pay up. I wonder how much she is worth to him?

TALIA HENDRIX | THIRTEEN

✕✕✕✕

Delia appeared, gently stroking my face until my eyes slowly opened. Was I dreaming? As she nods I sense trouble..She is trying to warn me. Why am I here? I was just laying with him..She continued gently running her fingers through my hair as her eyes welled up with tears. She wants to protect us both. What's wrong? She revealed the locket in the palm of her other hand and pointed to the picture of my sister. Trouble...How can I find her? Cow? What do you mean cow? I don't understand....

I wake up in the arms of Grant, who is in the process of carrying me to bed.

"I don't know what the cow means…" I mumble in my sleepy haze.

Grant leans down and kisses my forehead, "The cow will be fine, let's go to bed."

He gently places me on the queen sized bed, then pulls the covers over me.

"Goodnight, babydoll," he says kissing my lips.

He fixes the other side of the comforter and begins stripping to change into his pajamas. White t-shirt and some plaid blue and orange boxers. Couldn't go wrong with that.

I peek at him through slanted sleepy eyes. He is so sexy. I catch a brief glimpse of his chiseled abs. They make me want to trace each and every one of them with my tongue.

I smile to myself. "Grant will you hurry up, I'm cold and I need you. I think I may stay warmer if you keep that shirt off…."

"Yes, impatient woman. All you had to do was ask," he says sliding off the fresh shirt.

"Is this better?" He asks as he runs his hand up and down his chest briefly..

"Mmm, hell yes it is. Come here please," I shiver.

Grant slides into bed and pulls me tightly against his chest. The warmth of his body is such a comfort. I can't remember the last time I actually felt safe. I turn my body so we are face to face with one another. He wraps his strong arms around me and rests our foreheads on one another.

"Talia…" he whispers to me.

"Mhmm," I mumble.

"Do you believe in love at first sight?" he asks. I stare deep into his eyes and before I can stop myself I tell him;

"I've never been in love, so I wouldn't know. If I had to have a comparable moment of what love would feel like it would be you."

Grant tries to hide his smile as he nuzzles my neck. He lightly caresses his nose up and down against my neck. I let a small moan escape my lips. It's been so long since I've been touched by a man like this…He gently runs his hand through the ends of my hair lightly trailing his index finger down my face. I smile as the possibility of someone loving me doesn't seem so far fetched anymore.

I lean my face into him and gently plant a kiss on his neck.

"I'll win you over, you'll see babydoll. I'll make you mine," he smiles.

Still very much half asleep I mutter; "I love you too, Grant. Goodnight.."

He smiles, probably blaming the wine for my sudden confession. I won't remember it in the morning.

I drift off to sleep in his arms.

I looked around for her, I couldn't find her. Where was she? She was always here.. maybe it's the trouble she spoke of earlier. I concentrated on Delia, everything went blurry and suddenly I was not in my own dream anymore. She was watching over a woman who was laying on her back. I wasn't able to see who it was before it all faded to black..

GRANT THOMAS | FOURTEEN

✗✗✗✗

As I carried her up the stairs she started talking in her sleep. It was really adorable. I tried not to wake her, but with every step she seemed heavier. I pretended to understand what she was talking about. It was something about a cow, as if maybe she grew up near a farm or something. She would explain later, I'm sure.

I thought it was kind of funny that she felt the need to ask for me to remove my shirt. Luckily I take pretty good care of my body and don't mind showing it off from time to time. I climbed into the bed with her and pulled her to me. This girl has me whipped. I don't know how she is doing it, but I think I'm falling for her. I know guys aren't supposed to admit this type of shit, but I can't help it anymore.

I asked her if she believed in love at first sight, how cheesy of me. I hope she doesn't remember all of this in the morning, even though I'll never forget. She also let it slip that she loves me. That should scare the shit out of me, but looking into her mesmerizing emerald eyes makes everything better. They are so damn hypnotizing, I don't think I could tell her no if I wanted to. As much of a class act as I portray myself to be, if she wanted me, I would give her exactly what she wanted.

I *think* I love her too. No, I *know* I do. She doesn't realize it yet, but she loves me too.

I let her warmth take over me. I haven't had a girl in bed with me in months. The last real serious relationship I've had was with a girl freshmen year. We dated for two years, and I was sure she was the one. On the night I had planned to propose to her she cut me off and told me she wasn't happy with me anymore. She had been sleeping with someone else and she wanted to be with him. Guys don't talk about how they feel when women break them, but I was devastated. Especially when I found out it was Graham she was sleeping with...

That's actually when I started coming to visit Uncle Mike. He loved the company and I needed a distraction. I transferred schools to get away from Tiffany. I couldn't stand seeing her with anyone else. I sure as hell couldn't look Graham in the face, I probably would've punched him. What did I expect though? She was older than me, she was a junior and I was just some freshman that could make her feel good temporarily. I'm probably too nice. I worshipped the ground she walked on and she just walked all over me. Graham is the complete opposite of me. He uses them and then loses them. Women always love the bad boy, and that was Graham. You're supposed to count on family, but he's an asshole.

I'm really blessed for it though....If she didn't fuck me over I never would've met Talia. Just a mention of Talia's name makes my dick perk up. I'm not the type of guy who uses a woman, if anything I make sure she gets hers before I get mine. What can I say, I'm a rare gem. At least my mother raised one of us right.

I'm a family man, I don't imagine myself with a bunch of women. I just want the one that I can have kids and spend my life with. Tiffany never fit that description. You know what they say: you can't turn a hoe into a housewife... If you could everyone would be doing it. Graham's the poor bastard who's stuck with her, especially now that she had his son. She tried to pin that on me, luckily I got out with a *you are not the father*. A paternity test proved what I knew already.

TATUM EMERSON | FIFTEEN

xoxo

Danger… My mother woke me. She kneeled down next to me stroking my hair gently. I open my eyes and see her clearer than I ever have. Her white and blonde curly locks flow down her shoulders into a loose fishtail braid. She's dressed completely in a white flowy dress, but her eyes shine a bright blue. Delia. What are we doing here? What happened? You passed out…You're safe for now, my love. Your sister. Find your sister. She tells me with her eyes. A tear rolls down her beautiful angelic face. I reach up to wipe it away and my hand feels like ice. I'm dreaming, this is all a hallucination. This isn't real, is it? Yes it is. We communicate. I'm not sure how but I know exactly what she is saying without even hearing a word. Have you seen my sister? How can I find her? Kingsley…

"Tatum, Tatum! Are you alright?" Kendrick pleads.

I slowly open my eyes, "What happened?"

"You must've passed out from all the craziness. We are safe now. Marcello lost the person who was following us and has gotten us back to the estate," he explains.

He's holding an icepack on my head, I'm really glad, because it hurts right now. I must've hit it pretty hard on something.

"You really had me scared. I thought something had happened to you," Kendrick confesses.

"I'm fine, it's just a bump on the head right?" I cringe.

"Yes, thankfully it's just a bump on the head. I almost called our personal doctor to come have a look at you," Kendrick fretted.

I look around, realizing how differently the two of us live. He had a grand hall, a chandelier while I had a leased vehicle, a crappy little apartment and my roommate. I love my best friend, but I'd kill for a mansion like this. Something has changed about him since earlier. He seems genuinely concerned for me. I like his personal attention. It feels good to have someone take care of you sometimes.

"I'm having my security team look into who was following us," he announces.

"So far all we know is that the car was stolen from Scranton, Pennsylvania. A Julian Monroe has reported it as stolen. He said in the police report that it was most likely his ex-girlfriend a *'Talia Hendrix'*. She disappeared a week or so ago. Nobody has seen her or heard from her since." Kendrick reports.

"I don't know who it was, but it was scary enough. They rammed right into the back of your car. Is she an ex-girlfriend you pissed off or something? I can only assume she was after you. I have no idea who that woman is…" I declare.

"Well the only thing I can be sure of is that you will be safe with me. Marcello can go pick up some of your clothes from your place. You need to stay with me tonight for safety's sake."

"I literally have known you for all of two seconds and now you want me to stay the night at your luxurious mansion? Am I dreaming right now or something? This only happens in movies. For all I know Kendrick, you could've staged this whole thing so I would sleep with you…" I accused.

"Sweetheart, you already went down on me in the restaurant, why would you assume that I need to go to such lengths to get you into my bed?" he says smugly.

"WOAH! I can't believe you just went there. I'll remember that. Sorry I thought you were different. Obviously you're not Mister Right," I snort.

"Tatum that's not how I meant it…I meant I've had plenty opportunities to get you naked. You were just passed out in my house. I'm not a pervert, I like my women to enjoy the experience as much as I do. I'm sorry that I came off so short and harsh with you," he says, his eyes seering a hole through my soul.

"I just need to sleep this off. Do you have an extra bedroom I can sleep in? I mean obviously YOU DO, your house is a mansion...Which room is mine?" I grimace.

"It's the one right next to mine. I'll show you," he says as he wraps his arm in mine and helps me up.

"Does your head feel okay? You're not dizzy or anything right?" he asks, obviously concerned.

"It just hurts a little bit but I think I can make it."

I open the door to enter one of his many bedrooms. Upon entering the room, the first thing that draws my attention is the large four poster bed. Dark Mahogany wood, polished with a shine so bright you could see the chandelier in it. Whoever decorated for him had a delightful violet, grey and white intricate pattern displayed over the comforter. It's accented with pillows to match. At the end of the bed is a chastise that is the height of the bed. The top of it is silky in a beige color with small buttons criss crossing the design. The wall behind the bed is painted a slightly different darker shade of grey. It has a black and white photograph of books on a shelf. I'm not familiar with the artist but I love their work. To my left is a fireplace that is made of what appears to be marble and brick. Looking to my right I see the beautiful bay window with a built in readers nook. It's like this room was built just for me.

There are two other doors in the room. I open one to reveal a walk in closet that's mostly empty except for the linens. I walk in a little further and see another door. Who puts a door in the closet? That's strange. It has my interest peaked, that's for sure. I push the door and it opens inward. It looks like a hallway or some sort of hidden passage. Even though I know better, I continue walking through it and the door closes behind me. Shit! That's not good. The passageway leads me to another door, so I open it. I think I've hit the jackpot! The passageway has lead me into what appears to be his personal library. It looks like it could be almost as big as the public library. I wonder: does he even come in here to read at all?

Almost as if he hears my thoughts, Kendrick clears his throat.

"I'm glad you found it okay. I was worried when I didn't see you right away. I figured you would want to venture around. I told you about the library and here we are."

"Sorry I wasn't trying to snoop. Seriously though...Who puts a door in a closet?" I ask.

"When you don't want something found, the closet may be your best bet. It took you awhile to find it. So I would assume that it served the purpose. So what do you think?"

"Well, it's pretty amazing! Do you come in here and read at all? Have you read all these?" I question as I scan the many shelves.

"I come in here often. Especially after a hard day at the office. It's my place of solitude."

"You didn't answer my question completely...." I point out.

"No I have not read all of them. I'm a very busy man, when I'm not out saving damsels in distress," he smirks.

"I am not a damsel, and I am not in distress. You're over exaggerating! I'm not rich enough to have people after me," I add.

"You never know, maybe one day you could be Mrs. Sanders," he jokes.

"I'm pretty sure that's your mom's name...."

"My mother's name is actually Pearl. Can you guess her favorite gemstone?"

"I bet she wears a pearl necklace all the time too, right?"

"You've met my mother????" he chuckles.

"Sure have, every rich woman with whom I've ever made an acquaintance. I assure you I must know thousands..." I roll my eyes as sarcasm drips from my mouth.

"Sarcasm must be a second language for you. Would you be interested in visiting my home movie theatre? We can finish our date."

"You're kidding..You have a movie theatre in your mansion?? That's rich alright... To answer your question, yes I would."

"What movie do you have in mind? I can get anything you'd like to see.." he bites his lip, regretting the last part.

"Before we watch a movie, I need to call Aria and my boss. I'm scheduled tomorrow and I need to let my bestie know I won't be home."

"Your purse is on the end table by the bed. Your cellphone should still be in there."

"Come back to the library when your done with your calls. I'll see you soon!" he says as he walks out the way he came.

I walk through the passageway to my room again. Sitting on the edge of the bed, I rifle through my purse, finally finding my phone. I press the on button and find many missed calls from Aria. I first press it and let it ring. She picks up on the second ring.

"Tatum are you okay?! You aren't home. I've been so worried. I've been trying to get ahold of you but your phone went straight to voicemail!!! Where the hell are you?!" she says panicked.

"I'm fine, don't worry. I lost my phone, I'm at Kendrick's house. I'm safe I promise," I explain.

"Does Mister Right have room in his mansion for me to stay too? Tatum someone broke into our apartment... The police just left and I'm scared to stay here alone."

"Someone broke in? Are you okay? You weren't home were you? What's going on?" I gasped.

"I wasn't home...Tatum both our rooms are completely trashed. I don't know if they took anything or not. It looks like they were looking for something. I really have no idea...I just don't wanna stay here. Do you think he would be okay with me crashing? I can pack a bag now…"

"Let me ask. Pack your bag, fill one for me too and I'll call you right back."

I head back to the library looking for Kendrick. He is seated in his comfy reading chair.

"Kendrick, we have a problem. Someone broke into my apartment and it's completely trashed, Aria wants to know if she can come stay here. She's really scared to stay alone. Would that be okay?" I plead.

"I can't believe that! Of course she can stay. You both are welcome as long as you need. I'll send Marcello to get her."

I pull him to me and give him a big hug. I would never be able to thank this man, he's already done too much for me.

"Thank you, I don't know why this person is after us.. I'm really scared Kendrick. What if they find us here?" I whimpered.

"Honey, if by some chance this person did find you I have a full-time security team, including bodyguards. Marcello is my best, he's been with me the longest."

"I'll call her back. I told her to pack a bag, so I'm sure this will make her feel better." I admitted, grabbing the phone and pressing the button.

"Aria, he's sending a car to come get you. Be ready. He said we are welcome for as long as we need."

"I have both bags packed… How long will it take him to get here?" she asked anxiously.

"Should be about 10 minutes. His name is Marcello. He will come up to get you and our bags," I explained.

"I'll see you soon!" she said with relief.

Aria Morretti | Sixteen

xoxo

I just got done with my last class on campus and decide to head back home. I didn't really feel like staying with my parents. I was too exhausted for the drama that I would face there. Tatum should be home from her date by now, so we should be able to relax, gossip and snack when I get there.

The whole hour ride home went quickly, I was excited to hear how Tatum's date went. She had some instant connection with him. I hope she realizes I need to meet him to approve. Have to make sure he isn't a douchebag like Reed. She always had bad luck with men; they'd use her and abuse her. I wasn't having it, I'm really protective of her. She's like the sister I never got to have. I just got stuck with an older brother, Lorenzo.

My brother is what you would call the golden child. He can't do any wrong. Me, on the other hand, I have my fair share of wrongs. My love life isn't too great, and my ma tends to remind me every time I come to stay with them. I got tired of explaining why I was chronically single. She made it seem like life was going to end if I didn't meet and marry a nice Italian man. Let's not get started on the baby department, I can hear her voice in my head, *'When are ya gonna make me a grandma?'*.

I parked in my usual spot and I see Tatum's car. Good, I'm glad she's home. I head upstairs only to find our door broken open. Fuck! Why does this shit happen to me? I poked my head in the condo:

"I have a gun, so you betta get the fuck outta here!" I shout into the darkness.

I figure they don't know if I do or not. The place is fucking trashed. Why do people have to destroy shit that doesn't belong to them?! It looks like a hurricane just came in and wiped everything out. All of our pictures on the wall were busted. Looks like someone punched them. Who would do this? I try calling Tatum, she's not here. It goes directly to voicemail. I try again, same thing... voicemail...I try at least 10 times to get ahold of that bitch! I hope nothing happened to her. I don't know why the fuck she isn't answering me.

What if whoever did this comes back and what the hell were they trying to find? It doesn't look like anything is actually missing, it's just destroyed. I decide it's probably best if I don't touch anything and just call 911. With my hands still shaking I dial the emergency line. Dispatch lets me know it won't be long and keeps me on the line until they arrive, just in case.

TALIA HENDRIX | SEVENTEEN

✗✗✗✗

I wake up to the smell of sausage, bacon and eggs. Mmm smells like he's making breakfast. I pull my hair into a ponytail and go downstairs to the kitchen in my pjs.

Grant doesn't hear me, so he continues cooking a smorgasbord of breakfast foods.

This gives me time to admire his body. He's still shirtless. Oh shit! I asked him to take off his shirt, didn't I? I shake my head, what was I thinking? Besides the obvious I mean…

Grant's got a slight tan, no tan lines that I can see. He must work outside a lot because he doesn't seem like the fake and bake type. I move my eyes down his body to take a good look at him. I see his toned and sculpted forearms, then my eyes fall on his broad back. My eyes then trail to his tight, firm ass. It's sexy enough that it makes me wanna smack it, but I refrain and continue to study this *spectacular* specimen.

He grabs some orange juice out of the fridge. I watch him stretch slightly to grab it. I wipe the invisible drool off my face.

"Hey there lady!" Mike says, scaring the shit out of me from behind.

I jump and turn quickly. I have been discovered…

BUSTED! Damnit! I wanted to look some more.

Well, I suppose at least I can get some food now.

"Hey Babydoll, you been there long?"

I bit my lip and tried to hide the smirk; "Uh no, just got here. It smells amazing, doesn't it Mike?"

"Sure does. Didn't think Grant knew how to cook so well." Mike says, patting my shoulder.

"I take it you didn't try the lasagna from last night Mike?" I chuckled.

"No. I'm actually allergic to the cheese...What's that they call it? Cheese disease something or other..."

"That's awful, I'm sorry! Cheese is wonderful...Everyone should be able to experience its greatness," I say, realizing he is more aware of himself today.

"By the way Mike, I'm Talia. We didn't really get a proper introduction. Thank you for letting us stay here. It's really kind of you."

"I know who you are, I'm not that old. You're welcome, sweetheart. It's my pleasure. I really do like the company," he repeats what he said last night.

Grant smiles, "Do either of you plan on eating? Or are you going to chat the morning away?"

"No need to be sassy, fix me a plate, please?" I stick my tongue out at him.

Grant hands a full plate of food to Mike and hands the second plate to me.

I turn my head and make direct contact with his eyes. I wiggle my eyebrows at him.

"Thanks, it looks wonderful, honey."

"You're welcome. I'm planning on taking you to Salem today. We can have some fun, take in the sights and then head to Salem Willows to see the sunset," he says while his eyes remain fixed on mine.

"Sounds wonderful. I'll eat my food and then I'll go get ready," I smile.

I take a bite of the scrambled eggs he had prepared. Mmmm he is such a good cook. Why is he single again? Remind me to find this out. Taking a sip of my orange juice I look over at Mike. He looks content this morning, less agitated. He appears to be enjoying his food as well. He probably didn't eat this well when he was alone.

"Grant where did you learn to cook so well?" I was intrigued.

"My mother taught me. She said I needed to learn how to woo women the right way. I've never met a woman that doesn't appreciate great food."

"Damn right! Women love food. Then again so do men… " Mike stammered.

I chuckled, "I love the way you think, Mike."

"I'm glad to see when I leave Grant will be taken care of by such a wonderful, knowledgeable man. Not many can figure a woman out the way you have," I say with a wink.

"You're welcome back here anytime…. Well shit! I suppose you're welcome wherever the hell they put me…" his eyes sadden.

I reached for his hand, "I'll make sure to come visit no matter where you are Mike."

"I'm glad he's met someone special like you, sweetie. I hope he knows how lucky he is."

Grant chimes in, "Yes I am very lucky. I hope she won't grow tired of me."

"Tired of you? Never Grant. Especially if you keep cooking me food….Are you as good at baking? A woman can't resist dessert!" I smile. I couldn't remember the last time I felt this way.

"I did make some cinnamon rolls, too. Do those count?" he lifts his eyebrow at me.

"Oh HELL YES! I love cinnamon rolls! With cream cheese frosting??" I cross my fingers…

"Yes, it's actually homemade cream cheese frosting. Made it from scratch, I hope you like it," he chuckles.

69

"Where are they?? Now I want one…Pretty please?" I beg…

He grabs the spatula and puts two piping hot cinnamon rolls on my plate. YES! Score! Yup, it's official, I love him…..I mean Food.. I love FOOD..Grant is good enough to eat though...

I take a giant bite of the cinnamon roll, getting frosting all over my face. Wiping my face with my napkin, I take in the cinnamon gooey goodness. If he keeps this up he may send me into a sugar coma in no time. This frosting was super creamy and rich. I'm eating too much, my stomach is too full. I belch...Oh shit!

"Excuse me, sorry about that," my cheeks flush with embarrassment.

"It's natural; everybody does it, I mean am I really supposed to believe that women aren't full of gas?" he jokes.

"No, we don't 'fart'; we toot. Don't you know anything?" I try not to smile.

"Alright, I better not slack off anymore. I'll head upstairs and get a shower," I tell them.

I head up the stairs, grab my bag and head into the bathroom. I didn't have a lot of time to get ready. He probably wanted to head out. I was excited to get to see Salem for the first time. I've heard wonderful, magical things about the town. I hope that I stick around long enough to see Salem in October next year. I hear they have wonderful festivities for Halloween. I really wanted to meet some real witches and see all the amazing shops I've heard so much about.

TATUM EMERSON | EIGHTEEN

XOXO

I was waiting for Aria to get here. Kendrick had to take some calls in his office, so I stayed out in the foyer waiting for them. The door finally opened and Aria came running at me. She pulled me in for a bigger than usual hug.

"I'm glad that you're in one piece," Aria worried.

"I'm here. I'm glad that Marcello got you.. Where is he, by the way?" I question.

"He's doing his rounds….You didn't tell me he was *gorge-ous*! He's fucking hot. Why didn't you tell me?!" she whines.

"First off, I didn't tell you because I haven't spoken to you all day and I just met him TODAY. Secondly, I didn't know I needed to send you an alert every time a good looking guy is around…" I cringe.

"Yup, I expect that.. I am single….available..and alone.." she winks.

I cut her off, "Yes I'm very well aware, and horny too I see."

"No judgement zone, remember?" she whines.

"I'm free of judgement, especially with all the sex toys you try to hide in the closet." I laugh obnoxiously.

"Shhh! What if your boyfriend hears that? Can't let him know that.."

"He's not my boyfriend. We were on our first date tonight," I state.

"Sounds like boyfriend material to me. I've never had a first date that invited my friend and I to stay in his swanky mansion," she encourages.

"Hell, I've never had a first date that had a mansion!" I blurt out.

71

"I just can't believe all this, people breaking into our home, people following you and crashing into the back of Kendrick's car...Did they find out who it was?"

I shook my head. "No, not really just that the car that followed us and then hit us was stolen.."

"That is very strange that they haven't found anybody. Did the car disappear? Did anyone follow it? I hope they found out who did this. It's really upsetting!" She frowns, a deep sadness in her eyes.

I hugged her tight."I know, but we get to stay here at Kendrick's in the meantime. At least we will be safe here. I'm sure you could get to know Marcello a little better. I'm not sure if he's available or not. Better find out!" I try to change the subject.

"That's true, can't get sexy if he's got a wife around. I don't do that shit, I'm not a homewrecker. I prefer my men unattached, the only ring they need to have is one to put on my damn finger!" She declared with absolutely no sugar coating.

"You crack me up Aria, you know that right? My life would be so boring without you and someone trying to chase us." I laugh probably harder than I should've. Laughing was better than the alternative, which was crying. Crying was more messy.

"It's not my fault! I'm only celibate (sell-a-bit) so he can buy a bit," she threw her head back laughing.

I couldn't help but laugh myself , neither of us realized it, but Marcello had heard everything.

He smiled from ear to ear at us, "Ladies, for the curious minds, I am *unattached* as you call it," he then turned and winked in Aria's direction.

I've never seen her face turn that shade of red before. Hmm, maybe this would be an interesting turn of events for her.

"Marcello, you're like a fucking Ninja...I like it," she retorts while biting her lip.

"Thank you Miss Morretti. I'd like to think that's a compliment. You're a sneaky minx yourself, if you don't mind me saying."

"Well if you're prepared enough, do you wanna go spend some time together?" She raises her eyebrow slightly as if challenging him, daring him to say yes.

"Of course Miss Morretti, I would love that," he challenges her right back.

"Aria, my name's Aria. You're Marcello or should I call you Mr...what's your last name? If we are going to get to know each other, I would like us to be on a first name basis."

"Of course, Aria. It's Anzalone" he says staring deep into her eyes.

While they weren't looking I snuck away. I wanted to give them time to learn more about each other. They looked cute together. I wonder if they realized that.

I crept through the house and started on a search for Kendrick's office. Eventually I found the door to what I thought was his office. Turns out it was his home theater. I walked in and made my way down the red velvet carpet to the front row and plopped my body into a seat.

The seat reclined so I stretched out and got myself comfortable. Next thing I know I see the projector turn on. I turn to see Kendrick heading down the red carpet, hands full with two drinks and a big bag of popcorn.

I turn around and realize he has a whole concession stand in the back of his theater. Wow...

"Hey sweetheart, thought I'd find you in here. Sorry about going off and leaving you alone," he said his voice lulling me into relaxation.

"It's perfectly fine, I think Aria and Marcello are *'getting to know'* one another. I hope that's alright, I may or may not have encouraged it."

I bite my lip.

"That's interesting for sure. Everybody deserves to be happy." He slides in to the seat next to me and hands me my beverage.

"Hope you don't mind sweet tea. The soda machine is being maintenanced and the popcorn has chocolate and white chocolate drizzled in there."

"You're wonderful… that's heavenly." I pop a few pieces into my mouth. Mmmm.

"You sure know how to please a lady don't you?" I smile.

"The only thing I wanna do right now is please you…" he whispers while holding my gaze.

I lean close, close enough to feel his breath against my skin. Our lips touch then embrace in a passionate kiss.

I'm the one to break our kiss. Didn't want anything getting too carried away, I came in here to watch a movie, not star in one…

"So what are we watching?" I pause and look at the screen.

"You drive me crazy woman. I love it, you challenge me in ways no woman has."

"*The Notebook*! I love this movie! So far tonight you've managed to guess at least three different things I love. How do you do it? Did you bug my apartment or something?" I laugh, then I realize he probably could if he wanted to….

"This is actually my mother's favorite as well. I think the two of you would get along." He says as he pops a few kernels into his mouth.

We move the armrest in the middle so it is out of our way and we snuggle close. He puts his right arm around me and we begin watching the movie..

We get halfway through and the blubbering starts. Tears streamed down my face, I wanted to be a bird! I look to see if he saw me ugly crying and if I didn't know any better I'd say he was tearing up himself!

He grabs our popcorn bag and drinks. He walks up to refill them not taking his eyes off the screen. I was impressed. Never did I think Mr. Hot Shot would ever be blubbering on a first date with me. It's clear he had wined and dined before, but this was a new level for him.

"Here babe, I put lots of both chocolates on this batch," he smiles, handing me the popcorn and my replenished tea.

I may have to keep him around...I was feeling like a queen and I liked it!

"Are you crying over there?" I turn to look at him.

"No, I must have something in my eye..." he says wiping his eyes.

"Uh huh, sure." I snuggle closer to him. I was okay with a sensitive man, that means he probably considers how I feel, I hoped.

"Must've been some dust or something," he tries to hard to explain. Looking around there's no way this place has even seen dust. It's immaculate. I'm sure his maids take good care of the house.

TALIA HENDRIX | NINETEEN

✕✕✕✕

I finished getting ready and head down the stairs. I'm excited to go on this adventure.

I grabbed my bag and headed out the door to meet Grant at the car.

"Looks like you're ready to roll," he says smiling big as he opens the door for me.

"Yes I am! Let's do it," I say while sliding into the passenger seat of Mike's black *Volvo 850.*

I buckle my seat belt waiting for Grant to hop in.

"Our drive to *Salem Willows* is going to be like 41 minutes according to the GPS," he informs me.

I smile over at him and place my hand on his thigh with a supporting squeeze.

"So tell me more about your family, Grant." I nudge.

"Well my parents live in Gloucester. It's just a short 45 minute commute up north. Maybe I'll take you there one day to meet them, if you're lucky," he laughs a heartfelt laugh.

"So what are their names? Are you guys close? Any siblings?" I was interested, almost more than I should. I just couldn't help it.

"My mom's name is Selena. She's one of those mom's that sends you care packages more than you care to admit."

"Did she write your name in your underwear as a kid?" I burst out laughing.

"She may have….and my dad's name is Gordon, he was pretty great too.

Unfortunately he's not supportive of my dreams for my life."

"The dreaded dream killer Mister Gordon, huh? You turned out okay, though. He didn't fuck you up that bad." I nudged him, letting him know it was a joke and to relax.

"I have two siblings…. a brother and a sister. My brother is twenty-five the same age as me, and my sister Mandie is in her early thirties. I don't really get along with my brother and my sister lives in Plymouth with her husband Shawn and their kids. I haven't spoken to my brother in a long while. He was screwing my ex-girlfriend and got her pregnant. That makes me an uncle, I'm afraid," he says in monotone.

"WOW! That's awful, but it sounds like he did you a favor. If she slept with your brother that easily then you know she wasn't worth keeping around. My ex did the same, minus the getting her pregnant part. I've been cheated on a lot," I say, my tone sounding more serious now.

"So what about you, babydoll? Tell me more about you.."

"Well let's see….I'm a gemini, I love walks on the beach and I love being spanked," I smile.

"We should play 20 Questions at this rate… We would learn a whole lot about each other then. Are you game?" he encourages.

"Okay, shoot. What's question number one?"

"Let's start with something simple: what's your favorite flower?" he challenges.

"That's easy, you'd never know it but I'm more of a snapdragon type woman. I love the red ones best."

"Your turn babydoll, what's your first question for me?"

I thought for a minute then asked, "What's your favorite color?"

"That's easy, the color of your eyes. Emerald. I can stare into them all day, they are so beautiful.."

I laugh out loud, "I don't know, should that answer be accepted? The jury says Ding Ding Ding YES!"

"Well now you know my favorite color, what's yours?"

"Red, the color of my favorite kind of wine," I announce with a wink.

I was running out of regular questions. "Favorite holiday?"

"I'd have to say Thanksgiving because of the family time and the food. I go to my parents' house and help my mom with the cooking. We make a whole day of it. Traditions, maybe you should come this year? It's not too far away," he hints at the suggestion of me staying longer.

"Maybe, but I'm not the settling down type Grant," I pout.

"You could be, with me… let's not get too far off topic, it is my question after all…."

"Then go ahead and ask away..I'm ready for whatever you throw my way." I say as I stare out the window.

"Okay, wild card: favorite sexual position?" he wiggles his eyebrows at me.

"I like to be on top. I can control everything from there and I can watch their face as they are begging for more. The pace is up to me; it can be fast and hard or soft and slow...that's what I like," my tone was more playful and light.

"Well hot damn!"

"Yes I know I'm hot, don't have to tell me twice."

"You're welcome… that's all I can say. I hope I'm lucky enough to find out all about ummm… all of that."

"Are you part Irish? You'd have a better chance of being lucky then. The luck of the Irish wasn't ever really good luck, I don't know why people think that," I sigh, slightly annoyed at what I had pointed out.

"Babydoll, I'll be whatever you want."

"I like the sound of that, babe," I cajole trying to provoke a response.

"I do too. We are here. I just have to find a place to park."

I look around amazed: the willows overlooks the ocean. The wind is blowing my hair everywhere and I can smell the salty ocean air. It's so calming, the waves crashing on the shore. We park as close as we can to the dock, so I can see the water more than anything. Then we can explore the arcade games they had inside the buildings of the Willows. We walk hand and hand towards the tough iron gate that reads, '*Salem Willows*'. The gate doesn't open, so we have to go around it. I practically drag Grant on the sidewalk. We go straight to the old wooden dock. It isn't crowded, but I figure it will get busier later in the day. I climb up the dock and lean over the side just fascinated by everything I see. I hear the wood crack.

The ledge gives way and I fall head first into the ocean.

"TALIA!!" I hear Grant's muffled voice from under the water.

The water is cold and the waves keep hitting me, keeping me from coming up. I'm gasping for air and I can't catch my breath. The more I try, the more water comes rushing into my nose and mouth. I try to yell for help, but I can't shout because my throat is restricted. I can't think. I feel the water splash and I keep trying to fight until I begin to lose consciousness.. All I can see are the colors of the ocean as I keep sinking. It feels like forever.

Then I see her.... *Delia. Survive. Fight. Safe. Her mouth meets mine and she breathes air into my lungs. Giving me one more breath...* then it all goes black.

Grant dives in and swims towards me. He puts my body over his shoulder and pulls me out to the rocks that are close by.

He starts CPR immediately, and begins pressing his mouth to mine to force air into my lungs. As soon as he gives me the first breath, I begin choking up all the salty sea and try to catch my breath. The water feels like lava, burning my throat and stomach.

I just lay here trying to calm myself. The sooner I calm down the sooner I will be able to breath. I feel like my lungs are collapsing, the world is closing in around me. It's then I realize I am having a panic attack.

I can't focus. Grant is talking, but it doesn't make any sense to me. All I can do is cough and wheeze. My body is numb. I could've died! I couldn't function... it was if the life had been sucked from me.

"Baby, are you alright?" He queried, as he held my body close to him.

I was shivering and he tries to warm me by running his hands up and down my arms. My teeth chattered against his chest.

Why did I never learn how to swim? I guess nobody ever wanted to teach me. Even in high school during swimming I ditched. I didn't want to get made fun of because I couldn't swim.

"You scared the hell out of me babydoll," he gasps, the look lingering in his eyes. He had almost lost me. A tear slips from his eye.

My body stiffens as the warmth fills my body and it occurs to me: "You.. saved me…" I stutter.

I've never had someone have such concern for me, especially since my mom.

"Yes, and I'd do it again in a heartbeat. Whether you believe it or not, I care for you."

Grant had me cradled in his arms like an infant. I took in his love, accepted it and gave it back.

Every set of eyes at the Willows is on us, everyone so concerned, asking if 911 assistance was needed. Grant declines help and explains he had it from here.

The crowd dwindled and continued on with their day. I continue to breathe deeply, enjoying every delicious salty beach breath. I wasn't going to let *almost* drowning ruin our date.

"Do you mind grabbing us some food? Almost drowning takes a toll on a lady."

He helps me to take a seat on the bench.

He puts his hand on my shoulder. "I will, I just want to make sure you're alright first."

"Yes, but I'd like food please. What kind of food can I get here?" I probe.

"Let's see we have *Pizza,* ice-cream, *Hobb's Famous Popcorn, Chinese food.* Which sounds good?"

"Mmmm…..Jumbo slice of pizza, some of that popcorn and of course ice cream! But maybe not in that order. Yes, can we get that, please?" I smile weakly.

"What kind of jumbo slice do you want?"

"Cheese and Italian sausage would be wonderful, I also want some *Molasses Popcorn Brittle.* I'll work on that for now. And a drink; anything but water," I rattled, still shaken up.

"They don't actually call it Italian Sausage. Here it's just sausage. I'll be right back. Stay put, please!"

Grant jogged up to the window, ordered, paid and waited patiently for our food. He continued to look back every so often at me, making sure I was still doing okay. I watched with wonder as he diligently got everything I asked for and brought it back.

I start slowly wringing out my clothes, letting the water seep out.

"Here's your pizza, the *not* water, popcorn and molasses brittle," he smiles proudly with a thick undertone of worry.

"Thank you, babe. This is great. I'm sorry I scared you back there. Ooh! Is that salt water taffy!?!?" I wondered out loud, feeling giddy with excitement.

"Sure is! I got you a box. I didn't know what you would want, so I got a little bit of everything."

I took a giant bite of my pizza and I was in a state of bliss. It was so good to get the salty taste out of my mouth and replace it with something tasty instead.

I turn to Grant with admiration."This is the best first date I've ever been on.

81

Thank you!"

He smiles, impressed with himself, "You're welcome, babydoll."

I break off a piece of the brittle and bite into it. It is delicious; a combination of sweet and salty. Even though I almost died, I love this place. I couldn't wait to visit the arcade... I wanted to play some skee-ball..

Tatum Emerson | Twenty

xoxo

I'm on his lap kissing his sexy, smooth lips. Passionately entangling our tongues, exploring each other in a movie chair. We're like teenagers, so hot for each other. I wrap my arms around his neck and push my body closer to his. My nipples hardened through my shirt and he knows it. He slides both of his hands under my shorts, grabbing my ass tightly. I shouldn't do this, but it feels so right...

I pant against his ear, letting him know his hands feel glorious against my body. A moan escapes my lips.

"Mmm Kendrick…."

He kisses and nibbles from my earlobe down to my neck. Running his hands roughly through the back of my hair he gives it a little tug.

He allows me to pull his shirt off over his head, then he gets to work on mine. I put my hands up and practically tear it off. His eyes are admiring the lace that is now exposed to him. Goosebumps cover my body as I run my hands down his abs. Taking time to enjoy each part of his six pack, I lean down and run my tongue over each indentation. His eyes close, a clear sign that he is enjoying this torture as much as I am. His breathing becomes more of a heavy pant. I slide up to his neck and bite along his shoulder, trailing down his chest again. I unbuckle his belt and release the button on his jeans. I feel his hands running up and down my back, reaching for my bra. I gladly reach back and unfasten my bra with one hand.

He lets out a chuckle, "That was impressive and sexy as hell." He takes a nipple into his mouth and leaves me both speechless and breathless at the same time.

He then makes a decision for the both of us. He cradles me in his arms, our bodies so close they feel entwined. He takes us through the secret door into my temporary bedroom. He playfully tosses me on the bed and continues to finish what I've started.

I can't believe this is how I will lose my virginity.

I was ready, I have waited long enough. I throw my pants to the floor and use my finger to entice him to join me.

He climbs up my body like a wild animal stalking his prey…..Tasting every inch of my body and everything it has to offer.

I can feel his erection against me as his body slides up and down in rhythm with mine. My mind wonders if only for a second. *Should I tell him it's my first time?*

"Wait! I need to tell you something…" I stumble to find the words.

"Is everything okay, sweetheart?"

"I'm..uhh….I'm a virgin" I blurt out.

"Oh shit! We should… uh stop…" his eyes now bulging.

I think I may have just fucked myself. I should have never told him…

"Uh yeah… okay. We should probably call it a night. I'll see you tomorrow."

He grabs his pants and slides them on.

"Yep, tomorrow for sure," he says as he hurries away as if the building were on fire.

I feel tears stinging my cheeks. I'm stupid to think a man like Kendrick would ever be interested in my virtue.

I feel rejected and tossed away like a piece of trash.

I pull my t-shirt back over my head. I let the tears continue to run down my face. I need my best friend, Aria.

I decide it's a much safer bet to text than risk running into Kendrick.

I begin the text message: *"Please come to my room...I'll explain when you get here."*

She replies: *"Be there in a few minutes."*

I drop the phone on the bed and cry into my hands. I can't believe I was stupid enough to tell him the truth. It's not like I could hide it. I just thought we had a deeper connection, but I guess I was wrong.

I keep replaying in my mind the look of horror on his face. I guess me being a virgin turned him off.

I hear a little tap-tap on the door. Aria opens and then closes my door.

She practically sprints to me "Oh Tatum!"

I put my head against her shoulder and sob. My cheeks stain with streaks from the black mascara.

"Tatum what happened? Let's talk about it…." A look of concern on her face as she pats my shoulder.

"He knows...we were on the bed...and I told him I was a virgin…." I say between sniffles.

Her eyes sadden, "I take it he reacted poorly.."

I rub my eyes, "Yeah, he acted like I had a contagious disease….he looked like a deer in headlights. He couldn't get out of here quick enough.."

She grabs the box of tissues and offers me one, "It's his fucking loss! If he doesn't want my beautiful best friend then he's a rich piece of shit!"

I smile weakly, "Thanks for always being here for me. I'm sorry that we are stuck here now with him."

"Well, I can call my parents and we can go stay in Beverly. Fuck him and his hoity toity mansion! He can't treat my best friend like this….I'm gonna beat his ass!"

"I'm sure he has a swanky ass lawyer that protects him..I don't want my bestie going to jail because I almost gave it up to the wrong guy…" more tears fell.

"Trust me when I say, the right man will wanna be your first and last. Cherish your v-card while you have it. Sometimes I wish I could start over. Don't pressure yourself, you started liking him and sometimes great things happen. Other times they suck ass; either way you will survive. I will ALWAYS be here for you."

I hugged her tight, so glad I had her in my life. She made my life less unfortunate.

"Get some sleep, Tatum, I'll check on you in the morning. Whatever you wanna do, it's up to you. Don't forget you are loved girl! A*vere un po 'di fede*!" She smiles and sneaks out of the room.

I smiled softly to myself, she wanted me to '*have a little faith*' and for tonight I would. Tomorrow would be better, it just had to be. I slid myself under the comforter, my head hit the pillow and I attempted to fall asleep.

I hear another tap on my door. Instead of saying or doing anything I just lay under the covers listening and waiting.

The door creaks open;

"Tatum, are you still awake?"

Tears roll down my cheeks. I know exactly who it is.

"Look, I'm sorry for the way I treated you…."

He sets on the edge of the bed, I feel the weight of his body at my feet.

The air feels hot and thick, I can feel my body tense at the sound of his voice. Tension so thick I could cut it with a knife.

"I didn't run away because I didn't want you, Tatum. I wasn't thinking. How could a beautiful woman like you be a virgin? It didn't seem possible, and I wouldn't want to steal that from you without a real connection attached."

"So you don't fucking care at all?" I spat, my words like venom, hoping to poison him.

"You are awake then," he says almost with a chuckle.

"My pain is funny now? A second ago you said you were sorry. I'm glad I'm leaving this place tomorrow so I'll never have to see you again!"

I feel the pressure move from the foot to on top of me.

"Get off---"

His lips crush against mine and my words muffle. The tension in my body relaxes as I accept his tongue into my mouth. I want him, even if he doesn't want me.

"That's exactly what I plan to do," he whispers. His voice husky and full of lust and sexual innuendo.

"Well then, if that's your intention then fuck off!" I murmur, trying not to be subdued by him.

He leans down and tugs at my shorts with his mouth, dragging them down. Getting fed up with how long it's taking he rips my lace booty shorts in two. He slides my tank over my head and his lips immediately glue to my nipples. He makes sure to take each one in his mouth and nibble ever so slightly. My body tingles with anticipation as I let him have his wicked way.

He slides down his pajama pants to reveal his hard and ready cock. I lick my lips as my mouth remembers the taste of him. He reaches down for a foil package from his pants that are now scattered amongst the floor.

He rips the foil packet open, and slides the condom down on his amazing erection.

"Are you ready, Tatum?" he questions, before rubbing the tip between my now wet pussy lips.

I moan in anticipation. I've had orgasms before manually, but having him bury himself in me would surely make me skyrocket.

He wastes no more time and pushes himself deep inside. I feel my body stretch to accommodate him.

87

I wince at the slight sting of pain, mixed with amazing amounts of pleasure. He pulls almost all the way out and pulls me to him. I wrap my legs around him and I moan passionately in his ear..

"Don't stop.. keep going…"

He slides back deep in me. "So right and so tight baby," he whispers satisfied that he's balls deep in me.

I rake my nails on his back as I draw closer to my peak. He moans at the surprise of my fingers gently tracing the now red claw marks I've left behind. My nipples pucker and rub roughly against his smooth defined chest. I wrap my arms tightly around his neck and thrust my body against his, pushing him further. He slides his hand down and takes my wet nub between his fingers and works his magic.

"Oh god…" I moan, needing the release that is about to take me over.

"Mmm that's it baby, cum for me," he continues pounding into me as the climax washes over both of us.

Shivers take over me, it's then I realize I am completely naked…

He is taking in every inch of me. He lays me down flat. He climbs on top of me just studying my body.

He leans in and kisses me gently on my lips.

"That was amazing, Tatum. You are amazing."

"I've never felt anything like that. You're right, it was amazing." I let out a soft groan.

He grabs a tissue, slides off the proof of our recent activities and wraps it up carefully to dispose of it.

He runs a hand over my mound. "Sore? Let me run you a bath."

He scoops me up into his arms and carries me into the bathroom.

ACCIDENTALLY IDENTICAL

The bathroom attached to my room is huge. My attention immediately goes to the claw foot tub. This particular one looks big enough for two. It's way better than the one at my place. I love it. He lets me gently hang over his shoulder as he turns on the hot water and the steam immediately begins to fill the room. He drops some oil and what I can only assume is bubble bath in the water.

I smile as the sweet aroma of vanilla and lavender fills my senses. I immediately relax.

"Ladies first," he nods to the bathtub. He takes my hand and helps me slide into the luxurious water.

"You're joining me?" surprise fills my face.

I close my eyes and sigh as my body is enveloped in sweet smelling liquid.

He smiles, glad he caught me off guard. He doesn't answer me, instead he slides in right behind me.

TALIA HENDRIX | TWENTY-ONE

✗✗✗✗

Once my strength has regained I practically drag Grant to the arcade area across from the small parking lot.

He smiles and leans in with a kiss on my forehead. "I'm glad you're feeling better, babydoll."

I smile from ear to ear. "Let's play! Who's getting the tokens?"

"I'll get them, this date is on me," he proclaims.

"I'll have to thank you properly tonight," I say with a wink.

"Woman, you can have whatever you want...it's *all* yours."

I laugh as I cling close to his side. We walk together over to the token machine. He puts in a ten dollar bill and it spits out several tokens all at once.

We rush to grab the tokens as they come flying out, cupping my hands under keeping the coins from falling. He uses one hand to guide the rest into my hands.

Half of the change goes into my pocket and we head over to the skee-ball area. I slide two tokens into the slot, and six balls come crashing out of the ball-hop.

Grant gets the machine next to mine and follows suit. I take the wooden ball and underhand it, aiming for the 100 point bulls-eye. Instead it hits the ring labeled 10 and goes in. I roll another ball, hoping for the best this time. It makes it to the 50 ring. Closer than I expected originally. Grant pumps his fist as I watch his ball fall into the 100 ring.

"Damnit! Where did you learn to play skee-ball?" I whine.

"I never told you I didn't know how to play," he licks his lips as he tries not to smile.

"Well I still have four more balls. I bet I can still whoop you!"

I practically launch the third ball, I'm not used to losing. It bounces off the 100 ring, bounces a second time and misses again. Damn, I must be out of practice.

I decide the only way I can win this is if I cheat. I crouch down and heave the ball from a closer position with my hand almost under the thick plastic covering.

"Hey now! I saw that!" he points accusingly.

"I don't know what you're talking about," my eyes avoiding his, playing innocent.

He moves closer to me and tickles under my arms. I lose it and laugh, nearly peeing myself.

"OKAY OKAY!!! I'm sorry! Stop or I'll pee on you!" I shriek.

He stays behind me, leans into me and grabs one of the balls.

"Here give me your hand, I'll show you how to win...." he smiles against my neck.

Our hands entwine as we hold the ball together and he leans in and throws it.

It hits every ring, looking more like a pinball machine than skee-ball.. It bounces like magic and sinks into the 100. He quickly grabs the last and final ball and tosses it. Hole in one....Wait that's golf. He was better than I thought.

"Did you play little league when you were younger? Inquiring minds want to know."

"Maybe. Okay my brother and I played. We were on separate teams, so it was pretty competitive."

"How well did you and your brother get along as kids?" I ask as this peaks my curiosity.

"Well, when we were kids we did a lot of shit. There's one piece of information I forgot to tell you about my brother and I…" he sucks in his bottom lip as he hesitates.

"What else do I need to know?"

"My brother Graham and I are twins, so as kids we would switch places. Teachers never even knew what was happening. I'm sure when were babies our mom even had difficulty telling us apart. That's saying something."

My jaw drops as I try to respond.

"That's… interesting. Why wasn't that one of the first things you told me?" I said with my brows crinkled.

"I didn't think it was important since I never intend on you two meeting. I don't want to chance him thinking he can steal you away."

"If I plan on staying in your life, information like this would be the need to know kind. What if I can't tell you two apart? Wouldn't we run into him at Christmas or Thanksgiving?" I overlook the part about his possible jealousy towards his brother.

"I know I should've told you sooner, but I was afraid it would affect how you thought of me. I don't trust my brother at all."

"You have nothing to worry about. I'm all… I mean I'm interested in someone. I don't think Graham is my type anyway, no matter how sexy he may be.." I say, teasing him.

"Oh so is it everyday you let other men take you out? Since you're interested in someone.." his voice was thick with jealousy.

"You know I'm talking about you right, Grant Thomas?" I poke his chest, letting him know it's him I'm thinking about.

"Do you really mean that?"

"Of course I do. *Sono solo tuo.*" I answer, letting my Italian roots come out.

At least I think they are my roots. I can't be sure now.

"*I am only yours*? Is that right? I took Italian briefly. If that's the case, I am yours as well."

I laugh, "You are very good...That is impressive. I'm pretty fluent, not sure if I'm truly Italian or not but I can speak the seductive language of love. Speak to me in Italian, lover boy."

"*Penso che mi sto innamorando di te.*" (I think I'm falling in love with you.)

"Aw that's so sweet. *Forse lo sono anch'io*" (Maybe I am too.)

"I hope I said that right and didn't say something humiliating. I didn't say I fucked a dirty sock, did I?"

I couldn't stop myself- I had to giggle at him. "You *fuck* socks, huh? Is that one of your many hobbies?"

"No definitely not, I prefer *bellisimo* women, like you."

"Your Italian is better than you think it is. I'm impressed." I lean in for a kiss.

"So maybe I know more than I let on.." he whispers against my lips.

I could feel the heat radiating off this man, with his lips pressed firmly against mine. As we have our moment a kid behind us comments;

"Gross, get a room. You'll get cooties from that, ya know?" the boy says.

We both roll our eyes and laugh together. He hugs me tight.

"Sorry kid, you'll understand when you get older," Grant chuckles.

"Are we ready for our next adventure? I promise you won't have a chance to drown this time."

"What do I do with my other tokens?" My voice was serious, he didn't need to waste money.

"Keep them so we will have to come back sometime soon," he reaches for me and throws me over his shoulder, practically running back to the car. I gently bite on his shoulder as he puts me down. I slid back into the car and fasten my seat belt.

TATUM EMERSON | TWENTY-TWO

XOXO

I've never showered much less taken a bath with any man. This was one of two new experiences I've had since meeting Kendrick. He stayed in the bath with me for a little while but then got out and left me to soak my sore muscles. I'm glad he made sure to leave me a robe to slip on once I've finished. Aria is never going to believe what happened tonight. It went from awful to amazing. How does that happen to someone? I'm not sure what this man's intentions are with me, but I really want to find out.

How does a man go from leaving me hanging to ravaging my body and taking my virginity for keeps?

The water turns chilly against my skin, and I unplug the tub and slide out. I stand in front of the mirror looking at myself. Did I look any different? I sure felt different: my body was still sore but all in all I felt empty. My body is empty without him inside. I smile at myself as I comb my hair with my fingers. I feel more alive than I had in the last twenty three years.

My small travel bag is sitting on top of the vanity. I hadn't noticed, but Kendrick probably brought it for me when he hung the robe. My hand skims through the bag to grab the leave in conditioner. I spray the thick lotion into my hands and work it through my hair. I towel dry the rest to bring my waves back to life.

I stare at myself for a second, running my fingers over every place he has touched. I could still feel the heat; my body shuddered from the memory. I feel the soft, silky material of the robe on my skin as I slide it on. It's oversized and very comfortable, I love the way it caresses my skin. The robe is my favorite color, lavender. I wonder if he knew that? Probably not, but it's marvelous anyway.

I walk back into the bedroom and flop myself on the bed. I'm exhausted, so sleep will definitely be easy. I spread my arms out and just lay there. I wonder what Kendrick's doing right now.

KENDRICK SANDERS / TWENTY-THREE

XOXO

I can't believe I managed to pry myself away. What kind of man walks away from a woman who throws herself at him? I just became her first, but I hope she doesn't think this means we are together or something now. I had to get out of there and clear my head. Being around her is intoxicating and I can't think clearly. She makes me second guess myself and feel things I'm not sure I should be feeling.

I went into this for one reason, but now the conquest is complete. I don't want it to be, though. Hell, I don't know what I even want. It shouldn't be this big of a deal. As I sip on my glass of scotch, I wonder what the hell is wrong with me? I down the rest of the scotch and refill my glass. This is exactly why I didn't want to get too close to her. Get in, get out and get gone. The only reason I'm letting her stay is because someone is trying to hurt her and her roommate.

I have to be real with myself: I'm not a hero. Far from it, but maybe this one time I can do some good with my money and prove I'm not a completely selfish prick. I'm thinking too much. I hear a knock on the door of my office.

"Come in!" I bellowed.

"Sorry to bug you so late, Kendrick. I just wanted to check to make sure everything was in order before I head to bed." Marcello states casually.

"Sit, sit! Come have some scotch with me" I demand.

"Alright, I've done my rounds so I can only stay for one drink."

I get right to the point, "What do you think of the two women?"

"Aria and Tatum? I can't speak for Tatum, but Aria is one I would like an opportunity to get to know better," he declares.

"We are friends, aren't we Marcello? Can I speak candidly?"

"If you mean in the sense that I work for you and would take a bullet for you then, yes" he smirks.

"That woman... she's just so seductive. I don't know how long I can stay away from her. I can still taste her.."

"Really? That's very forward of you. When did this happen?"

"After she went to her room, I tried to keep her at arms length, but I ended up needing her."

"What exactly are we talking about here?" His expression hardens.

"I stared into those emerald eyes and fucked her."

Relief washes over his face. "Yes she is quite the woman."

"Glad we are in agreement, but she's mine. I've laid claim to that one."

"Oh that's not going to be a problem. She isn't my type," he responds, his eyes telling his true intentions.

"Good Marcello, because if she was, you would be out of a job." I smile with my million dollar smile.

"My sights are set on the other one, boss. I want Aria. There is just something about her. I can't put my finger on it, but I need her."

"You can have her. Anything I can do to help increase your odds, my friend?"

"Yeah, don't fuck her," he let out a gut busting laugh.

I laugh with him, "You have my word."

"Good, cause I actually like my job. I wouldn't want to have to fight you for her, but I would in a heartbeat."

My curiosity was spiked. "So what do you know about her? What's so special about her?"

"She's the type of girl you can bring home to mama. The one you can have a family with, would do anything to make you smile and bring you happiness."

"It's that serious, huh? You sound like you're ready to put a ring on it. You just met her, buddy. Don't go getting your heart broken too soon."

"Well she doesn't know I feel this way, so I can't quite screw it up yet. Give me time, boss. You just worry about not screwing it up with Tatum, at least until I find out if Aria is the one."

"There's nothing to screw up, because I'm not in love with Tatum."

"I'll let you believe what you want, but I don't think even you believe yourself when you lie anymore."

I can't admit it out loud, but he's telling the truth. I've been so busy falling head first into the company that I haven't had time to get my own head out of my ass.

"Even if did feel anything, it's not like I could actually follow through. I don't know how to have a normal relationship. All I know is how to fuck them and leave. I guess I'm just supposed to leave that lifestyle and suddenly *love* someone?"

"You make it too complicated. It's more of a day at a time thing. I think you've already got a few hypothetical days under your belt already," he says simply.

If he only knew where my 'belt' had been. It was just on the floor in Tatum's room. He doesn't know anything about that, and in this specific moment I am glad. It wasn't the judgement I was afraid of, rather the fact that I wasn't ready to share it with anyone... yet.

"While you continue to ponder how this is all going to work, possibly overthink and screw things up, I'm going to head to bed and get some rest. Goodnight, Sanders."

"Thanks again for the talk Marcello. Have a good night," I utter in response.

I take a swig of the last bit of my scotch and think on everything we had discussed. I stand up and grab a book from the shelf close to my desk and crack open the pages. I run my fingers over the antique pages of a business book my father had given to me. I run my fingers up and down the page and cannot focus on what the pages say.

I was so deep in thought that I didn't hear her enter the room. Startled, I make eye contact with those beautiful, jewel like eyes.

"I didn't hear you come in." I say, almost in a whisper.

"Sorry, I didn't mean to scare you. I just couldn't sleep and was wondering if maybe you were having the same issue." Tatum licks her bottom lip and bites down.

"It's fine. I'm glad you found me. Come here," I request.

She sits on the edge of my desk. I can't take my eyes off of her. She is so effortlessly beautiful.

"Just a second." I hold a finger out to her as I walk towards my door. I look back at her as I click the lock, so no one will disturb us.

. "Are you sure you were a virgin? I only say that because you are most definitely making a habit of turning me on. If I didn't know any better I'd say you were trying to seduce me again," I say with a lighthearted chuckle.

TALIA HENDRIX | TWENTY-FOUR

✳✳✳✳

We hadn't been driving for long when we reached our destination. We park and begin walking hand in hand down the brick road. I smile to myself. Is this what having someone care about you feels like? It scares me and makes me happy at the same time.

"Here we are!" He points to a big building with brown siding and brick marked *Witch Dungeon Museum*.

"So our next spot is a Witch Museum?" I say, holding back my enthusiasm.

"I know museums don't come off as fun, but you wanted to get to know the town of Salem. Humor me, then we can go on a guided tour," he cups his hand under my chin.

I can't resist myself, a smile breaks through.

"I trust you, I want as much of Salem as you can give me."

"I wanna show you Salem in the most tourist way possible. We can even visit a psychic if your down with that," he smiles.

"Yeah, but first I want a picture of us in these wooden stocks." I smile and ask a passerby to take our photo.

We both make goofy faces for the camera whilst pretending to be locked in the stocks outside of the museum.

I can't imagine being in these for real. It's so tragic what people had to go through just because they were different. I've never met a real witch before, but if I did I'd treat her like anyone else.

We both slide our hands and heads out of the old wooden stocks. Since this area is popular for tourists there are a lot of people out and about.

"Here ya are, I took a couple for you." The woman hands me my phone back.

"Thank you very much. We sure appreciate the kindness."

"Not from Salem, I assume? I can tell tourists when I see them. Enjoy your stay, and be sure to come inside the Museum. We show you how the events truly happen." The woman smiles and nods as she enters the building.

"Do you think she could've been a witch? Is that a qualification for working here?" I have many questions, not sure Grant could answer them.

"Not everyone from Salem is a witch. There are quite a few around but not everyone is." He corrects me, calming the tourist part of me down.

"Let's go see what they offer, I'm sure I will learn a lot!" I can barely hold it together, I feel at home here and I can't figure out why.

We enter and Grant pays for our tickets. The woman who took our picture for us is at the desk. I smile at her, she nods in my direction and comes out from behind the desk to put on yet another hat that she wears. Tour guide.

"To add to the many thoughts you are having, also manager and owner of this wonderful establishment," she says with a knowing tone.

"Are you also a psychic? Or am I that easy to read? I was seriously just thinking about that?" My face and voice both displaying the shock.

She smiles, displaying her smile lines from what I can only assume are from a life of light and laughter.

"My name is Melora and I will be your tour guide for the day. If you have any questions during the tour, please hold them until we are finished," she says knowingly.

Grant pulls me close as we follow Melora through the museum. We walk into the room where the re-enactment takes place. As we sit in the back and watch, we realize it is the trial of a beggar woman, named Sarah Good. Imagine being back in

1692, Salem Village. That's exactly where we were. Sarah Good was one of three who were first accused of witchcraft. This was her trial, her life. It was raw and real. The other two women were Sarah Osborne and Tituba.

I felt for these women. They had been accused and nobody believed otherwise. Even Sarah Good's family had believed she was a witch. As the tears fell from my eyes, I realized I knew how it felt to have your family turn against you. Grant squeezed my thigh in an act of comfort, after obviously seeing the tears fall.

After the re-enactment was through, we found out that she was sentenced to death by hanging. They pardoned her until the birth of her child, who died with her in jail.

"Are you okay my dear?" Melora asks after the re-enactment is over.

"Yes, it's so sad, all the hate and judgement. I'll be fine, it's just making me a little emotional." I wipe the tears from my eyes.

"Now we head to the dungeon, where they kept those accused of witchcraft," she says, leading the way.

In the dark gloom of the dungeon we were told of the story of Sarah Osborne. It was told that Sarah had been placed in the Boston jail and had died inside it's walls. The scene of what it was like to be trapped in a jail accused as a witch in the 1600's was eye-opening. The conditions were highly unfavorable, filthy, rat infested, and some accused were bound and tied up in the small cells. The cells had no bedding and no bars, but the only way to describe it or even come close was to call it hell on earth.

I couldn't handle it anymore. I had to get out, I needed to breathe. Overcome with raw emotion, I scramble to find my way to the nearest exit.

When I get outside I collapse near the stocks and put my head in my hands.

"Dearie, dearie, dearie! What are we going to do with you?" Melora's voice sounds magically in my ears.

Before I can answer she asks me a question I was not expecting.

102

"Have you found her yet?"

"What? Found who?" I try my hardest not to give anything away.

"Sorry, I mean your sister. You're here looking for her," she smiles.

"How do you-" before I can finish she stops me.

"Did I know? You made a wonderful observation earlier. I know a lot of things, some I've seen and some that are brought to my attention by a higher power."

At this point I'm sure my mouth is gaping open. I'm at a loss for words and am very confused.

"I also believe I know your mother, or should I say *mothers*. Both Delia and Amelia," her eyes shone almost a shade of purple.

"How is that even possible?" I stammer.

"Magic, my dear. I've been sent to look after you while you're here in Salem. Delia doesn't just visit your dreams, she frequently appears in mine as well."

"Does that mean what I think it means?"

"I'm pretty sure you know that answer. You knew before it slid out of your mouth."

"What are we? Witches? Psychic?"

"None of those. You are part *Empathxana*. With practice you could do very well."

"What does that even mean?" I look around to see if Grant has come out.

"I have a helper keeping him busy right now. If we can go to lunch together I can explain everything," she points.

"Where?"

"*The Ugly Mug Diner*. Meet me in 15 minutes." Melora directs before disappearing.

I stand there scratching my head. What the fuck was a, um what did she call it? *Empathxana*? Sounds like a panini press to me. I rub my temples. How was I going to keep Grant busy while I find out about my mysterious lineage?

I see Grant exiting the building I fled from several moments earlier.

"Hey babe, is everything alright?"

"Yeah, it's fine. I want to explore for an hour on my own to clear my head. Can you go purchase us tickets for something I read about? It's called the Schooner Fame: it's a ship. They take you for a ride in the ocean. Before you ask, I'll wear a lifejacket, but I really wanna go!"

"Will you be okay by yourself?" he looks into my eyes, full of concern.

"I'll be good. Melora offered to go to lunch with me, then I'll meet you in an hour. Pick me up at the *Ugly Mug Diner*, please?"

"Sure will babe," he leans in, kisses me and then heads towards the car.

Now I just have to find my way to the *Ugly Mug*. It isn't too far away. Jogging all the way there only takes about 10 minutes. I arrive in front of the black and white building, the sign on the window tells me I'm at the right place. I can see Melora sitting in one of the chairs by the window. I walk in, her eyes meet mine as she waves me over.

TATUM EMERSON | TWENTY-FIVE

XOXO

The sun peaking through the window blinds me. I flinch as my eyes try to adjust to the brightness. I try to wake up, rubbing my eyes. I don't remember how I got back in this bed. I remember Kendrick taking me from behind on his desk but can't quite remember how I got here.

I stretch my arms out hoping to relieve some of the stiffness I was feeling this morning. I can't believe I was a virgin yesterday and now I've already had sex twice! I hope it's not awkward at the breakfast table, assuming there was breakfast waiting. I stand up stretching my arms in the air. Even though I don't remember coming to bed, I feel well rested.

Before I woke up, I dreamt of her again. She wants me to search for my sister, but I have no idea where to look. Am I supposed to use some telepathic communication to get into her head and find where the hell she is? How can I even be sure I can?

I pull my dark orchid tank top over my head, slide my shorts over my hips and head out towards where I thought the kitchen would be.

The kitchen is easy to find. After going down the long hallway of doors, I walk into the open arch of the world's cleanest kitchen, where I now have three different sets of eyes on me. I quickly examine a room of beautiful oak cabinets that wrap around the whole kitchen. The stainless steel appliances all shiny and the countertops in a lovely white carrara marble. In the center of the kitchen everyone is seated at a counter-productive table, I believe they call them islands. They are all sitting in some leather sitting chairs that looked like they could be in an expensive pub. This man has money to burn, and he has amazing taste for decorating. I turn quickly, shaking away all my wonder, and greet them all.

Aria and Kendrick are eating omelettes, fruit and bagels.

"Morning!" I try to hide my blush as Kendrick's eyes linger, as he's undressing me with his eyes.

"Good morning bitch!" Aria smiles. Bitch is her word of endearment for me.

"Yes, good morning, Tatum. Did you sleep well?" Kendrick smirks.

Asshole! He knows damn well I slept well after all that happened last night. Of course he's going to make breakfast awkward.

"Slept wonderfully! Thanks again for letting us crash here until we can be sure we are safe."

"Yeah Kendrick, it was awfully nice of you to offer" Aria chimes in.

"Excuse me Ma'am, what would you like for breakfast? I can make you anything you'd like," the other woman queries.

"Could I please have waffles, scrambled eggs and some sausage links if you have any? Oh, and a glass of orange juice please." I smile, glad to have someone else make breakfast.

I haven't had breakfast in a long while. I stay quiet, trying not to bring any more attention to myself.

"Kendrick, I need to be completely honest with you. Your an asshole! I know what you did to Tatum last night and honestly I'm disgusted," she frowns in his direction.

He laughs loudly, "Oh are you now? I hardly think fucking her senseless is disgusting, but if that is what you really think. I'm sorry you feel that way. She was on board, practically begging me for it."

"Oh My…. Oh Shit.." I bite my lip so hard I think I may have drawn blood.

I haven't had a moment to tell her that he came back into my room.

"YOU DID WHAT?! First you discard her like she's trash and then you come back and fuck her? What the hell is wrong with you, dude? Tatum is an amazing person, and when she cares for someone she gives them her all. I can't believe you'd take her virginity knowing damn well you had no intention of being with her long term," she fumes.

My eyes gape out of my head, this is not good. I didn't think she would be pissed off that I finally got what I wanted.

"Both of you STOP! We had sex, Aria. I had intended on telling you. He came back, we talked, one thing led to another and I don't regret it. Please don't take it out on him. It was my decision too. I have feelings for him. I really shouldn't but I do and I can't deny how I feel."

"You have feelings for me?" he marveled.

"Yes Kendrick, I do. I'm sorry. I needed to say it, but I didn't mean to blurt it out."

His hand reaches across the marble and grabs mine. Aria stares at both of us as the confessions keep coming.

"I know it's not really something I should say, but I have feelings for you as well," he concedes.

"Aria, I love you. You're the best friend I could ever have. Thank you for always defending me and having my back." I smile in her direction.

Kendrick looks over at her. "Is there anyway we can put this in past? I care for Tatum and you obviously do too, so can we call a truce?"

She sighs loudly, "I guess we can. If Tatum has feelings for you and you do for her then I'm happy you both figured it out. If you hurt her again I'll fucking kill you!" Her lips met in a straight line.

"I'll never hurt her again, I would never hurt her on purpose," he vows as he brings my hand up to his lips. He places a gentle kiss on the top side of my hand.

The chef has my plate ready and steaming hot. She places it in front of me along with my glass of orange juice.

"Chef... What's your name? Can I make this orange juice a mimosa?"

"You can call me Chef Marazzi or Jewel whichever you prefer, Miss Tatum."

"Okay, Chef Jewel can I please get a mimosa? It's already been a crazy morning," I pronounce.

"I'll have one too if you don't mind," Aria joins in.

"I guess since the ladies are liquoring up this morning I better join too. A scotch on the rocks please, Chef Marazzi." Kendrick says, all attention focuses on him.

I smile at Aria. "Liquored Ladies for life, bitch!"

"Hell YES! That's the best thing I've heard in a long fucking time."

We both giggle, bringing a little of our craziness into Kendrick's home.

"You ladies are nuts! Do you wanna have a pool party?" he asks, trying to lure us into the water.

"Let's do it! I have my bikini upstairs, and I have one Aria can wear if she's down."

"Oh, you know I am" she retorts.

"Okay, we need to go get changed then. Which way is the pool? Wait, isn't it too cold to swim?" I squeak.

"Indoor pool, sweetheart," he assures me.

TALIA HENDRIX / TWENTY-SIX

✱✱✱✱

I sit across from Melora hopeful that I will be getting answers.

"I have an hour, tell me what I need to know please," I plead.

"Where would you like me to start, my dear?"

"What am I?"

"As I said before you are part Empathxana," she clarifies.

"What does that even mean?" I urge her on.

"Empathxana means you are part empath and part xana. An empath has the ability to feel the emotions of others. You feel what others may not even comprehend. You can control the emotions, and you can influence others', making them happy with just your presence or transferring your own emotions to someone else. That is why you feel such a strong passionate connection with Grant. You each have what the other lacks. A xana is a little more complex. You are the first half breed of a xana, which is completely unheard of. Xanas are always beautiful, blonde and have curly hair, but they have great gifts.. They tend to live in or near water, drawing from its natural powers. Some xanas are evil and bad natured, but this is not the case with you and your sister. Your twin."

I sit in shock, trying to comprehend what she just told me. I'm part mythical fucking creature? I don't know how I feel.

"Dear, are you alright? I know this can be overwhelming, but I have much more to tell you. We still haven't talked about your mother."

"Go on, tell me more. I'm in shock, but I need to know these things. I also need to know how to find my sister," I coax.

"Your mother and I met right before she met your father. Your mother was full blooded Xana. Your father Alistaire is mortal, human, however you want to see it. Delia got pregnant a year after they married. Xanas cannot raise children, they can't produce the milk to nourish the young. All of this goes against the primal nature of a xana. Delia fell in love, and she chose Amelia and Victoria, both of your mothers."

"Holy shit! How the hell do you know this, Melora?" I exclaim.

"Delia comes to me in my dreams. She's been waiting for you to find me. Her wishes are that you find your sister and I know how to find her. You aren't safe apart. Together you can protect each other, but alone you risk it all," she hums.

"I don't even know her name...where is she?"

"You do know her name darling, remember the woods? Someone calling out for Tatum? Sound familiar?" she chuckles.

"Are you following me? Wait, we've established that you have psychic abilities, so obviously you've seen it. My sister's name is Tatum? So together we are Talia and Tatum? Is she older than me? Am I older than her? Are we identical?" I murmur.

My list of questions continues to grow as she speaks.

"You are indeed identical, and you have an older sister by 20 minutes I'm told. Your birth was complicated and the labor was hard on your mother. As I told you, xanas were not supposed to be able to conceive, let alone survive labor. Both of you are lucky to even exist. Delia gave her life for both of you. Xanas each have a life force inside, conception and labor were never meant to take place. She died a week after your birth, but not due to just excessive bleeding. She transferred any power of her being, just to protect you two."

I feel the tears well up in my eyes. "Where is she?"

"She's in Boston. She's safe with a man and another young woman. I believe her name is Aria," she continues.

"How do I find her?" I sob.

"His name is Kendrick Sanders. If you find him you will find her. Please be careful my dear, there is someone after you. He wishes nothing but harm to come to you, even to the point of death. "

"Who is after me?" I groan.

She rubs her index finger to her temple as if to envision this person.

"Amelia's husband" she deadpans.

"Fuck. I'm sorry, I need to find Grant. I have to go, Melora. How do I reach you if I need you?"

"I'm just a dream away, my darling. All you have to do is think about me, concentrate on me, and I will find you."

"Thank you, Melora. I will find Tatum. That's what mom would've wanted; for us to stay safe."

"*Namaste*, my darling." She clasps her hands together and bowes her head to me.

I look around before getting up, then exit the diner. Once outside I inhale deeply: my world is full of chaos. I look towards the road just as Grant is pulling up. Thank God, I can feel somewhat safe again.

"Hey babydoll, I was just gonna come in to find you. Figured we could eat here if you haven't eaten yet. "

"I just wanna go home, Grant. Can we go back to Mike's please?" I plead.

"Sure, anything you want. Get in, let's go." He leans over to unlock the door for me.

Anxious to leave I jump in the seat and quickly buckle my belt. "Let's go please."

I'm silent for the ride home. I know he is wondering what has happened, but I don't think it's safe for me to tell him the truth. He knows enough already, I don't want to put him in danger.

"What happened today? Did that lady show up to meet you?" he questions.

"I went in and waited, but she never showed. Guess something came up." I lie.

My stomach churns. I don't want to lie to this man, but it felt necessary. I hope he will forgive me when I finally tell him the whole story. He will probably run away from me. It was then I remembered something Melora had said: *You can control the emotion of others.*

I concentrated on the emotion I wanted to expel on him. *Euphoria.* I kept thinking over and over. He can't resist me; he needs me.

Nothing happened, maybe I didn't do it right. His hand slides ever so gently on my thigh. Oh shit, it worked. The goosebumps own my body. He slides his fingers up and down gently against my skin.

I smile at him, "Behave yourself! I don't want to get in a car wreck," I lecture.

"Okay! I get it, but can I finish what I started once we get back to the house?"

"Yes, I think it's about time we got to know each other a little better," I say with a wink.

"Dollface, you have no idea how hard I am right now."

"I bet I have an idea…"

I smile in his direction, I can't wait for what's in store when we got back to the house. Apparently he is just as excited, since he is speeding the whole way back.

We get to the house, he parks the car, climbs out and meets me at the car door. He opens it smiling. I slide out and grab his hand as we run towards the house.

I really love this man. It's about time I give him another piece of me: my body.

I jump on his back, wrap my arms tightly around his neck and he piggy backs me the whole way upstairs.

He leans back and drops me on the bed. I spread my arms out as if I am flying.

The bed is plush and soft. I push the oversized pillows onto the floor as he pulls his shirt over his head and heads to lock the door.

"We're all alone now..."

I motion to him with my index finger. "Come here."

He moves slowly towards me, anticipation building. He hasn't even touched me yet and my panties are soaked through.

My nipples hardened as his tan skin brushes against mine, my hands reach for him. I gently caress down his shoulders and then gently rake my nails down his back. He leans in for a kiss and I oblige, opening for him, massaging my tongue against his. He ravages my mouth, steals my kisses and sucks hard on my tongue. I suck and gently bite on his bottom lip, as his hands explore my body. First my shoulders, then he moves to my breasts and palms them hard, moving his mouth down he takes one in his mouth.

I moan, all the sensations were slowly driving me crazy. Grant pins my hands above my head as he licks down to my navel. His long fingers trail down to my hidden heat. He spreads my lower lips and slips a finger deep inside. I shudder and long for the feeling of his cock buried deep in me. It's just begun and I need him now.

I whisper and pant into his ear, "Grant, I need you."

"Patience, babydoll.." he utters while sliding another finger inside.

I wiggle my body trying to get free, but the weight of his body has me pinned. He pulls his fingers away, leaving me feeling hollow. He stands up, unbuttons his pants and gives me my first glimpse of his sexy thickness.

"Like what you see, doll?" he smirks.

"Fuck yes I do, now come bury it in me," I lick my lips.

"That's so hot... you're gorgeous. Your body is amazing I can't wait to feel you."

I stand up and pull off the rest of my clothes, putting on a show for him. I slowly touch my body, my hands reach for my mound. I slowly finger myself, it gives me pure satisfaction. He's watching and it's killing him.

He groans, his pupils dilate as he watches me intently. Every feather like stroke, every plunging finger: he is watching.

My head leans back as I pleasure myself.

"Baby come here now," he commands.

I bite my lip and do as I'm told. He picks me up and I wrap my legs around him aching to feel his cock deep in me. He pulls us both together on the bed, he lays on his back flat against the bed and pulls me on top. I lean in and kiss him hard and rub my pussy against his stiffness. I spread my legs and position them on either side of him and thrust down on him, stretching to accommodate him.

"Mmmmm, you feel so fucking tight love," he groans.

I love riding his cock, bucking my head back in pleasure. I could do this all night and into the next day. He feels so good, we are so in sync, this was meant to be.

He entwines our hands together as he pushes upward to penetrate me deeper. The friction becomes too much and before we both know it we are being wrecked by our orgasms.

We collapse next to each other, both panting from our passion.

I turn to face him and utter, "I love you."

He can't hide the cheesy smile that appears on his face.

"Dollface, I love you too. I'm glad I met you that day on the train."

"I am too, Grant."

"I want to take you to meet my family in Gloucester. Is that okay with you? I know it's soon but I just feel so connected to you."

"Yes, when do you wanna go?" I pick my fingers anxiously.

"We can go now. It takes a little over an hour and my mom actually invited us for dinner. I just needed you to say yes," he says as he searches my eyes for answers.

"Let's go! I've never been to Gloucester. What else do we need? Should I grab overnight clothes? Or are we just staying for a few hours?" I question.

It wouldn't hurt leaving town for a day or so. When I come back I will try my best to find Tatum. It is time I meet my sister.

"Just pack an overnight bag and we can head out," he says as he pulls a duffle out of the closet.

I run upstairs and grab the necessities and when I come back down I toss them in the bag with all of his things. He tosses his bag over his shoulder and we wave goodbye to Mike as we head out the door.

TATUM EMERSON | TWENTY-SEVEN

XOXO

We walk through long hallways and finally I see it.

The biggest indoor pool, well the only one I've ever seen in person. Looking up I realize the room appears dome shaped. Every inch made to look like a personal beach, down to even the sand that is now between my toes.

I gaze down at my average body, nothing spectacular but my breasts look amazing in this bikini. It fits me like a glove and hugs my body like a second skin. It is my favorite shade of purple, lavender. It ties behind my neck with vertical pockets covering my unmentionables. It has a string on the bottom connecting everything together. The bottoms hug my curves enough to show just enough of my cheeks to keep Kendrick drooling. I can feel his eyes scanning my body, taking in every curve and loving every inch of my body. I chuckle to myself and continue giving a little shake of my hips. I bask in this indoor beach paradise. I wiggle my toes in the sand that's covering a beautiful flat rock. Palm trees are surrounding us and the pool is a beautiful aqua color. There is a tiki bar to the left, with Marcello behind the bar wearing a Hawaiian style shirt.

"Hi Marcello!" I wave, pulling Aria along by the arm.

"Hello, Miss Tatum!" He smiles before he catches a glimpse of Aria.

I can see his eyes filled with lust; he wants her.

"Aria, sit here and keep Marcello company. I'm going to cannon ball off that giant cliff there." I smile as I point off at the rocks above the waterfall.

I make a run for it, knowing Kendrick is right behind me. I climb up to the highest part of the waterfall and with no fear into the water I go. I hide myself behind the waterfall, watching and waiting and then *SPLASH,* he cannon balls in the water. I swim over to him with us now facing one another and wrap my arms and legs around him. He swishes me around in a circle in the water as I hang on for dear life. He's so easy going right now, carefree. I love being able to be myself around him, maybe this is the world's way of telling me I found my Mister Right.

"What are you thinking about, Tatum?" He asks as his eyes search my face for a possible answer.

"I'm thinking about how good we are together. I just hope we stay this way," I sigh.

"If I could get away with asking you to marry me right now, I would." He says with a smile.

"Tell me why you wouldn't get away with it?" I murmur.

"You would think I was crazy. I can't explain it, but I'm so drawn to you."

"If you ever plan on asking me to marry you, at least have a ring to propose."

"Guess I need to do some shopping," he winks.

Out of the corner of my eye I see Marcello and Aria sneaking away.

"Where are they headed?" I whisper.

"I would say probably the hot tub."

"Hot tub too, huh? What does this house not have?" I scrunch my nose.

"Pretty much has everything. What's even crazier is I live here alone, minus the people that work for me."

"I could see myself living here, I'd never want to leave." I try not to smile.

"Definitely going to have to do some important shopping. If I can help it, I'd never want you to leave."

My face is flush, I quickly go under water to keep from being found out. Did this man really want to marry me? I could see myself sharing forever with him. Did he?

"Tatum, come back." Kendrick murmurs.

I pop up out of the water, "Why would you wanna marry me?"

He smiles and thinks to himself for a minute. The time may as well have been a lifetime; it felt like it was.

"My life is great, but it's been that much better with you in it, having you around these last weeks makes me realize I want this more than I've wanted anything."

"You're crazy Kendrick. If you mean it then you'll know I deserve a better proposal than that," I tease.

"Yes I know you're worth more than some off the wall proposal. You won't see it coming when and *if* I do," he smirks confidently.

I smile and look around his version of paradise. Catching a glimpse of something my jaw drops, but pride fills my heart too.

"What's wrong?" Kendrick asks.

All I could do was point in their direction, Aria and Marcello were locking lips. Very passionately, if I did say so myself. They were now seated on some of the rocks surrounding the pool, so I swim closer to spy on them.

Marcello is running his fingers through the locks of her long black hair. Aria's arms are wrapped around his neck and she is on his lap now. I watch as the two of them seem to melt and mold together. I was happy for my bestie, but I still owed her for the mall.

Turnabout is fair play right?

"Hey ARIA!" I yelled as I climb up the rocks.

They quickly pulled apart and Aria's face is several different shades of red.

"Uhhh.. shit! Tatum.. Hi!" she stutters trying to find her words.

"So what's going on up here? Looks like you two are getting along *really* well." I raise my eyebrows at them.

"Sorry Miss Tatum, I couldn't help myself, your friend is so ravishing," he apologizes profusely.

I pat him on the back, "Don't worry about it, as long as you make her happy. If not, I'll hunt you down and kill you." I say clearly trying to intimidate him.

He smiles, "I understand and accept the consequences. I will make sure she's happy at all times."

Aria sits there, her eyes bulging and her jaw dropped. I know I couldn't take on a trained bodyguard, but it was the principle of the thing. She's like my sister, even though she's older than me I still have that insatiable need to protect her.

"Are you planning to get in the pool, you two love birds?" I coax.

Marcello scoops her up and all she can do is giggle. I smile big and jump off the ledge into the pool. Joining us, he drops her delicately into the shore line of the pool.

"I have an idea!" I shout excitedly at them.

"What do you have in mind?" Aria gives me a death stare.

"Chicken Fight!"

"What the hell is a chicken fight" Kendrick questions.

"Shoulder war? You've never played? That's cute, so sheltered. Aria and I will get on our partner's shoulders and try to push each other in the water. First one to fall off loses. The guys on bottom are the vehicles, the ones who move us and we are the attackers. So is everyone down to play?" I entice.

"Anything you want, sweetheart, let's kick some ass!"

"I always knew you were my favorite." I lean in for a kiss to reward him.

"Yeah, we will play," Aria smiles and nudges Marcello.

"Let's do it!" he taunts.

We swim to opposite ends of the pool and mount ourselves on the shoulders of our men. Kendrick makes sure his grip on my thighs is secure, and Marcello tucks Aria's feet under his arms. The men start full speed at each other, their heads barely above water. Aria and I meet up top and grab each other's hands, struggling for power. I push my weight forward trying to knock her down. The only problem with being best friends is we know each other a little too well. Anticipating my push she moves slightly to the left, avoiding the assault. I almost fall head first, but Kendrick grabs tighter and pulls me back.

"Oh man, LOOK!" Aria points to the waterfall.

"I'm not falling for that" I am determined not to lose focus.

Next thing I know I'm being pulled straight down into the water, by Kendrick.

"SABOTAGE! That's not fair, babe don't expect to get any tonight!" I pout.

"You and I both know you won't do that," he chuckles.

I shrug, this man already knows me inside and out.

"I guess you're right." I grimace.

"It's okay, Kendrick. There's one thing you should know now: Tatum hates to lose," she interjects.

"Fuck off, Aria!" I laugh.

"You do enough of that for the both of us, sister." She cackles.

"And like you aren't planning on seducing poor Marcello tonight?" I blurt.

"Oh shit, man! This is really funny," Kendrick encourages.

"I won't say no." Marcello deadpans.

"We all know you're going to fuck tonight, that's how you roll." I chirp.

"HA HA HA! Tatum, so funny…" she grumbles.

120

"I know, that's one of my best qualities: I'm funny. I should've been a comedian. The only reason you're even giving me shit about it is because you know it's true. Just remember, your room is right across from mine. I don't want to hear you in the throws of your passion," I joke.

"Aria, you know I love you! I'm just teasing you." I try to look like I'm sorry.

"Yeah I know. I love you too, bitch." She sticks her tongue out at me.

"If that's love I would hate to be your enemy," Kendrick smiles.

"Damn right, baby!" I bubble.

"Let's go check out the indoor grotto," Aria interrupts.

"I still can't believe my boyfriend has his own grotto!"

TALIA HENDRIX / TWENTY-EIGHT

✳✳✳✳

We stop at the gas station to fill the tank before heading north to Gloucester.

Grant smiles as I sing to almost every song that hits the radio.

How else would I survive a long car ride? The trip is about an hour and a half and it's anxiety filled the whole way. What made me think that I was ready to meet Grant's parents? I was filled with questions that didn't have answers. What if they didn't like me? Did I want them to like me? What was this thing between Grant & I?

As if reading my mind he says, "It will be fine, doll. They will love you just like I do."

I try to hide my smile. "How did you know what I was thinking?"

"I didn't, it's written all over your face right now," he smirks.

"Well shit, that's embarrassing. Sorry, I do really want to meet your parents. I'm just super nervous, that's all. I don't even know your parent's names," I confess.

"To refresh your memory, my mother's name is Selena and my father's name is Gordon" he laughs.

"Selena and Gordon, got it! Do you think your dad would let me call him Gordo?" I joke.

"Maybe, but I wouldn't try it at a first meeting, though." His face turns serious.

"I was kidding Grant. I promise I won't call him Gordo." I put my hand on top

122

of his.

"I know you won't. We will be there soon so just relax for the next 10 minutes. Can you do that?"

I pull my hair up into a ponytail and wrinkle my nose at him.

I turn up the radio and jam out when my favorite song comes on.

Grant even sings along with the words, I turn and smile big at him.

"I didn't think you even knew that song, Grant!"

"I'm only a year older than you! I'm not that old, of course I know it," he pretends to be offended.

I stick my tongue out at him.

"Better be careful. I'll bite it," he reminds me.

"Well, I never know what to expect out of your mouth."

"Same here, but we will have to get back to that later. We're here," he announces.

We pull onto a street named *Clarendon,* and the first thing I see is the beautiful tan two story house with a beige wrap-around porch. The front of the house displays the beautiful bay windows that overlooks the ocean. The front door is a burnt orange color on the outside and has a swinging wooden door with an intricate design on the outer.

We stride up the stairs together hand in hand as the swinging door opens. A beautiful older woman comes to greet us on the porch. She has raven hair that flows past her shoulders, with natural highlights of white throughout. Her eyes are bright blue, just like Grant's.

"Grant! I wasn't expecting you. It's wonderful to see you, honey." She pulls him in for a long overdue hug.

She pulls back from the hug and peers at me.

My cheeks immediately flush, not sure what's going to happen.

"Who's this lovely lady, Grant?" she smiles in my direction.

"This is my girlfriend Talia," he gestures lovingly towards me.

"It's so great to meet you, my dear. My name is Selena, or you can call me mom. Whichever makes you comfortable," she greets me by pulling me into an embrace.

My body stiffens, not sure what is happening, I let my arms wrap around her as well. I didn't want her to think I didn't like her, but I wasn't used to such loving touches.

"I'm really glad to be here. I've met your brother Mike as well." I beam with pride.

"Yes, my older brother has his moments. I'm glad my son has been taking such good care of him until my sister can move him to Salem."

"Salem is beautiful. This is my first trip to Massachusetts. I'm not familiar with all the beautiful settings just yet but I hope to call this my permanent home soon," I chatter.

"Where are you from, darling girl?" Selena questions.

"I'm from —" I try to answer.

"Come in, come in," a man excitedly booms through the door interrupting.

He is a very tall, muscular man, his eyes are chocolate brown and his hair is cut short with hints of his salt and pepper hair still showing through.

We all make our way into their home. Everything is white and beige in color. To the left of us is their white elaborate stairwell with white carpet. I have no idea how they keep it so clean. We walk through and into the kitchen where we all took our seats.

"My name is Gordon Thomas." The man holds a hand out to me before sitting down.

I offer my hand. "I'm Talia Hendrix. It's nice to meet you, Gordon."

"Would you like something to drink? We have pink lemonade, sweet tea or soda." Mrs. Thomas offers.

"To answer your question, Mrs. Thomas, I'm originally from Scranton, Pennsylvania and sure, I would love a sweet tea please." I nod.

"You came all the way out here to visit my darling boy? Please call me Selena," she corrects. She heads towards the white double sided fridge and grabs the glasses from the top cabinet. She pours four glasses of sweet tea and brings them to the table.

"Thank you, Selena. Meeting your son was a wonderful but happy accident. We met on the train into Boston," I smile.

"That's so sweet, and you two hit it off that well? How long have you two been together now?" she quizzes me.

"My love, give them a second to catch their breath. They've only just gotten here. I'm sure they don't want to sit here and answer to your curiosities," Gordon interjects.

"I'm sorry if I overwhelmed you both. I'm just so happy Grant has found someone he cares enough to let us meet. The last girl he brought home was---"

Grant cuts her off. "Ma, let's not ruin this with talk of history. Talia and I plan to live for today."

"It's okay Grant, everyone has a past. Including me, I won't hold any old stuff against you in the present time." I take a sip of my beverage and my eyes meet his.

He moves his chair closer to mine and wraps his arm around me, "See, this is why I love this woman. She's amazing."

"You love her?" Selena asks, now looking at her son.

"I do, mom. I love her. Even though we haven't known each other long I feel deeply connected to her. I hope she feels the same for me."

My cheeks flush bright red as Grant confesses to his parents that he loves a woman he's just met. I'm lost for words. I can't say I saw this coming.

"Are you alright, Talia dear?" Selena asks.

"I'm great, I just uh- it's a little warm in here. I'm feeling flushed." I say, feeling slightly insecure and embarrassed.

Gordon stands and turns on the ceiling fan above us.

"Hopefully this makes it a little less stuffy in here," he assures.

"Thank you, I just want you both to know I really care for your son."

"Is it okay with you if we talk about you a little more, Talia?" Selena wonders.

"Ask away, you're Grant's family. You are important to him, and I hope that you become just as important to me."

"So you said you are from Pennsylvania. What are your parents' names?"

"Well I was adopted when I was a week old. My adoptive mother, the only one I've ever really known was Amelia. Her husband Charles wasn't so nice to me after she passed away. I'm not trying to air my dirty laundry, but he was abusive towards me. That's why I came to Boston, to get away from that life," I murmur.

"Oh my! I'm so sorry Talia, I didn't mean to drum up bad memories," she apologizes.

"I understand, but you want to get to know me. That involves both the good and the bad. I got into trouble, and I know better now. I want to be upfront and honest with you."

Selena stands up and comes up behind my chair and hugs me from behind. This woman and her hugging...I was definitely not used to this show of affection.

"Honey, are you hungry? The universe is telling me I need to take care of you. Let me cook you a meal, I'm an executive chef, depending on who's kitchen I'm in sometimes I play the role of the sous chef. We have our own catering company. What can I make you?"

"What's your specialty?" I smirk.

"I can make anything dear, are you a vegetarian?" she queries.

"I'm not a vegetarian, so I would be satisfied with anything meat like," I gush.

"I'll make some beef stew, and mashed potatoes with brown gravy. Gordon can go down to the wine cellar and bring up a bottle, we are celebrating."

"What are we celebrating?" Another voice sounds in the doorway.

"Graham, what are you doing here? We weren't expecting you. In fact, we specifically told you that your brother was here this weekend," Selena gave him a fierce gaze.

"You didn't answer the question mom, what are we celebrating? Did Grant finally grow a pair of balls?"

"Fuck you, Graham" Grant fumes.

"Boys, this is no way to act in front of company! Graham please tell me you didn't bring that wretched woman with you…" she pleads.

"No Tiffany isn't with me. I only deal with her when I have to." Graham turns his attention my way.

"Who is this beautiful lady?" Graham winks at me.

"No thanks.. My name is Talia and I'm with Grant. Just because you share faces doesn't mean I'd ever be interested in *you*." I defend Grant.

Graham smirks,"That's what they all say."

I swing my open hand and make direct contact with his face.

"You're a cocky bastard and obviously a shitty human being," I spat at him.

Grant pulls me close, "Graham, you need to shut your fucking mouth now. I have no qualms with using your face as a punching bag."

"Do you always let your woman do your fighting for you, brother? Didn't think you were that much of a pussy," he baits, clearly trying to get Grant to fight.

Gordon comes upstairs from the cellar hearing all the commotion and grips Graham by the neck.

"Son, I love you but you're a fucking jackass. You need to leave now. You can't cause problems like this. We have company and you've obviously insulted both your brother and his girlfriend," Gordon fumes. He keeps a firm grip on his son and leads him out the same way he came.

I yelled after him, "Don't let the door hit ya where the good Lord split ya!!!"

"I'm so sorry about my other son's behavior. Beautiful women bring out the competitiveness in him. That's no excuse, but I'm sorry my dear," Selena apologizes profusely.

"Selena, it's not your fault. I'm sorry for my reactions as well. Let's continue where we left off: Dinner! I can pour the wine but that's about all the help I can offer." I smile sweetly, knowing I needed a drink as soon as possible.

"I'll get the glasses and set the table Ma," Grant announces.

I pop the cork on the Red Bordeaux wine and pour all four glasses full of the sweet nectar. I take a huge gulp of wine and feel the tension being released from my body. This is going to be one hell of a weekend.

XOXO

As I sat down in the seat next to Marcello, I couldn't believe they set me up like this.

"I like your shirt; very festive and colorful of you," I chuckle.

He licks his lips. "I could always take it off. I bet you would enjoy the show."

My mouth goes dry, "Ahem... I mean, I don't know about all that, but it depends on what you're hiding under your Hawaiian shirt."

We both look in the direction of our friends as Marcello grabs my hand and we run behind the rocks of the pool. The spot we pick is hidden from the rest of the pool area. He looks at me lustfully, but all I can do is bite my lip.

He slowly unbuttons his shirt, never taking his eyes off me. As I admired his tan skin my attention turns to his chiseled midsection; all of his muscles are toned and buff. He is the perfect example of an Italian Stallion. He leans back on his shirt and pulls me to him. I stare into his gorgeous chocolate eyes that match mine. The scruff covering his cheeks from what I assume is from a day or two of not shaving. I reach out, needing to feel it against my skin, I trace his jaw with my fingers softly. He pulls me directly onto his lap and I can feel his erection pressing against me through his swim trunks.

I smile as he leans up and meets my lips. We taste each other for the first time. He cups my face as we passionately kiss. I can feel the heat of my center, and the wetness through my bikini. I moan my frustration.

"You are so beautiful, like a ray of sunshine that's been hidden under the clouds," he whispers in my ear.

I suck my bottom lip, feeling a tear roll down my face. I had built up a wall and just like that he knocked a hole in my armor. I've been through my share of bad men: ones who cheated, stole from me and just fucked up my life.

Marcello wipes the tears away and leans in to kiss my neck. Just like that he made me forget the pain, I let a moan escape my lips. His hands rub my shoulders, down my arms and to my back. I feel his hand wander to the tie on my top. With one hand he undoes it and releases my voluptuous breasts. Marcello's mouth grasps onto my now hardened nipple, and I moan at the sensation. He releases it and stares into my eyes again.

"Aria, I'm not going to have sex with you here but when we do, it will be incredible."

My eyes saddened, "Oh… I get it, you don't --"

He cuts me off by placing his finger over my mouth. "Don't ever think that! I want you so bad, but I want more time to worship your body. That doesn't mean I won't make you cum.."

He wastes no time putting me on my back and trailing kisses down my stomach. Marcello yanks at my bottoms and presses two of his long digits deep inside. I close my eyes, arch my back and let out a passionate moan. I bite my lip, begging him to let me climax.

"Not yet sugar.. I wanna taste you," he whispers.

"Oh my…" I whimper.

He slides the bottoms off, and wastes no time putting his face against my wetness. He gently kisses my lower lips, spreading me for his own gratification. Licking and lapping up my sweet juices, he takes his time to lick every inch before working on my clitoris. Slowly flicking his tongue, driving me absolutely crazy. He grabs my nub gently between his lips and sucks as he continues penetrating me with his fingers.

"Mmm, Marcello…Don't stop." I beg, squirming against him.

He doubles his efforts and before I know it my body is convulsing from pleasure.

He comes up with a smile, "Mmm sweeter than a peach, and I do love peaches."

"That's one way to get to know me…"

"My goal is to please you. Of course I want to feel you, but not until we at least go on a date. Plus, I figured I owe you a couple more screaming orgasms," he winks at me.

"I hope they didn't hear me. I'm not ready to have to explain myself yet."

"They're too busy with each other right now. Nobody even knows where we went. There are cameras in here, but I'll make sure to edit this footage," his eyes met mine.

"You mean to tell me my pussy has just been recorded on some surveillance camera?"

My face reddens with embarrassment, I can not believe my best friend's boyfriend may end up seeing my vagina. I could cry right now.

"I promise, I will take care of it. I'm the head of security. Don't fret, sugar."

"Okay...I trust you. Please make sure nobody sees," I plead.

He kisses my lips, "I'll be right back, I'll do it now."

I watch him quickly disappear from the room. I couldn't stop thinking about what just happened. It was incredible, but not if it was on a fucking camera! I wish he would've told me beforehand, but would it have even made a difference? Probably not. I wish more had happened. Definitely didn't want that on film though.

I grab my bottoms, pull them back on and readjust my bikini. I can't be caught naked and they could find me any minute. Once I had calmed down and gotten everything back to the way it was originally, I headed back towards the tiki bar. I needed a drink after of all that. I climb behind the bar and began mixing my own drink. I figure I may as well get a little tipsy while I'm waiting on the news to see if

I made porn star status or not.

I make an extra potent *Sangria* in a fishbowl type glass. My body is still tingling from his touch. I sip my drink and look in the direction that Tatum and Kendrick had been, but they weren't there anymore. Maybe they were doing a little peach eating of their own.

I giggle at the thought. I'm glad my bestie is happy. After about ten minutes Marcello returns with a smile on his face.

"So??? Did you do it??" I pelt him with questions.

"It's done, but I'm not saying that I don't have the only copy," he winks again.

"You're kidding, right? That's a joke right?" I frett.

"Nope. I want to remember this moment forever. The day I first tasted that sweet peach."

"Fuck...If you show anyone I will end you!"

"Never my intention, it's only for me," he grinned.

"You are lucky that I like you.." I growl.

"Oh... you're sexy when you're mad, Peaches," he quips.

"Now I have a nickname...that's just rich. You don't think eventually someone is going to realize why you call me Peaches?"

"Let them figure it out. If I have my way nobody else will ever taste you again," he vows.

I couldn't help but smile at him. He thought he had me all figured out. Little did he know that I don't trust men easily. I've been burned before and every time sex was involved they got off and got out.

I couldn't say I felt that vibe from Marcello, but he's a man, after all. I can't trust so easily.

"What are you thinking about, Peaches?" He challenges.

"I have trust issues, that's all. Every man I've ever met has lied, cheated or stolen from me. I don't plan on letting history repeat itself. If you just want to use me for sex Marcello, then get it over with," I rasped.

"This is exactly why I didn't have sex with you. I'm not like the others. I have all the time in the world to prove it to you. It will be difficult to resist your captivating beauty, but I was raised to respect women, especially ones who attract my attention."

"I'm sure your mother would be proud of you, keeping a video of me hostage," I joke.

Before I know it, his lips are on mine again. That's one way to shut up a Morretti. He kisses me with such passion that I don't realize we are being watched.

Graham Thomas | Thirty

✗✗✗✗

I leave my house and head to visit my son, Branson. I never got a chance to help, let alone choose his name. At least my last name was on his birth certificate, which attached him to me forever.

I never made it far from Gloucester, but I did make it to Beverly. Tiffany lives not far from where I stay, which suites me because I want to be accessible to Branson. Unfortunately Tiffany didn't see it that way. She calls whenever she wants. She thinks she owns me, but in reality if I didn't want to own up to being a father I would've gotten out already.

At least something good came from knowing her. When I finally made it to her house, she is standing with her hands on her hips waiting for me on the porch.

"Where's my son? I came to visit him," I demand.

"He's not here, he's at my ma's," she slurs.

"What the fuck, Tiffany! You knew I was coming over to see him. Why even let me waste my time coming over?" I spat.

"I thought we could have some fun, Graham baby. You know it's been forever since you've had me," she winks.

"I don't have time for your nasty ass today. I want to see my son. If he's not here I'll come back later. I don't come to visit your STD having ass!" I growl.

"Fuck you, Graham, you know you like this," she gestures to her body.

"Nope, I'm out! Fuck this!"

I walk back to my truck and get the fuck out of dodge. My tires squeal as I peel out of her driveway. Fucking bitch! I would never sleep with her again. The first time was a mistake, I actually feel bad about hurting Grant, but he never will accept my apology.

My phone buzzes from the seat next to me. I grab it and press the talk button.

"Graham dear! How are you? How's my beautiful grandson? I miss him! You need to bring him up soon!" My mother squeaks through the phone.

"Hi Ma! It's good to hear from you. I didn't get to see him today, Tiffany's being a... Well, she didn't let me see him. As soon as I get him for a weekend we will come see you guys."

"Your brother is coming to visit today. We miss you darling."

"Grant's coming to visit?" This peaks my interest.

"Yes, he's coming to visit! That's what I said. Graham, do you ever listen to your mother?" She scolds.

"Of course I do! I'm just surprised, I haven't seen him since Branson was born."

"I've got to get stuff ready! Feel free to stop by! Love you darling."

The line goes dead.

Guess I'm heading to my parents house. It's only a twenty minute drive from Gloucester. I'm already in my truck, so I head that way. I hope that maybe if Grant's in a listening mood that I can get through to him. I know we are in constant competition, and yes I have fucked almost every girl he's ever dated, but he's my twin brother. I love him and I am sorry. I wasn't always the asshole player and I hope one day Grant can forgive me.

When I finally get to my parents I see Uncle Mike's vehicle in the driveway. Grant must've been at his house. I'm the black sheep in this family for many reasons. They don't keep me updated, but ma calls every now and again to check in on me and Branson. I run a hand through my hair and head for the door. I sneak in unnoticed, but I hear voices coming from the kitchen.

135

When my ma sent my dad down to get wine, she said they were celebrating. I find out quickly what they were celebrating. Grant brought a woman home, a sexy blonde babe with emerald green eyes. This is problematic: My testosterone kicks in. He always knew how to pick them. Why did they all have to be so fuckable? I feel bad for the thoughts, but my jeans get a little tighter below the belt seeing her. I bet I can make her mine for a night. Grant and I end up in a pissing contest and it only took about five minutes of being in the same room. I was going to try to apologize, but before I got the chance my dad stepped in and grabbed me.

He pulls me outside and tells me to leave. Apparently I'm not wanted. Shit, I was used to that. I got in the truck and beat my steering wheel before taking off. Now I need to go burn off my sexual frustration. Tiffany is easy enough. I start to dial her number...this was a bad idea.

TALIA HENDRIX | THIRTY-ONE

✕✕✕✕

"Cheers!" I raise my glass to the family.

"Salude" they say in unison.

I was on my third glass of red and I was feeling gooood. My body was full of warmth and I was feeling susceptible to almost any suggestion.

"My darling, is it strange finding out about Grant's twin?" His mother rattles on.

"It was surprising at first, but I'm a twin as well."

I immediately freeze, why did I say that….Fuck!

"What do you mean, Talia? I know you said you had a sister.. you didn't mention you were twins, did you?" Grant furrows his brows at me.

"I don't believe it came up... " I stammer.

"How do you know you're twins if you've never met??" Grant was fishing for answers and I wasn't sure I could lie right now.

I run my hand nervously through my long blonde hair.

"I haven't met her, I just know. I can't explain it right now."

"We *will* talk about this later," Grant commands.

"So Mama Thomas, how was Grant when he was younger?"

Selena chuckled, "I like it, Mama Thomas. You are precious, my girl. The boys were normal boys growing up, except being identical twins they used it to their advantage. When they were younger they used to work together, thick as thieves.

They would switch places at school, Grant was good at certain subjects. They each had what the other lacked. The teachers had no idea, but I did when the report cards came home though."

"They switched places? They are so different, though. How long did they get away with that?"

"Into their late years in high school; junior year, I believe. No matter how many times I told the boys they couldn't do that, they did it anyway. That was until I let the principal in on their tricks," she bragged.

"You got snitched on by your momma!!!!" I cackled.

"I did. We got so much shit for that, too. Thanks, ma!" He says smiling.

"Don't sass your momma, boy!" Gordon interjects.

"Pops, you know I wouldn't do that."

I take another sip of my red. "Grant baby, I'm tired. Can we go to our room?"

"Yes, we all should head to bed. Early plans in the morning," Selena says.

"What's going on tomorrow?" I ask.

"Grant didn't tell you? We are having a little get together with some of our friends and clients. Our contact from Sanders & Son Investment Inc. will be attending. Mr. Sanders has personally invested in our Winery. "

"Oh my.. no he didn't tell me about that."

"Be up by nine, sweetheart. You can help me set up the picnic area out back."

We finish up downstairs, and once everyone has headed to bed we decide to do the same.

I lay back on the bed, thinking maybe I could distract Grant from asking again about my twin.

"Babyyyy, come see me." I slur.

"We need to talk Talia, and I think you know what about" he demands.

138

"What are you talking about?" I did my best innocent face.

"You being a twin for starters... "

"I figured it would be better if you didn't really know until I found out if she was real or not," my eyes sadden.

"What do you know Talia? And be honest with me."

"We are twin sisters...and that she's in Boston.. that's all I know. Did I hear that right, someone with the last name Sanders will be here tomorrow?"

"Don't change the subject" he warns.

"I'm not. When I met Melora she told me about a man named Kendrick Sanders. She said I could find my sister that way," I whine.

"Who's Melora? Wait, I thought you said she never showed. What else aren't you telling me, Talia? I've been so honest with you and you've been doing nothing but lying to me apparently," he growls.

"Fuck! Can we talk when I'm not so drink, I mean drunk. I keep saying dumb shit and I don't mean any of it, Grant."

"Drunk or not, you've been lying. Sleep it off, but I'm going to sleep downstairs. I need time to think." He walks out and closes the door behind him before I could respond.

I couldn't help but let out a sob. I wasn't trying to lie to him but I wasn't ready to tell him things I didn't understand yet. The tears flowed from my eyes. What if he never forgives me?

Here I was, stuck in his parents house and now we were fighting. How the hell was this going to remedy itself? Why can I never get it right? I need to go downstairs and make this right. I hope my explanation will be enough, but before I can move sleep overtakes me.

TATUM EMERSON | THIRTY-TWO

XOXO

The next morning came quicker than I thought it would. After Kendrick and I made love yet again last night I was hoping for some restful sleep. Didn't happen. Kendrick woke me up at six and told me I needed to get ready.

"What am I getting ready for, Kendrick?"

"We are meeting with a client on one of our investment projects. My father, Prescott, will be going as well. We will head to Gloucester in about an hour," he explains.

"Do I need to wear anything specific? I may have to go to my place for more clothes."

"Marcello can drive you and Aria to pick up what you need."

"Okay. When will we go, since I only have an hour?"

"Hold that thought. I'll be right back sweetheart, I have to take this call."

I pace back and forth, nervous that I was going to meet his father.

"Change of plans, my father is arriving a little later than I expected. Marcello will take you to your apartment now."

"Alright, I'll head downstairs to meet him."

Marcello is waiting for me by the door with Aria underneath his arm. I smiled, these two are just so cute together.

"Ready to go Miss Tatum?" Marcello chimes in.

"Let's go! Do we have enough time to clean up the house?" I question.

"No need. Mr. Sanders had a team sent to clean up the mess. Everything should be in order now. He even went to the trouble of changing the locks as well," he hands me the keys.

"Are you serious?" I say in shock.

"Dead serious. I still have to check the place before I let you in, but otherwise all should be well."

As we head for the car I can't help but wonder why Kendrick waited until this morning to tell me about this meeting. I hope they aren't snobs. I don't know if I have the energy to sit there and pretend to be interested in someone who's all about themselves.

We made it back safety to the apartment and wow, he wasn't kidding! They even put a heavy duty door on our apartment. I put my key into the door and go inside. I keep hearing an alarm, then I see Marcello typing numbers into a box on the wall.

"Security system too? Is this really necessary? I'm sure whoever broke in doesn't plan on coming back."

"Kendrick wanted to make sure you were safe. You are an important part of his life and this is how he wants to protect you." Marcello affirmed.

"That was sweet of him. I'll have to thank him when we get back."

I walk into the next room and open my closet. I have to find something that is proper enough to meet his dad and clients. I swipe through all the clothes in my closet until I finally find what I was searching for.

I find a long sleeve maxi dress in a dark orchid, that has a v neck giving just enough cleavage for the imagination. The dress dipped low in the back, so low no bra would be required. The length fell down to my ankles and had a slit up the left leg, showing quite a bit of thigh. This would be perfect for whatever was planned. I'd still be able to stay warm if it got a little chilly, and the thigh would possibly distract Kendrick. He wouldn't be able to take his eyes off me.

I jump in the shower, quickly wash my hair and body, continuing to get ready. I decide I'm going to leave my hair down, but wear it flat ironed. Kendrick hasn't seen me with my hair straight, but today he will.

I finish my hair and slide the dress on. *Gorgeous* I thought to myself. Sometimes it's good to give yourself compliments when faced with situations of judgement. I touch up the little makeup I had on and add some of my favorite pink lipstick. I swipe it along my lips and head back out to wait with Marcello. We are both waiting on Aria to finish up when I hear a knock at the door.

Marcello turned and headed toward the door. He looks out our peep hole and unlocks the two locks.

"Mr. Sanders." He nods as he opens the door.

"Babe! I thought we were picking you up?" I tilt my head, questioning.

"Once again, our plans have been altered. I'm so sorry sweetheart, my father's in the town car. I've been called out on an emergency, but I need you and Aria to go with my father for appearance sake. Marcello, I need you to come with me."

"Damnit! Are you serious? The first time I meet your father and you are leaving me?" I whine.

"I'm sorry sweetheart, business calls. It's more of a security issue. I can't get into much more than that," he kisses my forehead.

"So who is driving us, if Marcello goes with you?" Aria chimes in.

"I will be escorting you ladies and the senior Mr. Sanders to the event," an unfamiliar face interjects.

"This is Mr. Easton Nightingale, he is my father's bodyguard and driver. He's basically my father's version of Marcello." Kendrick introduces the stranger.

"Who are the beautiful ladies, Mr. Kendrick?" Easton asks.

"This is my girlfriend Tatum Emerson, and her best friend Aria Morretti. Please guard them with your life as well, Easton."

I smile at the thought, I am his *girlfriend* now. He has no shame and he is telling the world.

"Pleased to meet you, Mr. Easton." I held my hand out in greeting.

"Indeed, it's wonderful to make your acquaintance," he nods curtly.

"You should all get going. You wouldn't want to be late to this meeting," Marcello interjects.

"Before I forget, Tatum, you look stunning. Very beautiful and elegant. Don't be afraid, sweetheart, my father doesn't bite." Kendrick smiles.

I smile, but there is a sadness. I don't like the idea of being fed to the wolves.

Easton ushers all of us out of the apartment. Marcello makes sure the doors are locked and secure. Marcello and Kendrick head off down the road to his car and we follow Easton to Mr. Sanders' car.

Easton opens the door for us, and we slide into the backseat. Mr. Sanders was in the seat farthest to the window.

"Which one of you stunners is dating my Kendrick?" Prescott approves.

"That would be me, Sir." I announce.

"Maybe next time he won't complain about me taking him for seafood. Last time we went he caught you." Prescott smirks, trying to lighten the mood.

I hesitate, not sure if I should smile or not.

Aria is cracking up. "That's a good one, Mr. Sanders, I'm Aria, Tatum's best friend."

"I've heard of you dear, Marcello is very fond of you. There are no secrets in the Sanders family," he winks.

"Now I see where Kendrick gets his charm. You and your wife should be proud," Aria snarks.

Prescott glares in my direction, "How do you feel about my son?"

"I haven't known him very long, but I want to be straightforward with you. I love your son!" I gush.

"He's very lucky indeed, much like I am to have the love of my sweet Pearl. She is the light of my life."

"I hope to meet her someday soon. I have heard glowing reviews from her son."

"My wife is a wonderful woman, and I think she would like you very much. We will have to set up a day when my son and I are both available to have dinner at our home," he approves.

I smile, "Yes I would enjoy that very much."

I feel the car come to a stop. Easton gets out and opens the door for Prescott.

"Sir, we are at the Thomas Residence."

"We made great time. Thank you, Nightingale."

We both climb out behind Prescott. He reaches for my hand to help me out and I take it, grateful for the assistance. I grab Aria with my other hand before Easton closes the door.

We all head for the front door together, and Easton rings the doorbell for us. I have enough time to glance at Mr. Sanders' attire. He is wearing a dark pair of slacks, and a white dress shirt with a tie that is covered with his navy blue cashmere sweater.

I slide my sunglasses down to hide my nervousness.

A woman opens the door to greet us.

144

TALIA HENDRIX | THIRTY-THREE

✗✗✗✗

After crying myself to sleep last night, I wake up feeling like a mack truck ran me over twice. I snuck downstairs to find Grant, but he was nowhere to be found. I looked out the window and Mike's vehicle was gone. I don't know where he went. I hurried to get ready, but for what? If Grant wasn't here I was just going to stay in my room.

Fuck it! I'm getting ready. I'll go talk to Selena and ask her where he went. Maybe she would know? I put my hair up in a somewhat pretty ponytail, I don't want to embarrass the Thomas'. I throw on a pair of dark jeans and a dressy shirt then I head downstairs, hoping to arrive before the company.

"Hey Mama Thomas, good morning!"

"Morning, darling! How is my favorite young lady this morning?"

"I'm okay. Have you seen Grant?" I quiz her.

"I haven't. Did something happen between you two?" she asked, concerned.

"He's upset with me, I withheld some information and I think I really hurt him. I feel really bad. I don't know where he's at," I blubber.

"I'll tell you what; since you've had such a rough night you can get some rest upstairs. We can handle the Sanders' on our own. I will let you know if I hear anything from Grant. If I don't I'll be giving him an earful, don't you worry," she sighs.

GRANT THOMAS | THIRTY-FOUR

✗✗✗✗

I told Talia I was going downstairs to sleep, but that's not where I really went. I left the house very early in the morning, while everyone was sleeping. I snuck out, needing air. I headed to the last place I expected to go.

He answers the door. I think he is in total shock.

"What the fuck are you doing here, brother?"

"I probably shouldn't have come, but I needed to talk to you."

"What do we have to talk about? You hate me, remember" Graham growled.

"I don't. You are my blood, my twin brother: I can't hate you. Do I think you're a fucking asshole 99.99% of the time? Hell yes I do. It's been how long and I haven't been able to get over it?" I point out.

"You've heard me apologize how many times now, Grant?"

"I know, that's why we need to talk."

"Talia withheld something pretty important from me. I realized that because I never forgave you, I'm having trouble forgiving her."

"Well, come in, I suppose. I don't want all my business out for everyone to see."

"Thanks. I know you want me to forgive you. I want that too."

TATUM EMERSON | THIRTY-FIVE

XOXO

"Hello everyone! My name is Selena Thomas, it's good to see you again, Mr. Sanders" she says.

"Wonderful to see you again, Mrs. Thomas. My son could not make it today, as he had an emergency. However, I do have these wonderful ladies with me, Tatum and Aria," he introduces us.

"Wonderful to meet you Mrs. Thomas. I'm Tatum. Thank you for the invitation to come visit your home. It's beautiful!" I effused.

"Thank you, sweetheart. You look very familiar. Have we met before?" Selena asks.

"I don't believe so, Mrs. Thomas. I guess I just have one of those faces," I smiled.
"Shall we get on with business?" Prescott interjects.

"Yes, yes! I have the patio out back ready with food and a bottle of white waiting for us" she quipped.

"Mrs. Thomas, may I use the restroom?" I ask.

"Yes of course. It's upstairs, the first door on the left."

I head upstairs, really wishing Kendrick was here. What the hell am I doing here anyhow? Am I just arm candy? Once I get to the top of the stairs, I decide to do some exploring. I open the first door and peek inside. It appears to be a master bedroom. I have no interest, so I went on to the next room. I remembered she said it was on the left side. I open the next door and there is a blonde haired woman laying on the bed.

The door opening must've startled her, because she jumps.

"I'm sorry! I didn't mean to disturb you…"

"It's okay, not a problem. Are you lost?" she asks, not even looking directly at me.

"I was looking for the bathroom…" something felt strange.

"I can show you" she gets up and finally faces me. Her face turns pale.

"Uhh……..Uhm.." I stutter.

"How did you find me?" she questions.

"I didn't. I wasn't looking. Why do you look like me? Who are you?" I sputter.

"Well, according to our mother we are identical twin sisters," she concedes.

"Delia..our birth mom. I feel sick… What is going on?" My stomach churns.

"Here, sit down. We can talk for a few minutes, but if it's okay with you I think we should keep this between just us."

"No problem. Not like anyone would believe me anyway. They would probably lock me up and keep me in a padded room," I admitted.

I sit down on the edge of her bed.

"First things first, who are you? What's your name?" I needed answers.

"My name is Talia and I know who you are. I met one of our mother's friends, Melora. Eventually I would like you to meet her as well. She has a lot to explain to both of us. My question is: how did you get here? Did you arrive with the Sanders'?" Talia asks.

"Yes, I'm dating Kendrick Sanders. He's not here though, I'm here with my best friend and Kendrick's father."

"We don't have a whole lot of time, they will realize you are taking too long, and come looking for you. I know we don't know each other, but I love you. Here's my number. When you're ready to learn about everything, message me." She hugs me and points me in the direction of the bathroom.

"Before I go, what are you doing here?"

"I'm dating Grant Thomas, their son. Same as you."

"Do you believe in fate? I think we were meant to run into each other." I tell her.

"I do! Our mother has been visiting both of us in our dreams. We are in danger if we stay too far apart. Call me tomorrow. We can meet, but remember, you have to keep it a secret," Talia warns.

"Little secrets grow up to be big lies, I suppose." I frown.

KENDRICK SANDERS | THIRTY-SIX

xoxo

Leaving Tatum to fend for herself alone with my father isn't something I wanted to do. When I got the emergency phone call, I had to take care of some business. I received a threat, one that I had to take extremely serious. My security team has found the vehicle that tailed us, and whoever was driving wanted it to be found.

The driver left a photograph of a woman with a menacing message, which my team, including my mother's bodyguard Valkyrie, thought I should see it in person.

When I get to my office, which was where the car had been abandoned, I realize that wasn't all this stranger had left for me. My office had been broken into and ransacked. I'm not sure what they planned on finding, but if this was about Tatum, there was nothing they could find there. One thing this person could find though is the address of my estate.

My heart leapt out of my chest seeing the photograph: it's Tatum. The message says;

"She dies by my hand. Time is ticking.
She's MINE!"

"First things first... this office cannot look like this when employees arrive for work. Let's clean this mess up, Marcello. I suppose it's a good time to rearrange anyway."

Marcello pulls the trash cans to the middle of the room and begins throwing broken things away. I start picking up all the books from the floor, and placing them in their spots on the shelf. Luckily my laptop had been in my home office or this maniac may have broken into that as well. I grab a broken picture that had been

150

thrown from my desk. It's a picture from several years ago, when my parents had renewed their vows. Anger begins to take over me. This has to fucking stop, I need to find the prick who is destroying my world.

I slam my hand on the desk, but there is something I was missing. At this very moment I was glad that I had sent Tatum off with my father. Easton Nightingale was a former Navy Seal and there are only three members of my team I trusted with my love. Marcello, Easton and Valkyrie. All three would kill to save my family, my love included.

My body was going through the motions of cleaning, but my mind was miles away from there. I have a relationship blooming, and I need to make this place a safe haven for my love. She wasn't theirs…. she was mine and now I needed to prove it to the world. We had to go shopping, securing safety at any cost.

"Where to Mr. Sanders?" Marcello inquired.

"333 Washington Street" I beamed.

"Sir? You will have to do a little better than that, please," he smiles.

"Can't give away all my secrets just yet."

Tatum would never expect this from me. The message was enough to prove to me if something happened I would never forgive myself. Doing this makes her more protected.

"It'll take us about twenty minutes to get there. I will make the phone call so they know to expect us."

For the entire drive my mind flashes pictures from the scene at my office. The vehicle, the decimated room...none of it made any fucking sense. The only way to get on top of this situation was to stay diligent and tighten security.

"Boss we are here… is this the right place?" Marcello sounds puzzled as he pulls the car to the curb.

"Of course. I gave you the address, didn't I? Do you think this will make a big enough statement?" I question him.

"As your paid best friend Sir, I would say that is a definite yes."

I look up at the good sized building in front of which we are now parked. We are headed to Suite 226.

My senses are on high alert due to the break-in, so I am more nervous than usual. Before I headed to the elevator I needed to talk to her. I scroll through my phone, where I have her listed as sweetheart. I press sweetheart and it rings a couple times before her sweet voice sings into my ears.

"Hey! I didn't expect to hear from you so soon."

"Yeah I just needed to hear your voice and make sure you were alright. How is it going?" I ask.

"It's going alright. Prescott has the Thomas' eating out of the palm of his hand, so he says. They are very nice people, Easton has been keeping a watchful eye on the outside of the house. Every ten minutes he keeps at it. Besides that I'm doing great, I miss you and Marcello! Easton's pacing is driving me crazy. When are you coming to get me?"

"Soon, my love. There's much I need to explain. Just have to finish with some business, then I'll be headed out to Gloucester. I'm glad to hear my father hasn't done anything embarrassing yet. Give it time; he will."

I heard her chuckle on the other end of the phone, "I hope you hurry, I do miss you."

"Miss you too, sweetheart. I'll see you soon."

I end the call just as the elevator arrives. Now back to business.

Riding the elevator to Suite 226 the gravity of the whole situation starts to sink in. I know I'm making the right choice. It dings and we've hit the right floor.

We enter the shop and my godfather Adrian Harrington welcomes us.

"Kendrick my boy! It's great to see you!" Adrian smiles.

"It's always great to see you Uncle Adrian. I haven't been here in awhile. Not since I was a kid."

"Remember how after class you'd come here and spend a few hours working to help me out?"

"I do, but now I need your help. It's very important that I get this right."

CHARLES HENDRIX / THIRTY-SEVEN

✗✗✗✗

I get the information I need from my contact. I make Frank Riccio my bitch. He now believes Talia is missing and that she jumped bail. With just a little bit of information I was able to figure out where the rich fuck worked. Frank was my father in law's partner on the police force, and he is also Talia's godfather, so he was eager to help. What a dumbfuck. He's supposed to be some big bad police officer and he took the bait, like giving candy to a baby. He gave me the address and I head there in the vehicle I had stolen.

I fucked up rich boys little office, destroyed everything that may be of importance to him. I was trying to find more information, maybe a home address. No such luck, but I left him a little reminder that soon I will take her life like she took mine.

I take a photo out that has been in my wallet since I arrived in Boston and write on the back.

I need to get out, the buildings alarm system is blaring and I do not want to get caught by rich boys security. One thing I am sure of though:

He can't hide her away forever.

TATUM EMERSON | THIRTY-EIGHT

XOXO

I hurry back downstairs to make sure nobody has missed me. Everyone is deep in business conversation and the Thomas' have broken out the wine glasses. It seems I was about to miss the tastings.

"Oh Tatum, there you are!" Aria welcomes me back.

"Would you like a glass Ms. Emerson?" Mrs. Thomas asks.

"No thank you, Mrs. Thomas. I'm not a wine connoisseur."

"Selena please, Mrs. Thomas is my mother in law. What would you like to drink dear?"

"Water is perfect, Selena."

She pours some water into the wine glass and hands it to me.

I smile, "Thank you."

I hear a loud knock on the door. Mr. Thomas gets up swiftly to answer it.

I look toward the front to see who it is and I see a familiar face.

"Miss Tatum, we are here to pick up both you and Miss Aria" Marcello informs us.

My face lights up. I am so excited to be out of here; I didn't want to chance that Talia may come downstairs and reveal our secret.

We say our goodbyes to the Thomas' and head to the car with Marcello.

We slip into the backseat and I lean against Kendrick, glad to see him.

"You look amazing, sweetheart." Kendrick smiles as he eyes my body.

"Well thank you. Where are we going, babe?" I stare at him.

"It's a surprise."

"What if I don't like surprises? I'm not patient enough to wait…" I whine.

"Too bad, you will have to wait. Don't make me blindfold you," he teases.

"Oooh, I may like that!" I giggle.

"We are still in the car you know..." Aria snickers.

I turn to see both Aria and Marcello with big cheesy grins on their faces.

I watch as Marcello whispers something in Aria's ear. I watch her face turn a rosey shade.

"Anything you want to share?" I glare at the love birds.

"Nope!" I hear both of them say in unison.

"Kendrick, how long is it going to take to get to your mystery location?"

"We will get to *our* first destination in less than five minutes, then after that probably about an hour and a half."

"Hmm.. where would we be going that takes an hour and a half..Are we going to...Worcester?" I wrinkle my nose.

"No baby, I can't tell you. Just relax please," he gently runs his fingers through my hair.

"Do I have enough time to take a nap?" I smile sweetly.

"If you want to. I'll wake you up when we get there."

I rest my head in his lap and close my eyes. Where could he be taking us? I was excited but also terrified. I wasn't good with surprises. I just had to hurry up and wait.

Maybe if I pretend to sleep I'll catch him whispering to Marcello about it. My brain and body had other plans.

156

Delia was smiling; I preferred receiving her messages with a smile. She moves to the left and that's when I realize I was staring into a mirror. No, it isn't that at all: it's Talia. I reach my hand towards her...our hands meet and enclose in one another. My mother grabs our other hands and before I'm aware a rush of energy buzzes between the three of us. The ritual is needed to protect us.

The Trixana is the transfer of energies through three individuals. Once it is brought forth, all three are bound together. Our eyes close and our hearts open, we can feel the rush of our individual auras. Many shades of blue, and red and Delia's white ambience forming a purple effervescent flowing all around us. All of the colors intermixing making a beautiful mixture of amethyst.

My body tingles as I feel more connected, more energized. I can hear Talia's thoughts too as well as my mother's. My mother directs her thoughts towards me. Be prepared: your life is changing by the second, Tatum. I look into my sister's eyes: Talia, we need to meet once I get back. Where are you going? I don't know, Kendrick's idea. I look in Delia's direction. I know sweet baby, but I won't spoil it. Talia smiles at me: meet me in Salem when you come home. Meet with Melora, my sweet babies. You have much to discuss with my dearest friend. Get rest. She quickly kisses both of our foreheads and everything goes black.

I stir myself awake and I can still feel the weight of Talia's hand clasping mine.

TALIA HENDRIX / THIRTY-NINE

✕✕✕✕

I stretch my arms to the ceiling trying to shake the heaviness that is on my hand. My energy level is off the charts, but I feel better than I ever have. I need to prepare for when Tatum gets back to Boston. That meant saving and possibly storing all the energy I could. I still hadn't spoken to Grant. He never came back and I'm stuck at his parents house. I'm grateful they are such wonderful people. I have nowhere else to go, so I should be grateful. I start downstairs and stop in my tracks as I hear the door open. I sit down on the carpeted stairs, watching the door like a hawk.

Grant comes in the door with a little boy who looks a lot like him. I stay hidden making sure not to let anyone know I was eavesdropping.

"It's about time!" Selena says impatiently, while scooping up the little boy.

"Sorry mom, I had to fight Tiffany just to get him for the day. I wanted to bring him to see grandma and grandpa. Isn't that right, Branson?"

"Yes daddy!" Branson says excitedly, practically dancing in Selena's arms.

That's weird, why would this boy call Grant his daddy? Shit! It wasn't Grant, it was Graham! I should be able to tell them apart. I put my hand against my face. Then I see Grant strolling in after them.
"You are both here? At the same time? Do I need to referee again?" Gordon claps his hand on Grant's back.

"Where is Talia? I really should talk to her. I shouldn't have left like I did and I want to apologize and see if she can forgive me." Grant sounds sincere.

I keep my mouth shut, waiting it out. Was he really sorry? I wasn't used to a

158

man who apologized for things. I didn't even know they existed until this second. My energy was so high I wasn't sure I could do this.

I clear my throat.

"Talia! There you are, sweetheart! Say hello to Talia, Branson" Selena gushes.

"Hewwo Ta-leee-uh" he says, sounding out my name.

I wave at little Branson. "Hi there!"

Graham's eyes burn a hole in me.

"So what are we all doing here together?" I question.

"Yeah, what she said" Graham retorts.

Branson cooes as I walk over to him and offer my arms up to him. He jumps from Selena's arms to mine and wraps his little arms around me in a hug.

"He's not usually like this around strangers," Graham points out.

"I'd like to think I'm not very strange, but I'm definitely honored."

The little boy then did the strangest of things: he kisses my cheek, leaving a little baby slobber behind.

"Talia, can we talk?" Grant's eyes meet mine.

"I suppose we should."

I hand Branson off and head upstairs with Grant.

"You're good with kids, you know that?" He smiles.

"I am. I love kids, I hope one day I have some of my own. Branson's really a sweetie." I keep my expression serious.

"Talia... I'm really.."

"Really what Grant? You left me for two fucking days at your parent's house. I'm sorry that I didn't tell you the whole story. I should have, but it was just as surprising to me," I rattled on.

"I'm sorry. I had trouble accepting that you kept something from me. I should've stayed and worked it out and instead I ran away like a coward. I'm sorry, baby. I should've stayed, because you are the last person I'd ever wanna run away from," he confesses.

I felt the tears threatening to fall.

"How do I know every time we have a problem you won't run away? Where the hell did you even go? I have so many questions and not enough answers! I've been abandoned enough in my life; I didn't need the one person I actually felt deeply for to just leave. How can I trust you now?" I cry.

He grabs my hand. "I promise you I will never abandon you again. I went to Graham's. That's where I was, I needed to make things right with the last person who made me feel betrayed."

"You went to talk to your brother? I'm supposed to believe that? You two can't even be in the same room for ten minutes and you *talked*? I don't believe you."

"You saw us walk into the house together, didn't you? I realized that until I forgave him, I couldn't ask you to forgive me. He's my brother and I love him regardless of what's happened between us. Now I need you to forgive me. I'll do whatever it takes. I love you!" He vows.

"Everyone is always sorry. Until they do the same fucking shit again. It's going to take more than a 'sorry' and 'I love you' to make me think about forgiving you."

"I said I will do whatever it takes. I wasn't lying, Talia."

"You mean you weren't lying just now. You've already lied to me once. I'm not keen on second chances."

"You lied, too. I can forgive you for that, just like I need your forgiveness…"

I sigh "I know. I'm sorry. I'm not used to this kind of stuff. I don't usually have people care for me, or love me. I'm not used to people being sorry and genuinely meaning it. We can work on it, right?"

"Of course we can, baby, I meant it when I said I was sorry. In fact, maybe I should've gone to my brother for advice sooner. He told me if I loved you then I needed to man the fuck up and apologize. That I needed to make it right. He was right for once, so here I am."

"I need to be honest...I met her."

"Your sister? How did you do that if you've been here the whole time?" His expression turns serious.

"She came here with the Sanders' for the business meeting."

"Why would she be with them? That doesn't make any sense."

"She is apparently in a relationship with their son. I think his name is Kendrick. She came upstairs to find the bathroom and found me instead," I explain.

"Sounds like it was meant to happen. She had no idea?" Grant stares at me, unable to process.

"Yeah, I think it was fate. I'm glad you and Graham worked it out. He doesn't want to sleep with me anymore, right?" I laugh.

"If he knows what's good for him then no. Hopefully he doesn't ruin the peace between us."

"I'm sure he will be a complete gentleman. Maybe I can actually get to know him now instead of automatically hating him for you," I smirk.

"That would be nice, since my nephew has already fallen in love with you, there's only one person left for you to really get to know. Guess that would be Graham."

"I heard my name, are you two okay up here?" Graham pokes his head in.

Aria Morretti | Forty

xoxo

Tatum is fast asleep and I wasn't far behind. Somehow we manage to board the plane without waking her. Miracle, that girl could sleep through a fucking hurricane, I swear. I knew where the private jet was headed. I had to keep it hush hush because it was a huge surprise for Tatum. The flight was only an hour and half to New York City. I wasn't sure what we were doing here yet but I hoped Kendrick would confide in me. I was a pretty good partner in crime, if I do say so myself.

Tatum reaches for my hand in her sleep. I grip it and feel pure vibration surging through my hand. That's strange... I've never had that happen before.

"Are you okay, peaches?" Marcello whispers to me.

"She zapped me is all, static electricity...I guess from the high altitude," I quip.

He chuckles, "Not sure if that's a real thing or not, but I'll accept it."

"So do you know why we are going to you know where?" I nudge.

"Of course I do. If Kendrick wants to tell you then he will. I'm sworn to secrecy, Peaches" he smiles at me.

My eyes met Kendrick's and his pointer finger went to his mouth to shush me. I took this time of silence to look around me. I was on a private jet, and that doesn't happen. I've never been on one before. I was surprised to find out there were no seat belts like in a regular airplane. Now that I think about it I've never flown. I'm surprised I didn't have an anxiety attack during liftoff.

The jet looks like a very high end living room in the sky. If I didn't know better I'd think I was just sitting on someone's couch next to Tatum. It's a full size couch. It's amazing how different the rich people live.

I wondered if both Tatum and I would fit into this lifestyle. Marcello was obviously used to this, but I don't know if I could be. I couldn't help but feel like all of this was too good to be true. This never happens, we are never both happy at once. It's like the world has it out for us, only one of us is meant to be happy. If I have any say, Tatum will get her happily ever after, if it really exists. I hope for her sake Kendrick is the real thing.

I couldn't let that bullshit cloud my mind; we were headed to New York City and no matter what happens after this it will be amazing. I look out the window and can see the New York City skyline, then my eyes are drawn to it. Lady Liberty, she's a badass bitch. She has her own spot in the middle of the water. She's a queen everyone comes from miles away to just catch a glimpse of her. I smile and nudge at Tatum to wake her.

"Bestie, you have GOT to see this…"

TATUM EMERSON | FORTY-ONE

XOXO

I looked around expecting to see my mother. I saw another woman who was wearing a locket exactly like the one my mother had been wearing. We were in a forest and she was sitting on a fountain in the middle of the clearing. Her curly white hair was the only indicator to her age. She looked familiar, not sure where from. It was then I heard a familiar voice. I saw my mother: she was young and her hair was golden again, not white and grey as previous. Where was I? Was this a memory? This seemed like a moment in the past. I looked on, waiting to see if I would be discovered. I watched their exchange of words.

"Mother, I don't know what I'm going to do. There's this man, Allistaire, who says we are soul mates. He's a mortal and he could never understand. I need your help," Delia pleaded.

"Call me Eva...anything but mother. Darling, I prefer you not address me so formally. I may be dead, but mother doesn't do it for me. Mortals don't understand us and they never could keep our secrets. You're pregnant now aren't you?" Eva glared.

"If you already know then why do I need to justify that question with an answer?"

"Darling, you know what you must do. As a purebred Xana you cannot have a baby, and if you do you can't nourish it. That's if you survive childbirth. You know I didn't. I wouldn't change anything. You are still my baby and I am forever grateful to your mortal mother, Katherine for taking such wonderful care of you."

"Yes, I love my human mother but I also love you, Eva." She smiled sweetly.

"I have something for you, to pass on to your daughter," she unclasped the

164

locket around her neck.

Eva placed it around Delia's neck and clasped it shut.

"It appears we have company...." Delia whispered as she pointed in my direction.

"Oh shit" I muttered.

"Tatum what's wrong?" Aria's voice broke through.

I shook my head, trying to fight back.

"No don't! I didn't mean to!" I yell.

"Knock it off will ya?!" Aria almost shouts.

"Aria? Where am I?"

"Baby it's okay. We are on my private jet because I am taking you somewhere special" Kendrick tries to comfort me.

I let out the longest sigh. It was like I had been holding my breath and just now could let it go.

I let the tears fall from my eyes, I had so many emotions and I just couldn't handle them all. Kendrick reaches for my face to wipe them away, but I pull away.

"Sorry. I just felt stuck in a dream. It was about my mother," I sniffle.

"Sweetheart, whatever happened was just a dream. I'm here now and I have a surprise for you," he smiles.

"Yeah. Can someone explain why we are flying and where we are going?" I look around.

"You'll get to find out - we just landed," Kendrick winks.

He grabs a piece of silky material and wraps it around my head, covering my eyes. Everything was completely black, but I trusted in him.

"We are going to have to go down the stairs to exit the plane," he says as he scoops me up in his arms.

"You're going to carry me the whole way?"

"Just to the car, then you'll be able to climb in. I won't take off your blindfold until we are close to the location."

I hear Aria laugh. I'm assuming it was at me being blindfolded. I couldn't understand what needed to be so secretive. A blindfold?

"Is this really necessary?" I whine, pulling at the silk.

"Be patient for once in your life, Tatum" Aria asserted.

"Traitor!" I mumble under my breath.

"I heard that!" I felt a smack on my shoulder.

I am put down into the car. I feel the weight of someone next to me and hear the doors slam shut. We were on our way.

TALIA HENDRIX / FORTY-TWO

✶✶✶✶

Grant suggested we go out on the back porch where we could talk privately. Selena brought Branson outside and we headed out back with them. They had a beautiful wooden wrap around porch, stained to a dark oak. They also had a trampoline that was buried partially in the ground. That seemed like it would be safer that way.

"Where do we start? I never thought I'd be having a conversation with a set of twins" I chatter.

"I'm just glad that Grant and I worked shit out. It would be a shame not to be involved in the family. I really miss my family, and I'm really sorry that we had such a rough first meeting," Graham seems remorseful.

"Me too, brother. We wasted too many years. We shouldn't take any more for granted," Grant encourages.

"Agreed, tell me more about yourself Graham," I beam.

"I currently own a construction business, I actually built this deck we are on right now. I took a big hand in building my own house too," Graham smiles.

"Wow! That's actually impressive. This porch is beautiful, it seems to me that you do amazing work. How long have you been in construction?"

"I've owned the company for two years now. Previously I was working for the former owner and we built up the business together. He was an older gentleman who wanted to retire and offered me the company for a prime price. I couldn't say no. In total I've been in the business for about four years. What do you do, Talia?"

"Right now, nothing. I'm just going where the wind takes me. I hope to settle

167

down in Massachusetts soon. I can honestly say I love it here," I smile.

"I'm hoping the wind keeps her in my arms." Grant laughs and reaches for my hand.

"I've always been stuck between two very different careers: cosmetologist or selling real estate," I shrug.

"Real estate would be a good profession. I don't know much about the business of hair cutting, but I do know houses. Grant, are you going to tell her what we possibly discussed?" Graham stares at his brother.

"Which part?" Grant glares back.

He turns to look at me. "I'm going for full custody of Branson. There's a lot of stuff surrounding it but Tiffany has been withholding him from me, and on top of that I've seen bruises on him that she doesn't seem to want to explain."

"The other part he's referring to is…. me joining his construction company. He wants to co-own the company together. He's asked and I wanted to be the one to let you know his offer. I haven't decided if I'm going to do it, but it would mean staying in Gloucester," he hesitates, waiting for my reaction.

I couldn't help but smile. It was a wonderful opportunity for him to be able to stay close to his family, but what would happen to me?

"What are you thinking?" He inquires.

"I think it's an amazing opportunity. You should do it! I'm glad you two are getting along well enough to move into a serious agreement together," I reassure them.

"That also leads us to something you said earlier about being a realtor. Were you serious? Our plan involves you too," Grant nudges.

"We want to build the houses, and we want you to sell them. How do you feel about that?" Graham entices me with a hook, line and sinker.

"Uh..What the fuck? You're kidding, right? What am I supposed to say to

168

that? I don't even have my realtor's credentials. I don't even know how long that would take. I would hate to have you guys hung up waiting on me," I hesitate.

"Made in New England is the name of the company, and the Thomas brothers would like to formally invite you to be our realtor in training," he stares into my eyes. He would wait for me forever, no matter how long it took.

I sigh out loud. "Let's do it. You won me over. It's not like I have any concrete plans other than just today. I certainly don't have a job lined up, but how am I gonna pay for these classes or schooling?"

"It's a forty hour pre-licensing salesperson class at *Boston Realty Institute*," Graham chimes in.

"That doesn't sound too bad...you never said how much it cost though," I frown.

"It doesn't matter how much it is. We are paying for it and I consider it an investment, especially since you will be selling homes we build," Grant reassures me. Tears fall down my face. No one has ever believed in me like this.

"Baby we got this, don't worry about it. I promise."

"Okay! Enough business talk, I wanna jump on that trampoline," I effuse.

TATUM EMERSON | FORTY-THREE

XOXO

I couldn't believe my eyes, once the blindfold was off he revealed the most wonderful surprise. He flew us to New York City and now we were in an elevator, headed straight for the top of the *Empire State Building*. One hundred and two floors up, but I was told we were going to one hundred and *three*. I didn't have the slightest idea what was going on but I'm so glad Aria packed my Nikon.

"Say CHEESE, everyone!" I exclaim.

I snap the shot of all four of us.

"This is incredible Kendrick! What do you have up your sleeve?" I give him a questioning glare.

"If I tell you it wouldn't be a surprise. Do I need to put the blindfold back on?" he raises one eyebrow.

"That won't keep my mouth shut." I laugh.

"I could gag you with it, though." He smirks.

The elevator comes to an abrupt stop. As the elevator doors open we turn a hard right and there is a door to our left.

"So where does this lead?"

"You will see, sweetheart. Just follow me, we have one flight to climb and we will be where we need to be," he beams.

I smirk as I lean down to slide my heels off and take off running up the stairs. I manage it by simply pretending someone is chasing me. I was using muscles I hadn't used in awhile.

My jaw drops in shock.

All I see is a bunch of copper pipes. Where the hell was I? I take out my camera and start snapping pictures.

"Tatum, you didn't go far enough." Kendrick chuckles behind me.

"Where am I supposed to go?" my face scrunches in confusion.

"See those doors right there?" He points to a set of double glass doors.

"Where does it go and what does this sign mean?"

"You are full of questions. The only way to answer is to go and find out."

I push open the doors, ignoring the warning sign and immediately freak out.

"HOLY SHIT!" I yell.

Feeling Kendrick behind me, I turn to him.

"New York! This is indescribable."

"Welcome to the Empire State Building, the part that only important people get to see," he smirks.

"I'm special enough for that? I didn't even know this existed, I've never even been here."

I snap a few photographs of the view. The images don't seem to match the amazing sight before me. I am so caught up in the skyline that I don't pay any mind to what Kendrick is doing.

I hear Aria gasp and I immediately turn. Kendrick is on one knee smiling at me.

"What is going on? Kendrick, what are you doing?" My eyes widen.

"Tatum Katherine Emerson, I've never met someone like you. I know we haven't known each other very long, but it feels like I've known you much longer. I think I realized it the first day I met you. I want us to spend forever getting to know each other, building a family together...Tatum, will you do me the honor of marrying me?" He pulls out a box and opens it to me.

My jaw is on the floor, I never imagined this would be my life. All I can do is snap a picture of him in that moment. I was in shock.

Tears well up in my eyes. This is perfect, better than I could have ever imagined it. Kendrick's face is looking a little puzzled.

"Yes!! Of course yes!!" I squeal.

He stands, takes me in his arms and kisses me. He removes a gorgeous 2 carat round cut solitaire diamond ring with a stunning platinum band detailed with small tiny emeralds surrounding the center, from the box.

He slides the ring on my finger effortlessly. Aria at some point has weaseled my camera away from me and is snapping photos of us. Both Marcello and Aria are smiling. Aria never cries but she is right now. Hell I was crying, only happy tears now.

"I love you, Tatum. Thank you for making me the happiest man in the world." He rests his forehead against mine.

"I love you, too. I never imagined I would ever see the Empire State Building, let alone a secret floor. It's pretty but its not that spacious."

"Tatum, I need you two to pose against the railing. Be sure to show off that beautiful ring!" Aria gushes.

I snuggle closer to Kendrick's left side and put my left hand over his chest. Showing off my engagement ring, I was engaged now. Holy shit.

Aria snaps a few memorable photos for us. I'm glad we will be able to look back on this.

"Did you two know about this?" I look at them both with accusing eyes.

"I didn't know about this part, but I knew we were headed to New York City," Aria smirks.

"I knew. I took him to his Godfather's jewelry store. I didn't help pick anything out, but I knew what he was up to." Marcello mutters.

"I've never seen a ring like this, Kendrick. It's just perfect."

"It reminded me of your breathtaking eyes. A ring that perfect should be on the finger of the sexiest woman ever. I think I succeeded," he laughs.

"We are going to get married!" I smiled, admiring my new favorite piece of jewelry.

I couldn't help but wonder what my sister and mother would think of this all. Would Talia want to be involved? Want to meet my, no it's *our* other family members now. She didn't come in my life early enough to meet my father. He passed away a long time ago, but I'm glad my mom found Dani. They are truly happy together, and that would be the first call I would make.

"We need to tell our parents, Kendrick. What are they going to say?"

"Probably that we are crazy, but it's true. I'm crazy for you. Too cheesy? I don't think so," he smirks.

"When are we going to tell them?"

"As soon as you are done enjoying the sights here we are flying to meet my parents. They are already there waiting, but they have no idea what's happening. I just insisted they meet us there. I won't tell you where because it's much more fun that way."

"Can I call my mom? Before this somehow makes its way in the papers?" I frown.

It would be in the papers. We would have little to no privacy at all. Kendrick was rich, which meant everyone would need to have their nose in OUR business. That sounded weird; his business. It's not mine yet.

"Of course you can, but that would ruin the other surprise…"

"What surprise are you talking about, Kendrick?"

"Your parents; Victoria and Dan is it? They are heading to our next location," he kisses my forehead, almost as if he thinks it will make my world stop spinning.

I don't correct him, it's not important at the moment.

"You are such a stalker! How do you know so much about my family, about me?"

"I do my research, future wife."

I smile, lean in and whisper in his ear.

"If you know so much....what color are my panties?" I tease.

"That's a tough one..." he strokes his chin with his index finger and thumb.

"We are right here you know!" Aria's voice breaks the moment.

"Sorry! Let me take a few more pictures and then we can go," I say as I snap away.

I know they were being abnormally patient with me because my life was about to change in a big way.

TALIA HENDRIX | FORTY-FOUR

✗✗✗✗

After jumping around with my now favorite little boy I was ready for food and then possibly filling out my information for realtor class. I know nothing about selling houses. I hope these two know what they are doing.

"Are you all ready for lunch?" Selena chimes in.

"I'm starving, aren't you Branson?" I ask.

"Yeessss! Peenut budddaa and jelleee" he screeches.

"Yes my sweet boy, peanut butter and jelly!" Selena coos.

Branson slips away and into Selena's arms. Grant reaches to me and helps me up.

"Thanks baby, what's for lunch?" I smile.

"Chicken, it's honey butter chicken. I hope you like it babe," he pushes a piece of hair away from my face.

"Sounds amazing, can't wait to try it." I smile as my stomach growled.

We walk into the house to find Graham on his laptop at the table.

"Talia I have the website pulled up for the classes, I just need you to fill in your personal information. We will take care of the rest," Graham reassures.

I steal his seat and begin typing away, it seems to be basic stuff; name, birthdate, high school information, and a social security number. Shit it asks if I consent to a background check...they would find out about my history and it may screw everything up.

Grants' hand clasps my shoulder.

175

"It won't matter, trust me. You took care of it already didn't you?"

"U-uh well sort of..I paid my fine but the judge ordered community service, I left before I could complete, does that matter?" I swallowed trying to remove the lump that has now formed in my throat.

"Oh shit Talia… why didn't you say anything? This is bad, did they specify when your community service was to start?"

"I don't know, they didn't say anything. I could've gotten mail from them and I wouldn't know. I wasn't exactly able to take my time and check the mailbox," I frown.

"We need to call the courthouse tomorrow, in the morning. We need to get this sorted out, and you may have to go back and do the community service hours. That's just the worst case scenario."

"Fuck! I can't go back there, Grant! Charles will be looking for me. I can't just waltz in and be unseen. He has contacts. Shit!! What if he is looking for me right now! I need to leave, I don't want to put any of you in danger!" I tremble.

"Calm down woman, everything will be okay. I would never send you alone. I'd risk it all to make sure you are safe," he insists with his hands firmly placed on my shoulders.

"Seriously? That's your advice? I may have endangered your whole family and all you can say is calm down?" I screech out.

"You're panicking right now, you just need to remain calm. I know all this seems crazy, mostly because it is but we will take care of—"

"Done!" Graham interrupts again.

We both look in Graham's direction, our faces displaying the question we both need to know.

"Your community service hasn't been scheduled yet. Something about a conflict in your case. Looks like they have some other things here, Talia would you like to have a look?" Graham offers his seat to me.

I look at the computer screen having a staring contest with the words. I point my finger to the particular part where it explains a possible problem with everything.

"It looks like there might be a warrant out for your arrest, something about a stolen vehicle…." Graham mumbles.

"What!!! How can this be… I've been here, I haven't even driven anything in several weeks or longer! I'm so sorry I got you all involved…. I feel so helpless right now and I'm not sure what's going to happen to me," I stammer.

"I guess I'll be paying for it the rest of my life even if I didn't do it. I've made a lot of shitty mistakes but stealing cars is not one of them. The only person I've ever stolen from was Charles."

"Look Talia, we will just have to make a trip down to the precinct and get this figured out. I'm your witness, you've been with me this whole time I know you haven't done anything wrong." Grant's voice instantly calmed me, soothed every fiber of my being.

"Dinner is ready kids," Selena reminds us.

"Wow, Mrs. Thomas this looks amazing! What is all of this?" I wave my hand with amazement.

"Well for starters, my son wasn't correct. We have chicken braised in—"

"Let's not mince words and just eat darling. We don't want your wonderful dinner getting cold and it will if you explain everything," Gordon interrupts.

Plates of food are passed around like they would be at a Thanksgiving feast. It reminds me of the last one we had with my mom, Amelia.

We weren't ever able to celebrate it on the actual day because my mom was a nurse and was always on call. Her job was always keeping her busy and she saved a lot of lives. Back then Charles was the doting husband and even what I considered a father.

LAYLA MCFADDEN

We ran around all day prepping before Charles came home. My job was setting the table and then stirring the mashed potatoes. I made a total mess of it but my mom was never mad at me for it. She loved having my help and she was never critical of me. I remember watching her pull the freshly cooked turkey out of the oven, the smell wafting back to me even in my memories. Amelia would never fail to amaze me. I was eight years old then and I didn't understand the importance of treasuring every second, especially if we aren't promised tomorrow. I wouldn't make that same mistake again.

Tatum Emerson | Forty-Five

xoxo

Not sure where we are going or what we are doing, but we head back to the airstrip. My finger is definitely feeling heavier than when we got here, and I'm nervous to face Kendrick's parents. I haven't seen my mom and Dani in a very long time. I'm sure they will both think we are rushing into this big decision, but when you know, you know!

"My love, what is going on in that head of yours?" Kendrick's eyes meet mine.

"Just wondering how our parents will take the news," I let out a sigh.

"Flights not going to be that long, so we will see what they think shortly," he teases.

"Thanks, now I'm even more nervous! Can we go talk alone?"

"Of course, darling," he grabs my hand.

We head to the back of the plane to the master suite. He barely gets the door closed before I shimmy out of my dress. His face shows his surprise as the fabric falls to the floor, revealing that I had nothing on but lace orchid panties that matched my dress.

"Holy shit…. you are so fucking exquisite," he pulls me to him.

He kisses on the sensitive skin of my neck. A moan escapes my plump lips.

I feel the need. I need him. The heat between my legs and the anxiety is too much.

"Drop 'em, I need you" I breath into his ear.

179

He does what I demand and drops his pants, revealing his firm erection standing at attention for me and I haven't even touched him. I start to wrap my arms around his neck and he stops me. He falls to his knees, nuzzling my heat and nibbles at the lace. He tugs at them with his teeth and rips them down.

He kisses up my thigh to my center. I lift my hips toward him, begging him to take me. He doesn't. Instead he gets close enough he's almost touching and lets out a hot breath.

"Fuck me!" I command.

He stands up smiling but still not giving me what I want. I press my body against him and wrap my legs around his tight frame. I slide myself against him and tighten my grip on him.

His cock thrusts deep into my core and I feel him everywhere. His hands slide down to my ass where he now has a firm grip. He continues pushing me up and down, helping me ride his thickness. My face meets his neck and I bite down emulating a vampire. I wrap my legs tighter as my orgasm draws me closer to oblivion.

My fingers slide down his toned back leaving scratch marks.

He continues to pump himself deep, as I lose myself in his warm embrace. I climax first tightly squeezing him, milking him of his release.

"You are so fucking tight baby, this is crazy," he pants, clearly enjoying the death grip my pussy has on him.

"This is mine" I smirk as I slid off his now softening member.

"Forever and a day," he quips.

He begins cleaning himself up and swiftly does the same to me as he hands me my panties.

"We better get back out there," he smiles.

The plane must be close to the mystery location because the turbulence is causing me to grab on to Kendrick.

"What's going on? This ride is getting a little rough now, no pun intended." I nervously chuckle.

"Pull your dress up sweet cheeks, we probably just hit some turbulence," he smirks gently tapping my ass.

I pull my dress up and smooth out the wrinkles. Kendrick is to my right pulling his white dress shirt back on. He quickly buttons it and grabs his tie, never taking his eyes from me.

"I can help with that, *fiancé!*" I smile as I reach for the midnight blue tie.

I wrap it around his shirt and pop up the collar. I begin tying my best Windsor knot.

"Fancy. Where did you learn to Windsor baby?" Kendrick challenges.

"I learned from my Grandpa Verne. He was my mother's father. He taught me a lot when I was younger. I used to practice with his ties. He was a wonderful man. He also taught me how to play poker, have you ever played Kendrick?"

"Poker? Like the game of cards? I've played a few times. I can't imagine you playing though," he states.

"That's slightly insulting!" I huff.

I start to walk towards everyone else to take my seat, and possibly catch some much needed sleep.

CHARLES HENDRIX | FORTY-SIX

✻✻✻✻

The rich prick left with his security, but I didn't bother following. By some chance maybe he left his whore home alone. I could only be so lucky. Breaking into his guarded fortress wasn't nearly as hard as I assumed it would be. The place had fingerprint scanners, and luckily enough I had his fingerprints on file. The 3D printer did the rest, with his fingerprints on my fingers I gained access to everything.

Everything was pretty quiet. This alone made me question my decision, did richie rich have the upper hand on me? Did he know I was coming?
I snuck from room to room: nobody. I found his study, maybe he keeps his money here? I check the general hiding spots; behind picture frames, under the desk. It was then I found it, his Beretta he has safely locked in the false bottom.
I grab the handgun and tuck it into the back of my pants, even the second magazine was coming with me.

I needed to find the perfect place to put the cameras, I want eyes on them. I wouldn't have to worry about the assholes fingerprinting and figuring out who I am, all they will find is dipshit's fingerprints all over.

I drill a hole silently into the wood of the bookcase and place the micro lens, making sure it is perfectly set. I slither my way to the kitchen and hide one in the plant overlooking the whole floor plan. When I hear footsteps that is my cue I need to exit and now I would see everything!

XOXO

The love birds left the room and Marcello and I finally got to be alone.

"So are you going to tell me where we are going?" I question.

Marcello looks around to make sure they are completely out of earshot.

"Kendrick didn't want me to say...but he never specified about you knowing-" he hesitates.

"Well? Out with it already!" I coax.

"We are heading to Yellowknife. Kendrick has a surprise for Tatum there. The parents' are both waiting there, neither of them know each other or why they are there so we will have to escort them both."

"Where the hell is Yellowknife? You act like I should know, but I've never been anywhere like that. Is there even a yellow knife there?" I question.

"No Peaches. It's in Canada. It's located near Great Slave Lake, surrounded by mountains, nature and of course Native Americans. That's all I can tell you. I don't want to ruin the surprise," he clarifies.

"The only nature I enjoy is the beach. Tatum is terrified of bugs so hopefully we aren't too much into nature. I would definitely be interested to learn about Native American customs though, that sounds intriguing."

"Trust me, this place is worth the trip," he chuckles.

I scoff "Highly doubt it...I'm just there for the cultural experience!"

"You aren't in the least bit excited to go somewhere new? We are flying to Canada. Have you ever been?"

"I haven't, but we better stop talking about it before they come back," I hum.

"Very good peaches, are you down for some fun in the air?" he winks.

"What did you have in mind?" I question, curious to know his intentions.

He grabs me by the hand and leads me towards where I assume the cockpit of the plane would be. He slides a keycard into the access point of the door and it flashes a green color. The door opens revealing the outer shell for the pilot's quarters including his private yet luxurious restroom. Before I know it my bare ass is sliding all over the bathroom counter. Marcello's strong greedy hands vigorously trace my body while his slightly calloused fingertips stop at every curve. His greedy mouth devoured my neck down to my collarbone sending vibrations through my body. Without warning he slides a finger inside me, causing me to react.

"Shhh Peaches, we don't want the pilot to hear all of our fun," he whispers as he presses the very digit that was just inside me against my lips.

I take him by surprise and open my mouth sucking his finger in. I now know why he calls me peaches, my sweet juice touches my tongue as I take his finger in and out of my mouth seductively. I watch him intently as he bites his lower lip, showing what I already know to be his enjoyment.

My mouth makes a soft smacking noise as I release his finger.

"Did you enjoy that Marcello?" I smirk devilishly.

His lips crash against mine, he makes quick work of shutting me up. I've never wanted a man inside of me more than I want him right now. I reach for his belt. I unfasten and then pull it completely off, then tending to the button and his zipper. I pull them down and admire his erection through his briefs, I drop to my knees before he can stop me. I slip them down as well and glide my tongue against his throbbing cock. His breathing is heavier with every lick of my tongue. Let's see if he can handle more.

I take him deep inside my mouth so far I can feel him touching the back of my throat. A tinge of his mixture of sweet and salty lusciousness coats the back of my

184

tongue.

"Peaches, if you keep going I'm not going to be able to stop myself," he whispers breathlessly.

Instead of answering I plunge him deeper, taking every sizeable inch in my mouth. I slide my hand lower giving his balls a squeeze. I continue humming against his cock and feel his balls tighten as his release overcomes him.

"Mmm... peaches, how's that taste?" He smirks his expression sated.

I finish lapping his juices up and swallow it all down. I hear the door start to rattle, and a knock is followed.

"Who is in my private quarters?" a voice spoke out of nowhere.

Luckily Marcello was swift and locked the door after we made our entrance.

"Just a minute Captain!" Marcello bellows to the door.

"Whoever is in there you need to leave immediately!"

"Shit! We need to get in our seats" he whispers as he grabs my hand and opens the door.

"What do you two think you are doing?" he scowls as we side-stepped away from him.

"I was just helping uhh- Miss Aria here with her contact lenses. I uhh we need to get back to our seats!" He mumbles out as we run back to our seats.

Twenty-Five hours or so later…… HAHA!

After our six hour flight from Toronto to Yellowknife we had a black town car that was waiting on us and we all got in. Lucky for us we all ended up falling asleep through most of the flight. Tatum has her black silky blindfold back on and currently has Kendrick whispering what I can assume are sweet nothings into her ear. The location shouldn't be much further I hope, after several hours of flying. I'm really feeling the jet lag everyone talks about even on a personal aircraft. My mind was still buzzing from my encounter with Marcello, this was so out of my normal zone. I'm not used to a man genuinely being interested in more than my tits and ass, Marcello had me thinking. Future plans.

I run my hands through my almost raven locks and nervously twist a piece in between my fingers. I stare out of the window to witness the scene of winter and that alone sent a chill down my spine. I cuddle myself closer into the down jacket, it's length covering damn near down to my knees. The fur hood pulled snug against me, it reminds me of how much I fucking hated these long coats and even more the fur that I hoped was actually just fake. I had no way of knowing, it was a gift.

TALIA HENDRIX | FORTY-EIGHT

✳✳✳✳

Dinner was amazing, I've never thought I'd be a fan of spinach, but Selena paired it with cheese and I was spent.

"Dessert anyone?" she smiles, gesturing to her magnificent creation.

Lemon meringue pie. I've died and gone to heaven, my favorite! I don't remember telling Grant about that….maybe I mentioned it, but it could be coincidence.

"Yes please!!!" I belt out like a starving lunatic.

Selena smiles and scoops out a piece for me.

I take bite after bite, stuffing my face.

"It's so good!!! What's that extra ingredient I'm tasting? It adds a little something special" I question, feeling my tongue start to tingle.

"It's the strawberries, they give it a little more zest. I'm glad you like it."

I look toward Grant and his eyes look like they are going to pop out as he realizes at the same time as me….I'm allergic to strawberries.

"Talia, are you okay? Your face is starting to get puffy!" Graham's face now full of concern.

"Ma, she's allergic to strawberries!!!! We need to help her now!" Grant yells.

"Oh my gosh, I didn't know!! Let me grab the antihistamine" she cries.

"Baby stay with me, everything is going to be alright." Grant's voice sounds muffled and further away.

My mother touches my face, not Delia but Amelia. Her beautiful blonde hair pulled up just as I always remembered. Her chocolate brown eyes stare into mine and I couldn't help myself as I let out a sob. Mom, I miss you so much, I wish you could've stayed. I love you, Talia my darling, she coos. We will see each other one day, but not now my love. You must go back, now…

"*Darling* are you okay?" the voice whispers from my darkness.

"Mom… are you there?" I reach my hand out.

"I thought I lost you for a minute," Grant's face greets me with worry.

"Wh-hat happened?" I stutter as I'm coming back to my senses.

"Allergic reaction to the strawberries, but you should be as good as new in a few hours. The swelling has gone down drastically. Does your mouth feel any better?" Grant whispers as he brings his hand up to my face.

"I think I almost died…" I gasp.

"Another few minutes and you would've gone into shock…I can't lose you baby," he whimpers, his lips trembling at my cheek.

"I'm so sorry, my dear! I didn't even think to ask you if you were allergic!" Selena tears up as she places the wet washcloth on my forehead.

"I'm not that easy to get rid of!" I try to smile but my lips won't allow much of it.

Grant picks me up and carries me upstairs to the room we are staying in. His strong arms hold me tight as I can feel my body growing weaker. Maybe Delia was right, I need to connect with Tatum. The longer I go without doing it the more weak I actually feel, or maybe it's the fact that she's so far away right now.

I snuggle myself under the covers adjusting myself into the fetal position. I can feel Grant's weight at the edge of the bed. His eyes are drilling a hole through me, so I know he's keeping a watchful eye on me. I watched him through half closed eyes. He was still sitting, eyes now closed and his hands clasped together. It took me a second to recognize exactly what he was doing… he was praying.

I'd never seen anything like it before. I can't remember a time when I've witnessed someone praying silently, whether it was for a thank you or for guidance.

I reach my hands to his shoulders and give them a gentle massaging motion. I press my breasts close to his back and I know he feels when I do, and it's not just my nipples poking him through my shirt. My heart is beating fast and every part of my being is quivering. I need him to invade every inch of me. I lightly caress his face, he opens his eyes and his dilated pupils make contact with mine. I move my hand down slowly tracing over his nipple then down to his abdominals. I lean in close, using my tongue to trace each gorgeous line. He tasted of sweet peppermint cocoa and temptation. It made my mouth wet, but that's not the only thing. I trace every inch of him and find myself only wanting more.

"Let's see what we have behind zipper number one" I wink.

I release the pressure when I unbutton and unzip his pants, revealing his magnificent cock straining against the opening of his boxers. I press my mouth against the opening, teasing the tip ever so gently. I lovingly circled and smacked my lips on the head causing him to let out a low growl.

He pulls me on his lap and presses his lips against mine as his tongue requests entry. Request granted, we tangle our tongues together and I can't help but let a moan escape. I can feel his erection pressing against me and I start to feel overdressed.

I break our kiss and stand tall in front of my man, that sounds so different. I like it. I run my hands against my body as he watches my every move with his hand gripping at his cock. Pumping his hand up and down but never taking his eyes from mine.

"Hands off, lover boy, he's all mine" I gesture to his hand.

He rubs the tip where a bead of liquid has formed.

"Ah ah ah" I shake my finger as I lean down and lick away the pearl.

He stands tall before me as he lets his hands wander over my body. Pulling my sweater over my head and making work of quickly releasing my succulent breasts for his taking. His mouth devours my nipple, sucking and gently biting, sending chills down my body straight to my heat. I want him to know what he does to me, I slide my pants down and press his hand down in my panties. I bite my bottom lip as he discovers how wet I am, all because of him. His fingers invade my pussy, so deep it feels like he's touching my soul. I rub my face against his scruff and nibble on his ear while trying not to cause ear damage from my passionate moans.

"Grant I need you.."

Zero seconds later he pulls my panties down and does the same for his boxers. He plants me directly on his lap, I can feel his cock begging for entrance to my center. I straddle him and settle above his throbbing hardness, gliding my pussy against him. He wastes no time pushing himself into me, and I can't help but let out a loud moan.

"Talia you are so fucking wet, all of this is mine," he grits through his teeth.

I begin my stride, wrapping my arms around his neck I bounce up and down on him. Every thrust I can feel myself tighten around him, giving him a sexy hug.

Our chemistry was hot enough to melt the ice caps. Death couldn't keep me from this pleasure that he made me feel so deep. I ran my fingers down his back, digging my nails into his tanned skin. Marking his skin with the proof that this is real, he's mine. Those marks signified it.

I lick at his neck, tasting him while he's buried inside me. Our bodies continued moving in sync until his release took him. The energy from his orgasm was enough to bring me to my very own, my body shivering and quaking against this man. I'd only known him for a short period of time but he's melted me from the inside out.

He pulls me closer and lays a kiss right on my neck, I shudder at the touch. There's something about him I can't point out.

Tatum Emerson | Forty-Nine

xoxo

We made it to wherever the car was headed. I wasn't blindfolded anymore, but I couldn't tell where I was. All I could see for miles and miles was snow. It was everywhere. We had some snow on the ground back home but it was just a light dusting. This was several feet of snow.

"Sweetface, are you going to tell me where we are going?" I pout.

"Sweetheart, look around take it all in. We are here," he smiles.

I try not to panic as I look around seeing mostly water and a huge brown brick building that is about the size of a mansion. The sign in front reads *Aurora Lakeside Manor*.

"Where are we at?" Aria chimes in.

"Since we are here I think I can divulge a little to you all. We are at Aurora Lakeside Manor in the Northwest Territory of Canada," Kendrick informs us.

"The real question is what are we doing here?" I arch my brow waiting for him to answer me.

We pull up to the front of the gorgeous residence and I see two Mercedes Benz parked near the door.

"Well this is a hotel molded after a mansion. It was actually built to resemble *The Playboy Mansion* on the outside. We will be staying here for a few days, and I have another surprise waiting for us, so we should head inside." He grins mischievously.

Kendrick and I walk hand and hand into the stunning hotel, breezing past the front desk with Marcello and Aria leading the way. We veer to the right of the entryway, heading toward a set of stairs when I recognize someone. Easton Nightingale stands there guarding a door. His dark brown hair is slicked back and his chiseled jaw fixed in a straight line. His eyes are assessing the building, constantly keeping tabs. Next to him is a shorter woman. Her dark hair is cut short, shaved on the sides and the top is parted into two different french braids that she wears like a crown. Even with the weather as it is outside she is wearing a black sleeveless shirt, revealing her larger than normal biceps for a woman. She looks like she wouldn't hesitate to kick some ass. Or worse, slit your throat.

"Easton, it's nice to see you again." Kendrick nodded towards the man at the door.

Easton nods in greeting to Kendrick.

"Petrovich will you check inside the room once again. I need to go downstairs and gather the others." Nightingale reports and then quickly disappears.

"Sir, Give minute, I check for you" Petrovich addresses us with her thick Russian accent.

"Who is Petrovich?" I frown at Kendrick.

"That is Valkyrie Petrovich, she is my mother's bodyguard. Both my parents are here…. so are yours," he reveals.

"My… parents? Your parents? What is really going on here Kendrick?" I demand.

"We are here for a meet and greet. We are engaged now, you will be a Sanders soon, my love. Don't you think we should all meet and announce it together?"

"Who's idea was it to come to Canada and meet here? Don't get me wrong, it's beautiful, but I was lured here under false pretenses…" I sigh.

"Well.. I just bought this hotel as an engagement gift for you.." Kendrick smirks.

"WHAT?! You did what? You just proposed to me... what the fuck is going on!!" I belted out.

"Tatum Katherine Emerson! You watch your language! We are in a public place!" I hear my mother screech at me.

"Mom.. how great to see you! Hi Dani, how are you?" I smile smugly.

"You're Dani?" Kendrick questions, no doubt wondering why I didn't tell him.

"Yes I'm Victoria's wife Danielle, but you can call me Dani. It's nice to meet you, what did you say your name was?" Dani reaches her hand out to Kendrick.

"I'm Kendrick Sanders, it's a pleasure to meet you both. My parents should be along any minute now."

"Da, all clear. You may enter," Valkyrie interrupts.

I look around for Aria and Marcello and they are nowhere to be found. How the hell did I get into this mess. We walk into the room, and it's almost as big as my apartment. It's a whole house in one room, there's a large square oak dinner table to the right with a stainless steel fridge and stove tucked away in the corner. The bedrooms are off to the side and separated in three different rooms, thank goodness. They each appear to have their own bathroom suites attached to them. Kendrick had definitely thought of everything.

"Let's all take a seat, Valkyrie will make us some cocktails and we can get to know each other better," Kendrick nodded.

Everyone takes a seat and the 20 questions began to fly…

"So, Kendrick is it? How do you know my daughter and what is the meaning of flying us so far away?" Victoria snarks.

"Mrs. Emerson, your daughter and I are.." the door interrupts Kendrick's thoughts.

"Darling! There you are!" Pearl almost shouts.

"Mother! Father! Have a seat, there are some people I'd like to introduce you to," Kendrick grins.

Pearl and Prescott take the seats opposite my mom and Dani. They exchange casual greetings, both introducing each other.

Kendrick holds my hand underneath the table.

"To answer your questions, there's something your daughter and I would love to share with you."

I hold my hand up to show the four of them the beautiful engagement ring.

"We're engaged!" I smile, feeling the happiest I've been ever.

"Congratulations to you both" The Sanders reply.

"Tatum why is this the first time I'm hearing of this man? This is a little fast, don't you think? How long have you been seeing each other?" Victoria practically pouts.

"We've been together almost a month now. I'm 24 years old mom. I'm allowed to live my life. Yes it is soon, but we both feel so much love towards each other. If you can't be happy for us mom why are you even here?" I frown.

"We can't wait to have you as our daughter in-law honey! We can't wait for you to be a Sanders," Pearl gushes.

"I heard Kendrick here bought this manor to honor your engagement. This is a great investment " Prescott nods his approval.

"So when did you pop the question Kendrick?" Dani asks.

"Today actually… I took her to the exclusive top floor of the Empire State Building and proposed there," Kendrick replies.

"That's fabulous, but was this the only reason we were brought here?" Pearl interjects.

"No I have a surprise for the whole family. I hope everyone brought their winter gear. Are any of you familiar with the phenomenon of the Aurora Borealis?"

Kendrick asked as he rubbed his hands against each other.

I tossed back my drink, hoping it would loosen me up, this was awkward and my mother hasn't said anything since I spoke.

"Can I get another Vodka Cranberry?" I ask Valkyrie.

"Da, I get for you" she responds as she takes my empty glass.

Later that evening…

The eight of us make the trip down to Lake Aurora where we were met by Valkyrie and Easton. They have a fire started in the pit next to the very spacious deck. It's furnished with a large outdoor sectional with lots of colorful yarn infused pillows.

"Ladies, you'll find blankets set out for you that have been warmed by the fire. Hopefully they'll take the bite out of the crisp air we appear to be having." Easton gestures to the luxurious dark brown cashmere blankets placed around the seating area.

I didn't realize before, but Easton's British accent is very prevalent to me now. Not sure why I never noticed, I assume it's because he doesn't speak very often. I smile at him and he only nods back at me. I grab a spot on the left side of the U-shaped sectional for Kendrick and I.

I want to be far away from my mom right now, thankfully they sat on the opposite side as us. Kendrick snuggles against me and carefully drapes the cashmere blanket over us both.

"So what are we doing out here, sweetface?" I ask as I nuzzle myself against his neck.

Kendrick points to the sky across from the lake. It started off slow, but the colors began dancing in the sky. The closer to the trees of the forest the more lime green shows. The smokey waves became bigger and more bold on this chilly

195

November night. Before our eyes the other pigments layered and intertwined together. Alluring colors of green, purple, blues and yellows fill the night sky in continuous motion. The rays of white split through the vibrant waves, reaching for the heavens. I've never seen anything like it. I am in complete awe. The Northern Lights reminded me of all the wonderful magical things in the world. Marrying Kendrick would be the most magical moment in my whole life. In this moment my soul felt complete, and every bit of negative energy had been washed away.

As the colors continued, I felt my inner energy charge as if I needed this. I wish my sister was here, we could use this time to connect.

Two weeks later back in Boston…

I need to text my sister Talia and figure out a place to meet with her. Kendrick is busy with work, so a lie will not be necessary. That wouldn't be a good start to our engagement; this would be a very hard pill to swallow and with finalizing the wedding plans I can't risk it.

I message her:

Me: *We need to talk about meeting up.*

The dots of her reply make the hair on my neck stand straight up. What will she say? Does she really want to meet up with me and connect?

Talia: *Today. It has to be today. Grant's out and I know you are plan-free too.*

How did she know I was plan-free? Maybe the more we connect our powers will make us more susceptible to reading each other.

Talia: *Yes, I can read your thoughts. It's something new. Must be the clarisense that Melora was talking about. Meet me in an hour at Melora's.*

Me: *What was the address again?*

Talia: *The Witch House. 310 Essex. In an hour.*

I head into the kitchen, I just need to check with one of Kendrick's staff, Kiyah Galway. She is the resident redhead of the Sander's Mansion, she's also the youngest. Her short copper orange and yellow pixie spikes resemble something of a fireball. Her bangs are choppy, framing her face and her blue eyes, so bright and icey. At the young age of 20 she helps Jewel manage the kitchen mostly, but she is also the co-head housekeeper on Kendrick's payroll. She keeps everything going, I mean everything. She takes charge when Jewel is on vacation or on her days off. I don't know how Kiyah does it at her age. Kendrick has a soft spot for her, I'll have to remember to ask him about her.

"Hey Kiyah, is my car ready for me so I can head out?"

"Top of the mornin to ya, Tatum. Yes, it's ready. Would you like me to fix ya something before yous go?"

"No but there is something you can do for me. Is there anyway you can print out directions to The Witch House in Salem?" I ask her with a weak smile.

"You can do that yourself ya know" Kiyah smirks.

"Excuse me?" I raise my eyebrows.

"I mean to say, your phone is programmed for all of our wireless printers. I wasn't trying to be sassy, I'm sorry Tatum. Some time with me accent it's hard to understand. I'm just a young lass afterall. Apologies."

She's right, some of her words get lost in translation. I forgot to mention, she's straight out of Ireland and there are times I cannot understand a word of what she says. I read into everything, if it even resembles sarcasm I'm on it.

"Thanks a lot, Kiyah. I'll be back before dinner, let Kendrick know, please" I nod to her as the printer spits out my directions.

I grab the piece of paper and head out.

About 30 minutes later...

197

I arrive at The Witch House with twenty minutes to spare. I parallel park Ava on the street next to the massive black house with three levels to it. I examine my surroundings and try to take everything in.

The large house has three peaks meeting at the top with beautiful criss cross patterns on the windows. The windows that I assume belong to the attic are more petite in size, the round door is black as coal with a decoration hanging off it. As beautiful as it looks on the outside I am anxious to see what it holds inside it's walls. The historic significance of this building did not go unnoticed. It made me wonder why this was where Talia had asked to meet me, but it also gave me the creeps.

In the window closest to the door I could see a pair of violet eyes staring at me. I was scared shitless, but something kept drawing me closer to the door. It opened slowly without me touching it. I should've ran, but I needed to know everything Talia knew. I enter the building, looking to see who or what opened the door, but I see nothing until she wants me to see.

All I hear is the whip of wind as the door slams shut.

"Dearie! Welcome, I'm glad you made it. Sorry for the theatrics, but you never know who may wander up here when we are closed," she practically shouts behind me.

"I'm here looking for my sister and Melora… Can you help me?" I shutter.

"Of course dearie, I am Melora Vicari. Salem's secret keeper, and the witch of The Witch House. It's a pleasure to meet you Tatum," she smiles sweetly.

"Pleasures all mine, Melora. Where is my sister?" I survey the room expecting to see her.

"She's here now dearie, grab the door will you? I need to clean this place up" she winks at me.

I open the front door to welcome my identical twin into The Witch House. I

198

pull her into a hug and quickly close the door.

"Ladies, come come, sit sit I want to show you something."

"This is just a museum. Why did you choose this place?" I question them both.

Melora closes her eyes and covers them with her hands.

"Restituere ut original forma" she whispers in Latin as she waves her hands towards the walls. She opens her violet eyes, that are now glowing as she reveals to us her true dwelling.

"What the fuck was that Melora?" Talia questions, her face full of concern.

I look around and observe that nothing is the same as what it looked like a few seconds ago.

"You didn't really think I lived in a museum, did you?" Melora giggles.

"Uh.. well, yeah I did.." we both blurt out.

I smile, knowing my sister and I already have that connection...

Melora rubs the palms of her hands together and waves over the table revealing a plate of snacks and 3 cups of tea.

"How are you doing this... how is this even real?" I ask, the color draining from my face.

She then uses her hands and motions to our tea that is now stirring itself.

"That's it. I'm dreaming, aren't I? This is half past crazy o'clock..." I mutter.

"The museum is enchanted, only by me of course. To everyone else it looks just like you saw it when you came in. When it's closed, this is my home. I'm Salem's best kept secret. I asked you both here so I could explain more about your unique situation," Melora gestures to herself.

I sip my tea and try to make sense of this situation. I just watched a witch, something I never believed to exist before, magically make a museum into her own dining area. The whole area had magically transformed into something completely different. There was nothing left of the old museum except the fireplace, and as soon as I make eye contact with it, it lights up in flames.

"Don't be afraid, dearie. It's just a little magic. I know you don't understand right now, but you will see."

I sip more tea and as I do my vision gets a little more blurred.

"Don't fret, Tatum. I gave you maypop in your tea. Both you and Talia will sleep soon and we can *all* get everything out of the way," Melora cooed.

Somnum was the last word I heard before everything went dark.

Then I realize Delia is here..

"My girls! It's beautiful to see you together like this," Delia cooes.

"Thank you, Melora, for bringing them to me," she nods in her direction.

"Let's get this started. I would have invited your father, dearies, but your mother is still a little sensitive about that subject," Melora sighs.

Delia coughs and reminds us she is still there listening.

"Sorry mom.. " we say in unison.

"If you would like to know about your father I can tell you, I lived it. Allistaire Remington. That beautiful heart-breaking asshole. Even to this day I would fall to my knees for that mortal," she warms her hands and begins to show us.

Her hands move in several different motions, clearly tracing a figure of a man. With every stroke of her hand a piece of him magically appears until a clear image of this man can be seen. He couldn't be taller than six foot, with curly dark brown hair that had been tousled back and the most beautiful blue green eyes I've ever seen. His jaw was chiseled, but his face still an oblong shape. He looks like someone I should know... He looks like us. The general build of his face ever so slightly matched ours: the same noses, and the green tint in his eyes matched as well. I even noted that he shared the small ears we both have. How can we be so alike with this man I've never met and why has he never sought us out? I'm not even sure what happened between him and Delia, but I have a strong lingering feeling of dislike for this Allistaire, even if he is our father. As far as I'm concerned he was just a sperm donor.

"When I found out I was pregnant with both of you, I told him and he wanted us to run away together. He actually sought out Melora here to find a way to keep me alive through the birth of my gorgeous girls.." she continues.

"I wasn't successful, I'm afraid. I'm about twenty some years too late, but I know what to do now.." Melora admits sheepishly.

"You mean you figured out how to cure an Empathxana? To let them give birth without a horrific death?" Delia inquires.

"Yes. The only way for the mother to survive the birth is if all magic is bound and banished," she explains.

"What does that mean?" I spoke up.

"Yeah Melora, what does that mean?" Talia repeats my words.

"It means I would have to do a binding spell to strip the Empathxana of her unique abilities and that would make her mortal. She would be able to give birth naturally with no magic interfering," Melora murmurs.

"You're right, my friend. I wish I could've survived to raise my children, but I must say my sister didn't do a bad job as long as she was alive.."

"Wait... Who is your sister?! What did she do?" Talia screeches.

"I know I haven't told you girls, my full name is Delia Logan... Amelia is my youngest sister."

Bomb dropped. All of our jaws have dropped even Melora looks a little confused.

"Amelia Logan.... MY MOTHER?! Is your sister? She was my aunt? What the literal fuck!!!" Talia's rage could be felt in the air around her.

Delia sways her hand in a snake like motion in front of her. Amelia appears.

"Can you just call on spirits as you choose?" I growl through my gritted teeth.

"Sister, welcome. I'm sorry I took so long to summon you. Can you please talk some sense into your niece?"

"This is not what I intended, or how I wanted you to find out my sweet girl.." Amelia whimpered.

"How do you get off doing this to me, right now of all times? Bringing my dead mother here, only to tell me that the one and only mother I've known in my life was in fact my own aunt. This is too much. I want to leave. Tatum, are you coming or not?" Talia snaps.

I grab her hand; the way out is only one word away at all times, it appeared into my thoughts: Relinquo.

We were back in the Witch Museum, Melora wasn't back in her body, but we needed to leave.

"I'm done with this shit… I can't do this anymore." Talia sniffles.

CHARLES HENDRIX / FIFTY

✕✕✕✕

First lead since putting those cameras in. Finally Talia was going to leave the safety of asshole's mansion. I almost didn't check the kitchen cam, but I'm glad I did now. Not only did I hear the conversation, I was around in time enough to follow her. She drove into Salem; for what I'll never understand. Hopefully I can get her alone...

She parked outside a giant black house, the sign says The Witch House. I wonder what the hell she's doing here. I watch her walk up to the door, then I circle the block to try and wait her out. I park approximately 200 feet away from her location, right in front of The Salem Inn. My hand makes contact with the Beretta that is in my belt to make sure it is where I need it to be. She is going to come with me one way or another, and this Beretta was going to help me keep her compliant. I know I wouldn't even have to show her the gun, she would be afraid just knowing it's a possibility. She knows not to fuck with me,

It took me well over an hour to figure out how to navigate around this place. There's a lot of one way streets, but she hasn't left. I look around making sure no one is watching, then I slide and sneak over to her vehicle and begin working on getting into it. I find a paperclip in my pocket and bend it into the perfect shape to jimmy this car lock open. Military training comes in handy, more like the bullshit that happens when you lock your keys in your car and you are supposed to be on base by a certain time. I didn't wanna go back there. I wiggled and jiggled the paperclip up and down making sure to hit the pins in the lock and tada. The lock pops up and I make my way into the backseat. Before I do I make sure to relock the door and place a tiny camera up front so I can see her on my phone when she leaves the building. She should really clean this bullshit car, there's blankets and looks like laundry in the backseat. Perfect for me to hide under.

It took her about forty-five minutes to leave the building, and it took her another five minutes to actually make it to the car. Fucking women, I swear. I watch her as she looks around as if she is looking for someone. Did she know I was around? Shit I hope not. I wait for the door to open and close then just before she puts the key in the ignition I wrap my arm around her slutty neck. I tighten my grip on her neck as she struggles and tries to escape.

"I wouldn't do that if I were you..I'll kill that rich prick you call a boyfriend if you move a muscle," I push the muzzle of my gun against her temple in warning.

Her body went still. Good, she knew I meant business. I hit her over the head with the butt of my gun and she goes unconscious. I pull her limp body into the backseat and grab a zip-tie to confine her hands together. Once I'm satisfied I wrap several layers of duct tape around her wrists. Then I follow the same procedure on her ankles as well, I grab one of her socks and stuff it into her disgusting mouth and then tape over it making sure she can't scream for help. I open the console in the backseat that leads to the trunk and climb through, pulling her body with me.

I check her pockets, no phone. That alone was incredibly stupid of the douchebag. How can you keep track of your girlfriend if you don't give the bitch a cellphone. I use the emergency pull to exit the trunk. I cover her body quickly with a blanket and shut the trunk behind me. I open the driver's side door and start up the car. I'm going to take her where no one will find her, or what will be left of her after I was done.

TALIA HENDRIX | FIFTY-ONE

✷✷✷✷

This is bad...so bad. I had every intention of walking away from all of this. I hadn't got far from The Witch House when I saw him.. Charles was in the front seat of my sister's car and getting ready to drive away. I was frozen still: where was Tatum? I stormed out earlier and let my emotions get the best of me. My step father, or should I say my uncle has my sister and the only thing I can do is figure out where the hell Kendrick lives.

The only thing I know right now is maybe I should go back inside, face some demons and see if they could help me. I barg my way back into The Witch House. It is now clearly not under any sort of influence from Melora because it is back into its original form as the museum. Out of the corner of my eye I see it on the table. Tatum's cellphone and wallet. Why would she leave these here, unless she forgot them?

Luckily for me she doesn't have a lock on her phone. I'm able to get into it and discover she has several missed calls from Kendrick and a few text messages from Aria. I listen to the voicemails he has left.

Sweetheart, where are you? Kiyah told me you left on your own. You know that's not safe. Please call me and let me know where you are. I need to know that you are okay.

The other messages become more frantic: this man really loves my sister. I can't let him know what's happening, he doesn't even know me, he wouldn't understand. He would think I was insane. Yeah, Kendrick, uh my step father who we just recently found out is our uncle just kidnapped your woman. I can see that going over like a lead balloon. I can't explain this to him, so my only option is to be

Tatum until I can find her. I'll call him back and get him to come pick me up. I'll figure out how to explain the fact that her car is missing later.

I press his name in her phone and it rings once before he picks up.

"Where are you? It's not safe. Marcello will come pick you up, where are you?" Kendrick pleads into the phone.

"I'm fine baby, I'm in Salem. I had some car issues but I'm at The Witch House," I try my best imitation of Tatum.

"He will be there in twenty minutes. Stay put. I can't believe you just left by yourself knowing someone is after us. What the hell are you even doing in Salem?" He chastises.

"I wasn't thinking, an old family friend contacted me. She wanted to meet here, she had some addresses I needed for the wedding invitations," I admit.

It was only a half truth.

"The wedding invites were sent out 2 weeks ago, Tatum. What is wrong with you? How could you forget that?" Kendrick says.

Shit he's going to see through my charade. Think Talia, think!

"I know that baby, but I had them save me a few to personally give out because I didn't have the addresses to mail them. "

"Are you sure you're okay, Tatum? You don't seem yourself right now," quizzes Kendrick.

"Perfectly fine, couldn't be better. I'm just a little stressed, with the wedding coming up so quickly. I just know there's still a lot I need to do. I haven't even pinned down a dress yet."

"Sorry sweetheart, forgot to let you know… my mom, your mom and Aria are all taking you dress shopping tomorrow morning. I was going to tell you when I got back, but you weren't here," he sounds annoyed.

I needed to find a way to make him believe I was her. How was I going to

206

pretend to be my sister when I really didn't know her? I can only hope that Kendrick didn't know her that well yet.

"Baby, I'll make it up to you when I get back," I bit my lip realizing I never should've said that.

I can't have sex with my sister's husband to be. I had to convince him we needed to wait until our wedding night, and hopefully that would keep his sexual urges at bay.

"Mmm, sounds good to me sweetheart...can't wait."

"It's not what you think... I really wanna wait until our wedding night, to make it extra special. Can we my love?" My voice pleads with him through the phone.

"Of course, I'd be happy to oblige any and *almost* all requests my future wife has in store. I'm not saying that it's not going to be almost impossible, because you're not even here and I'm hard as fuck babe."

"So vulgar, Mr. Sanders," I chuckle uncomfortably.

"I like the sound of that... Marcello should be pulling up soon. Can't wait to see you. Don't think I won't hesitate to punish you for misbehaving though."

"I'll see you soon!"

I click the red end call button and finally exhale. This was going to be awful, I felt like I was betraying her and in some ways I was. I let my crazy step father get ahold of her, thinking she's me. She didn't deserve any of this. I hear the car pull up on the road behind me, instinctively I look to see who it is.

"Miss Tatum, are you ready? Do you have all your things?" Marcello questions.

"Of course," I slide into the sleek black car.

We were on the road for about half an hour or so it seemed.

"He was worried sick, you know," Marcello lectures me.

"I know, I'm sorry I upset him. I'm okay though, I should've been more careful and took someone with me…"

Good thing I was part Empath and good at reading people, otherwise I would be royally fucked right at this moment.

He nods in agreement.

"Mr. Sanders has several interviews lined up for bodyguards for you..Do you have any preference? I have to vet each and every one of them and sit in with the interviews," he says looking back at me through the rearview.

"He's making me have a bodyguard? Are you kidding?" I cringe.

How the hell was I going to find my sister if I had a babysitter. Better yet how was I going to tie up the loose ends with Grant?

"It's necessary, we can't have you out on your own. Especially with the wedding being a week away...I also know you lied to him about what brought you here. Is there anything you need to confess?" Marcello warns.

Fuck he knows… I'm busted.

"I did lie.. but it was for a good reason.." I pause.

"Tatum, you don't have to be afraid to tell him the truth. He's not going to be mad, especially if you wanted to go sightseeing or something."

"I was doing just that, I also wanted to find Kendrick a wedding gift.. He's a hard man to buy for. Any ideas for me?" I smile knowing I've gotten away with it.

"Something from the heart is always best," he smiled warmly.

"Do you know what time Aria and the moms are coming around to take me dress shopping?"

"As far as I know around ten."

"Like 10 PM? or 10 AM?" I question him knowing I am far from a morning person.

"Of course in the morning, I don't recall any dress shops open that late at night," he chuckles.

"Don't judge. I've never really spent much time in those types of stores.."

About 10 non-glorious minutes of banter later...

"We're back!" Marcello bellowed into the empty corridor.

A tall muscular man in a suit darts in my direction. I'm going to take a leap and say it's gotta be Kendrick. He picks me up and swings me around like he hasn't seen me in years.

"Don't ever do that to me again sweetheart. I was terrified something had happened to you," he leans in to kiss me, I turn quickly giving him nothing but cheek.

"Sorry Kendrick, I just wanted to site-see and not bother you with it. I've been dying to see Salem," I encourage.

He looks me up and down in his arms.

"How the hell did I get so lucky? I feel like I'm winning the lottery, I can't wait to officially make you mine on paper," he smirks.

As if he could ever "make me his" HA. That's a fucking joke. I will always be Grant's. He's got a lot of nerve. I have to remember I'm Tatum right now. I don't recall my sister using profanity, then again I don't know her that well. Let's test it out.

"Fuck yes, I'm so excited to be yours, baby…" I smile, and try not to accidentally cringe.

If I somehow end up getting through this without setting off alarms I'm going to run away and become an actress.

Kendrick's hand gently caresses my left hand and pulls it up examining it a little too closely…

"Why aren't you wearing your engagement ring?" Kendrick frowns.

"Well...uhm.. my car got stolen, I thought it was wise to hide my ring in the glove compartment. It's such a noticeably large gem, I didn't want someone trying to mug me for it. I'm so sorry, I don't know how the hell it even happened. I was inside the museum and I heard my car alarm blaring and then some man took off in it," I sniffled.

"Sweetheart why didn't you just tell me that from the beginning. I knew it wasn't safe for you to be alone. Don't worry love, don't you remember we had a duplicate made just in case this happened," he holds his finger up and then exits the room.

None of this makes sense, I have no clue what he was talking about. A duplicate ring? Is that what rich people do to protect their assets? Fuck. I felt my phone vibrate in my pants. I'm pretty sure I know who that is. Grant is probably worried sick... I need to tie that lose end up before I do all of this. It tore me up just thinking about breaking Grant's heart. I hope he can forgive me.

If I'm going to temporarily steal my sister's identity I need Grant Thomas out of the picture. I need to end it with him, I have to help family. She's the only family I have now, I have to put her ahead of my own selfish needs. My thoughts are interrupted as Kendrick comes back into the living room.

He picks up my left hand and slides a ring on my finger. The beautiful square emerald is surrounded by diamonds and is set on a gold band.

"I don't understand.. it was stolen. How did you?" I question him.

"We always keep your real engagement ring here. We had a duplicate made because you were worried about losing the stones. Don't you remember? Is everything okay, Tatum?" Kendrick's eyes meet mine.

"I don't know how I could forget that. Guess I have plenty on my mind right now. Speaking of which, Marcello informed me I'll be getting a bodyguard. When is this happening?" I showed my disapproval.

"That was the next thing I needed to make you aware of. I picked your bodyguard today. Her name is Wren Riott, and you will meet her very soon. She's on her way to the mansion. She and Valkyrie are acquaintances, she is trustworthy and she is very professional. She will be escorting you tomorrow for the dress shopping," he smiles.

"Is this because I left by myself? Some kind of punishment, Kendrick? I can't fucking believe you would do this without discussing it with me!" I pout.

"Sorry sweetheart, today was just the cherry on the bodyguard sundae. You need to be protected at all times and Wren will do just that for you. It's just something you need to get used to."

"I'm going to my room. I want to get a nap in before I'm forced to interact with someone I don't want around..." I huff, reminding myself to keep myself in check.

"I'll come wake you when she gets here. Love you sweetheart," Kendrick blows a kiss my way.

How the fuck am I going to find my room, It's not like I've ever been here before. I close my eyes and try to sense Tatum's leftover energies. At first I doubted it, until I got to her room. I lock the door then I sprawl out on the bed. Should I call or text Grant to tell him I can't see him anymore.. Of course a phone call..

I press Grant's name in my missed calls and it rings a few times before he picks up.

"Talia! Where the hell did you go? You just disappeared and didn't even leave a note..." Grant sounded sad.

"Hey babe, we need to talk.." I prepare myself for the heartbreak I'm about to lay down on this man...

"Oh shit, what's wrong? We need to talk is never a good thing..." he swallows so hard I can hear.

"We can't be together anymore..." I said feeling like I just got punched in the gut.

"Don't say that Talia... We are perfect for each other, I don't know what's going on but please give me another chance," he sighs.

"No Grant. We can't be together at all. I don't love you. I can't do this anymore. Don't try and find me, I don't want to be found," I click the phone off and the tears rage an assault on my eyes.

Fuck, he's never going to forgive me. I might've just sacrificed my only happiness in the world for my sister. I'm going to make sure Charles pays for this. I need to sleep, maybe I can figure out where Tatum is.

I lay on the bed and shove my head into the pillow as I violently cry myself to sleep over the love of my life.. *Grant Thomas.*

TATUM EMERSON | FIFTY-TWO

XOXO

What the hell is going on? I can't see anything... it's pitch black. There's something covering my eyes, distorting my vision. I can't move my arms or legs. The last thing I remember is someone wrapping their arm around my throat and choking me out. I couldn't breath, but I remembered what he had said to me. He would kill Kendrick if I resisted. I just found him... I can't lose him to this psycho. To my surprise I found my mouth was not taped shut...

"HELP ME!! I'VE BEEN KIDNAPPED HELP ME!!!" I scream.

I listen for a response, all I can hear is his crazy sounding laughter. He is laughing at me; this sick fuck thought it was funny I was yelling for help.

"FUCK YOU! Let me out of here! I don't know who the fuck you think you are, but you won't get away with this!!!"

"Who said my intention was to get away with it, *Talia?*" He spat at me.

"My name isn't Talia, you fucking jackass!"

"You're not a very good liar. The more you try the more you fail. You know what you've taken from me! You took my Amelia away, you stole many years I could've spent with her, taking care of her. YOU were the reason she died, she gave you everything you spoiled fucking bitch! Don't act like you don't know what you've done."

"Kendrick will come look for me! He's probably on his way here right now." I try to sound tough.

I'm not fooling anyone, not even myself. This guy is too far gone to negotiate with, maybe I can frighten him. Not likely but I have to try to get out of this.

213

"There's nothing left to find you bitch. Your car is abandoned and burnt to a crisp. Nothing left in there, no DNA, not a shred of anything pointing to me. You won't be alive to tell the story either," he cackles.

Before I can respond, something heavy and metal hits me in the face.

Mom, I need you. Help me, I'm in trouble! If you can hear me, please...

Tatum I'm here... I'm so sorry...this is all my fault. My sister hugs me tightly with tears in her eyes. This wasn't meant for you, he was looking for me. I know Talia.. Please tell Kendrick I love him and take care of him for me...This psycho is going to kill me. Make him talk about Amelia. It will keep him busy. I'm sorry we didn't get to spend much time together as sisters. Don't apologize it's not over yet. We don't go down without a fight. I'm supposed to be getting married in less than a week. He will be devastated when I don't show. I'll do it for you Tatum, I'll marry him. Then I can use Kendrick's money to give to Charles. He will let you go, it would be more trouble to keep you or kill you. Have faith in me sister, we are molded from the same cloth of life. I will not lose you. It's not an option, if given the chance to fight or escape, do so without thought.

I love you sister of mine... I love you too, Talia.

TALIA HENDRIX | FIFTY-THREE

✕✕✕✕

"Tatum wake up! You should've been up ten minutes ago" a voice practically yells in my ear.

"Okay, okay I'm up..I'm awake what do you want?" I hiss.

"We are going dress shopping with Pearl Sanders this morning, your mother ditched on us. What's your problem? Fall asleep on the wrong side of the bed? Kendrick not fucking you silly still? Or are you on your period this morning?" Aria glares at me.

I wipe my eyes and get my shit together. This must be Aria, her best friend.

"You are so funny, Aria. I just didn't sleep well. I had a rough day with my car getting stolen and all."

"What the fuck? Ava was stolen? Since when is she just a car to you. You are acting strange and you need to snap out of it. We are going to be riding together with Pearl & Valkyrie, so remember to act like you aren't a total nutter," she laughs and waves a hand in front of my face.

"Okay, I'll be down in like two seconds."

Aria slips out of the room and I change into Tatum's navy blue cold shoulder mini dress. At least that's what the tag says. The dress has cut outs that reveal my shoulders so it's only being held up by two thin straps on each side. The soft material flows down to my elbows at three quarters length, and almost touches my knees. Okay no, it didn't. It was shorter than I would ever wear in my life, it wasn't revealing unless I planned on doing something as simple as bending over. If I did my sister's mother-in-law was for sure going to see my ass, probably more than my ass at this point.

I finger combed my hair and pulled it up into a small bun on the top of my head. I felt like shit and that dream with Tatum last night did not help settle my nerves one bit. I open her side table drawer and find her makeup bag, grabbing for the volumizing mascara. I do a quick flutter, first on my left lash and then on my right and toss it back into the drawer. I better head down or I'll be in more shit..

One car ride later.

We pulled up in front of Boston Bridal. I could see the chandeliers from the car and the many mannequins dressed in wedding gowns. This was going to be a shitshow and everyone's eyes were focused on me. The only good thing so far about this morning was meeting Tatum's new bodyguard, Wren Riott. She's a beautiful woman, she looks like a total badass too. Her hair is dyed an almost bright orange copper color that is way past her shoulders. She keeps the sides braided back and the top is poofed up in a fauxhawk. She's taller than me, and she has dark brown colored eyes. Her nose is a button shape that goes great with her oval face. She most definitely is a riot, I didn't expect to enjoy her presence but it helped ease any of the awkwardness between me and Kendrick's mother.

"Mrs. Sanders, it's such a delight to see you again! Welcome back to Boston Bridal. As per your request we have closed the boutique just for your private party.
"

"Mara darling! It's such a pleasure to see you again. Please call me Pearl, Mrs. Sanders is my mother-in-law. I would like to introduce you to my future daughter-in-law, Tatum," she holds her hand out, waiting for me to take it.

"Good morning, Mara, I'm Tatum Emerson soon to be Sanders! This is my best friend and Maid of Honor Aria," I gesture towards her.

"Timothy! Drinks for the ladies please!" She shoos the short man away.

"Yes Ma'am," he scurries away, obviously in fear.

"Thank you for all of this." I whisper in Pearl's ear.

ACCIDENTALLY IDENTICAL

"You are most welcome, you are family now. You are the one my son has chosen as his life partner, so all of this is well deserved," she kisses my forehead.

I smile, I haven't had someone do that in a long time. Is this what it feels like having a mother around?

"Let's get to the dresses, lovies!" Mara gushes.

She shows me to the dressing room where she's pre-selected four dresses for me to try on. I can honestly say I have never even tried on such expensive clothing. These dresses were all over two thousand dollars, for a dress she, I mean I would wear once. That's nuts.

Dress number one was a *Vera Wang*. The dress was a spaghetti strap and slipped down my back into a v. The bodice was crystal-encrusted and had a close fit, showing off my curves. The bottom of this dress made me feel like I was engulfed in tulle, about 100 yards if I say so myself. It was full of volume and life. I felt like I was wearing a cloud, a very expensive, beautiful cloud. I held the bottom of the dress up as I walked out barefoot onto the stage.

The stage was huge, covered in white carpet with a bank of large full sized mirrors wrapping around. In this moment I now realize why they only serve champagne in here, no stains. Everything is white. On the outside they have plush white couches and chairs for the bridal party which now have Pearl and Aria filling them up. I smile and twirl for them. Modeling a dress that is not meant for me. I channel my inner Tatum and give them the show they require.

"Gorgeous!!" "Beautiful" "Delightful!" I hear from the crowd.

"Okay! Next one!" I smile at them.

I return again to the dressing room and wiggle out of the white ball of fluff and return it to it's hanger.

Dress two is more elegant, more rich. It's strapless, head to toe lace, it curves in right at my hips and then out in an a-line pattern. I feel like a princess. The back has tiny little buttons that I have no hope of getting to button by myself. Just as I did with the first dress I pull it up slightly so I don't trip and make my way out to the

217

grand stage. Mara stops me and uses some heavy duty black clips to hold the dress together so it fits me just right.

"Here darling girl, we have to finish the look," she smiles as she pins the veil in my hair.

I hear the "Awwwww's," in unison.

"I feel like a princess in this one," I turn to them and smile.

"Tatum I'm so proud of you! You look gorgeous!" Aria gushes.

"Sorry I'm late ladies. I wasn't sure if I was going to make it."

"Hi Momma Emerson," Aria waves her over.

"Baby, you look so beautiful, I'm glad I didn't miss everything," Victoria says with tears in her eyes.

"Thanks mom," I say while biting my lip awkwardly.

I hurry myself into the dressing area and I sit on the white chair in the room to think. Am I really going through with this? If I am then it will be a dress that I like, that I can see myself getting married in. I look at the third and fourth dress picks and I pick my favorite.

I step out of the other dress and slide my favorite delicately over my body. I pull the zipper up in back as far as I can before I look at myself. I never pictured myself in this position, marrying a man I didn't love. The only way this would work is if I could imagine that I was marrying the love of my life, picking my wedding gown for that day. In my head it was Grant I was marrying, and he would run his fingers down my shoulder, straight down my spine and admire the fact that this dress would be so easy to get off after the ceremony.

I really study myself for several minutes before I'm ready to show the world my choice. The bodice meets my breasts and hugs them in a heart shape that holds every inch of my body together even when I feel like falling apart. It is covered in white and silver glitter with diamond flakes and as it meets my hips, umbrellaed out with tulle into an a-line. The whole dress is dipped in glitter, like I had rolled around in it. I loved it.

"Hey Aria! Can you come help me please?" I call out for her.

"I'm here what do you....holy shit Tatum! That's gorgeous!!" Aria smirks.

"Can you finish zipping me up and find me some shoes that match this dress? I'm looking for a short heel but I want lots of glitter like this." I hand her the veil.

"Yes, this is the one, isn't it! I'd know that look anywhere!" she says as she finishes with the dress.

"I think so, but I don't wanna go out without the shoes..."

"Gotcha covered bestie. I'll be right back!" Aria squeals.

She isn't even gone for 5 minutes and she brings back the most beautiful fucking shoes I've ever seen in my life. They are from the Rene Caovilla collection, size eight, the heel was a little taller than what I was used to at four inches but I have to have these. Grant would appreciate these shoes, they were fuck me heels and I was in love.

They are open toed, metallic leather, with a crystal design unattached, flowing up the delicate skin of my foot. It was like a crown for my fucking foot! The back of the shoe climbed up the heel to a point, and it had the signature glittered outsole! I could never afford these normally but today I could. I stood there in the full length mirror admiring my own beauty now that my ensemble is complete. I think of Grant.

I touch my own skin gently, imagining Grant pushing my dress up to my hips and sliding my panties to the side to taste me if just for a moment before slipping them off and taking me hard from behind in my sexy fuck me heels. I'd lean over further and grab the couch and let him thrust deep into me and take me as his wife. As Mrs. Grant Thomas.

Reality wakes me up.

"Tatum, are you ready in there? Everyone's getting antsy," Aria peeks in.

219

"Yes, I'm ready," I smile hoping one day I can make it right.

GRANT THOMAS | FIFTY-FOUR

✗✗✗✗

She hung up on me.

I can't fucking believe what I just heard. After everything we shared together she just ended it without a reason over the phone. I rake my hands through my hair and wonder what the hell I did wrong for her to end it this way. She said she didn't love me. She doesn't fucking love me. I fell for someone I barely knew and she broke my heart to shit.

I need booze, lots and lots of fucking booze. I open my parents cabinets and find the vodka. I don't even bother with a glass, I screw open the top and guzzle the clear liquid down with no regrets.

Well, maybe just one, Talia Hendrix.

She was..is.. the love of my fucking life and it was so easy for her to tear me to bits. I should've never allowed her to get my guard down. Now I don't have to worry about my brother fucking her. No, that was the vodka talking... we were solid now, but Talia just fucked everything all to hell. I've never loved a woman like I love her

I take another huge swig waiting for it to numb me to this all.

"Brother, what's going on?" Graham asks as he enters the kitchen.

"Talia fucking broke my heart man..."

"What happened? Things were going so well."

"She called me and told me she doesn't love me and not to look for her...What the fuck does that even mean, bro?" I growl.

"It sounds like she's confused. I'm sure she will come around Grant," he nods as he pats my back.

"What if she just doesn't love me? What if it was all a fucking lie?" I worry.

"She loves you, I've seen the way she looks at you. No matter what you will get through this."

I down more of the vodka and watch as my asshole brother judges me.

"You should probably lay off the vodka. I don't want you to say or do something you might regret," Graham cringes.

"Fuck off Graham, I love her and she fucking ripped my heart out right in front of me. I can get fucked up if I want to," I groan.

I couldn't control myself. I put my head down and cried...something I haven't done ever in front of Graham and not since Tiffany.

Graham did something he hadn't done in a long time himself. He smacked me across my face.

"Dude, what the fuuuck!!" I slur.

"Get a fucking grip, man. She will come around, don't sulk... that's not the man she *loves*. She never fell for my shit Grant, she told me off. That means something," he reassures me.

How the hell does this shit happen? I didn't plan to fall in love.

KENDRICK SANDERS | FIFTY-FIVE

XOXO

Marcello, Easton, my father and I find ourselves at Boston's Men's Wearhouse for tuxedos. While the ladies are helping my sweetheart find the wedding gown of her dreams, we have to get our attire ready as well. Tatum's already picked the colors for us, she said she wants a color called Tahiti with a dark grey jacket and pants to match. The vest and tie would be this color she picked, I hadn't seen it yet. Hopefully it's a masculine color.

We all head into our separate dressing rooms. Marcello is of course my best man, so Easton was on his own security wise. I strip down and slide the dark charcoal grey slacks on and then button the white dress shirt. Once it's securely tucked into my pants I grab for the vest and then I realize something... Thanks sweetheart, it's totally not a masculine color. It's a lavender color....that's what Tahiti is. That's how I know I love this woman, she could put me in pink and I'd still think the sun rises and sets on her ass.

"Uh, son... is your's purple too?" Prescott mutters from the next door.

"We can thank Tatum for this later...but yes it's purple too," I try to contain my laughter as I imagine my father's reaction.

"Lavender here too," Marcello chimes in.

I pull on the jacket and adjust the pocket square, then I turn to the mirror and do a check of everything. Pants need a slight alteration but jacket fits like a glove as does the vest. I toss the tie around my neck and exit the dressing room.

"Looking good, son," Prescott pats my shoulder.

"Thanks dad. Has Tatum talked to you yet?" I question.

223

"Yes she has. She asked me if I would walk her down the aisle, I don't want to intrude and cause hurt feelings if perhaps Victoria and her wife want to walk her down the aisle?" He offers.

"She's not on great terms with her parents as of late and Tatum is a bit old school. If her father were alive he would do it. I know it would mean a lot to her if you said yes, dad."

"Of course, I will contact her right away and let her know I will be honored to walk her down the aisle," he smiles.

"Did you ever think I'd be getting married dad?"

"Son I knew when you met the right woman your whole world would be turned upside down. Did I know it was going to be so soon? No but I'm glad you're happy and your mother and I gladly welcome Tatum into the Sanders clan," he raises a glass of scotch to me.

I grab mine and clink his glass.

"Cheers pops!"

"To a long happy marriage!" Marcello chimes in.

"Okay let's get back into our clothes so the tailor can work on them I need to pick-up Tatum's wedding band from Adrian's."

TALIA HENDRIX | FIFTY- SIX

✗✗✗✗

It's the night of the Tatum's bachelorette party and Aria is under the impression that I have no idea about it. She's too obvious to surprise anyone with anything. She even picked my outfit for tonight. I guess I should be grateful- one less thing to decide, especially for someone else. My cocktail dress is coal black and it dips down in the front showing off my cleavage. The spaghetti straps are barely holding my tits up, and because of the straps I have to go braless. Hugging my ribs is a sheer material that criss crosses then flows down elegantly leaving the front at just above my knees and the back of my dress trailing down ever so slightly until it hits my ankles. I have to give her credit for trying, but I can't imagine this being Tatum's scene or dress.

Aria has so cleverly blindfolded me in the car with three other women, one is Wren and the other two I'm not familiar with. I'm assuming they are Tatum's other friends, but I couldn't tell you.

"We are almost there, ladies!!!" Aria screeches excitedly.

"Where are we going, Aria?" I pout.

"You will see, hope you are ready for your last experience as a single woman! WOOOHOOO!!!"

"I can't believe I'm getting married tomorrow," I gush, then realize I'm not, Tatum is.

Aria slides off the blindfold and gives me the biggest smile I've seen in the five seconds of knowing her.

"Tatum, I present to you the sash of Bride to Be," she hands me a large, bright

225

white silky sash that says Bride to Be in a gold metallic lettering.

I bite my lip and willingly slide the sash over my head to allow it to hang where everyone can read it. What the fuck am I getting myself into?

"Don't worry bitch, we all have them" she says, holding up the other sashes.

"Only you get the crown, bestie!"

I look at them and my attention turns to Wren, who is now sporting a white sash herself that says "Bride Squad". I can't help but literally laugh out loud because that's the funniest fucking thing I've seen in the last week. That's including all the times that Kendrick has tried to either get me naked or casually walk in when I'm getting dressed. You would think my sister never gave that man any sex. I've had to practically beat him away from me, I'm only getting away with it because of tradition. Tradition is saving my ass, because there is no way I'd ever cheat on Grant, not even for my sister. That would be a whole 'nother level of no fucking way.

We enter the building into a long hallway with a large line of women. The walls are all brick and metal and all I can hear is music blasting.

"Where are we again?" I yell over the music and obnoxious women.

"STRIP CLUB! WOOOOHOOO BABY!!!" I hear some random scream excitedly.

"What she said" Aria giggles.

"Wren, can you go let them know we are here and have reservations. All these other thirsty bitches will have to wait, the Bride Squad is here!" She beams.

Wren waves us up in her direction as we pass all the women who are pissed we are cutting in front of them.

"Back off ladies!" Wren warns.

They open the velvet rope for us and we dance our happy asses into the main attraction. There are many seats filled with women, not a lot of space to sit.

226

"Where are we going to sit? Doesn't look like there's room," I ask.

Wren leads us to an area directly in front of the stage with five empty chairs.

"You sit right here Bride to be!" Aria forces me into the chair positioned front and center to the stage, with the rest of the girls in our group on either side of me. We are only seated for a few minutes before the lights dim dramatically and the room erupts into cheers and shouts from every woman in the room, myself included. The male announcer starts to hype the crowd up even more over the loudspeaker when he shouts, "Hey, ladies! Are you REEAADDDDYYY??!!"

A loud siren blares and a burst of white light flashes bright as a heavy techno beat starts to play. Laser lights come to life and bounce frantically off of every surface in the room and on stage are now three very sexy men decked out in Marine dress blues.

They are standing at attention, stern expressions in place and looking very much the part. If I thought the room was loud before, it is nothing compared to the noise level now. As soon as we all see the men on stage, the room breaks out into a mini chaotic mess. Woman are out of their seats, jumping up and down, whistling and yelling at the top of their lungs, and our little group is right there with them. Dollar bills are already waving in the air and the men haven't even started dancing yet.

Their dance starts off slow and sensual then becomes more erotic. Their quick thrusting of their hips leads to each article of clothing making its way off their muscular, sweaty bodies. I swear if I didn't know any better I had accidentally slipped into the movie *Magic Mike*. There are hot, topless male dancers everywhere. Next thing I know they have ahold of my chair and are carrying me on stage. I try to enjoy it, hell it's been a few weeks now since I've had sex. I was feeling the pain.

One at a time each dancer does their sexy strip tease on my lap, grinding and gyrating against me. As the Marines' made me want to salute them the next dancers make their way on stage. The cowboys are next, their white wife beater shirts with those tight jeans that just fit so right on their sexy asses and of course their cowboy hats. It didn't take long before my crown was covered with one of the cowboy hats.

227

"YEEEHAWWW!" I call out and swing the cowboy hat above my head.

It goes on like this for an hour, Marines, cowboys, firemen and sailors. I'm so aroused now, I want to be Talia again. Talia would be able to fuck Grant when sexually frustrated, not me Talia pretending to be Tatum. I'm playing keep away with Mr. Sanders. Once I'm able I slide off the stage and head directly for the bar. I need liquor and I need it now.

"Wren will you order us some shots of fireball, I'm feeling frisky," I smile.

"Yep, I'll take care of it, Miss Tatum," Wren replies professionally.

"Just Tatum please! You're at my Bachelorette party I think we can cut the formalities please!" I beg.

She nods to me and gets the bartender's attention to order the shots.

"Wren, can I also get a Blow Job too? Oh and a shot of Whiskey please," I smirk, thinking how awkward it's going to be for my bodyguard to order that.

"She's going to hate you for that," Aria chuckles behind me.

"After this can we head back to the suite? I'm feeling exhausted," I whine.

"After you drink all your drinks," she winks at me.

TATUM EMERSON / FIFTY-SEVEN

XOXO

I don't know how long I've been here and I'm certain I will die here. I've been beat, starved and I can't remember how long a person can go without food or water before they die. From what I've gathered my capturer wants me to suffer. I've learned several things so far from my wonderful kidnapping experience, my captor, whose name is to be determined, thinks I am my twin sister. Part of me knows that this can't possibly be her fault, but the other part of me is fucking zip-tied to a chair. It also has me wondering what the hell happened to even get her in this situation.

My head is throbbing and I have no idea where I am... I've seen him come and go down through a yellow wooden door that seems to lead to a particularly small passageway. I wiggle myself in the chair to try and move, I can feel the zip ties cut into my wrists. Bad idea. Why is no one looking for me? I'm supposed to be getting married and I don't even know what fucking day it is, this is a wreck.

Be calm my dearie, Melora is here to save the day. She swings her arm towards Charles and his body is hurled across the room and he hits his head. Remember how I said I ran all the museums in Salem? He took you here to The House Of The Seven Gables. Mistake on his part.

VIDETUR!

The room transformed just like it did at The Witch House.

"Tatum, are you okay?" Melora asks as she pulls the tape off my mouth.

"I've been better," I mumble, as I rub where the tape was.

Melora snaps off my zip ties and then she waves her hand over my cuts and bruises.

229

"What are you doing, Melora??" I whine.

"I just took care of all your wounds. We have a wedding to get you to, don't we?" she smiles at me.

That's when I see it.. the man's lifeless body.

"Is that…. Is he.. dead???" I croak.

"He's not your problem anymore dearie,"

"You wish, you bitch!" Charles yells as he hits Melora over the head with a wooden board.

"No!!!! Leave her alone you piece of shit!"

The adrenaline kicks in and my body forgets that it's been starved for days. I go into autopilot mode to both protect Melora and save myself from getting trapped back in the chair. I push myself to do the only thing I can: I jump on his back and start throwing punches at him. It's me or him and I want to get out of here alive.

Melora's body begins to levitate, her eyes begin to glow and all she does is blow out a breath towards him. He goes flying, busting the door and hits the stairs so hard all you can hear is the crack of his neck as he tumbles down the hidden stairwell of The House Of The Seven Gables.

CHARLES HENDRIX | FIFTY-EIGHT

✳✳✳✳

I was attacked by a fucking witch, the last thing I remember is flying through the air and falling down the stairs. I try to get up but suddenly feel like something is wrong. I look around the brick stairwell and that's when I see it, my body. How is this possible? I'm dead? I never got my revenge on Talia. I feel a rush of sudden wind and a fog appears I can barely see before it goes completely black.

The next thing I see is mind blowing.

"Amelia? Is that you?" I whimpered.

"Charles? What are you doing here?" Amelia gasped.

"If I'm seeing you then I must be dead..."

"You are dead. I'm ashamed of all the things you've done to our daughter. I never knew your soul was so filled with evil," she frowned and looked down at her feet.

"I'm not my darling, that wasn't me. My life without you was unbearable. The loss of you blackened and broke my heart," I babbled.

"I know how hard it was on you and Talia both but you were all she had. You must redeem yourself or you'll be without me for the rest of eternity," she explained solemnly.

"I'm so sorry Amelia. Everything is my fault, the fact that we couldn't have kids that was my doing. I was selfish, heartless and abusive. I can't say I'm sorry enough. Is there anyway in this world you could forgive me? I just found you again I can't lose you," I confessed my sins.

I couldn't believe how much weight I had carried on my heart, it wasn't until I let it all go that I felt like I was free. I felt like my old self. My revenge trapped me in a world full of a darkness and I didn't need to reside there anymore. I had the light of my life back in front of me casting her judgement, thinking whether I was worth a second chance or not. I really hope that through it all she can see the good times, the ones I've since forgotten.

"The answer is yes, Charlie. Maybe you don't deserve it, but I want to give you a second chance to heal your soul. Not just for you, but for me as well."

I drop to my knees and cry. I have never cried over any woman, but my darling Amelia was worth every tear.

"Charlie, let's go. It's time for us to start our forever again," she looked down and smiled at me.

I reached for her hand and intertwined our fingers and disappeared together.

Together for always. Our souls as one.

Aria Morretti | Fifty-Nine

xoxo

Today is the day everyone's been preparing for. My best friend is getting married. There's just something I can't put my finger on though. She doesn't seem like herself even last night, maybe it's just the wedding jitters. We got shitfaced last night at the club and made our way back safely to the hotel bridal suite at the Fairmont to play some bachelorette games.

I flashback to what I could remember of last night.

We played this game called Dirty Minds. It was my idea, I also added the stipulation if you get the answer wrong you have to take a shot of vodka. The game starts and the first question is mine to ask.

"Okay ladies, first question; Your finger fits right in it. You play with it when you're bored. Once you're married, you're stuck with the same one forever. What is it?" I bust out in laughter.

"You each get to guess. I'll even let the bride guess last! Brenda it's your turn!"

"Pretty little pussy!" she cackled.

"Mandie your turn!" Tatum cheered.

"Uh-uhm...a husband's mouth!" Mandie beamed.

"Bride's turn!" they say in unison.

"A wedding ring?" Tatum smiled.

"Ding ding ding! We have a winner! The bride wins the first question! Mandie, Brenda take a shot!" I smiled knowing all of them are lightweights.

233

"Since I got the question right I get to ask the next one right? You can't get out of the game Aria!" Tatum snickered.

"Your party we can play anyway you want," I said handing her the paper.

"Question number two! What starts with "p" and ends with "orn" and is the hottest part of the movie industry?" Tatum poses the question to me first.

"PORN!" I belt out.

"Born! It ends in Ornn" Brenda squealed.

"Mandie what's your guess?" I asked.

"I'm think I'm done with this game, I'm not feeling so good" she belched.

"If you're going to puke use the toilet!" I screeched.

"One more then I'm done Aria, I need to get my beauty sleep..." Tatum whined.

"Who won that round?" I asked.

"None of you! The answer was popcorn pervs," she smirked.

"You have to be fucking kidding me, it was popcorn?" I frowned.

We could hear Mandie puking in the bathroom. I think it may have made all our stomachs a little queasy but we still had one more left and I was determined to make it interesting.

"Okay so change up, I'll read the last question but won't look at the answer so I can play too. Whoever gets the answer wrong has to take three shots instead of just one since it's the last question! Sound fair?" I stared at Tatum.

"Let's do it, what's the question?" Brenda asked.

"What goes in dry and hard and comes out wet and soft?" I snickered.

"It's gotta be a cock right? That's the only thing it can be!" Tatum shouted.

"Agreed, it's a cock. What's your answer Aria?" Brenda questioned me.

"My mouth? Let's see who's right....Fuck we all lose.." I muttered.

I started to pour all nine of the shots of vodka.

"Well what's the fucking answer? " Tatum barked.

"It's Gum," I said flatly.

"Yup I'm done I quit I can't believe it's gum…" Tatum huffed.

We all tossed back our shots and before I knew it the room started spinning..

That's what I remember from last night, honestly I've never seen Tatum ever get so aggravated when drinking, she's usually such a free spirit. It's water under the bridge though because my best friend is getting married today and I'm the maid of honor.

"Tatum, are you awake yet?"

"Grant just give me a few more minutes," she mumbles sleepily.

Well that's weird. Who is Grant? We don't know anyone by that name. I shrug it off and set an alarm for thirty minutes from now. It's five in the morning and the hair and makeup artist are going to be here shortly. I decide to let her get more rest, but before I hop in the shower I grab a bottle of orange Gatorade for her and some ibuprofen. I set it on the bedside table next to where she's sound asleep and head into the bathroom.

I turn the shower on and begin my daily routine. Luckily enough this hotel we are staying in has the professional shampoo and not that cheap shit so I can use that to clean my ravenous crazy drunk lady hair. Once I'm done I hop out and give my hair the best blow job ever. I slip on my nude colored panties and matching strapless bra and grab my bride squad silky black robe. Once it's wrapped around me I tie it in the front and go check on the bride.

"You feeling okay Tatum?" I ask.

"Yeah I'm great, starting to feel nervous. Thanks for the drink and the meds I have a killer headache. Hope the meds kick in before the ladies get here," she mutters.

"Anything for you bestie, if I were you I'd jump on in the shower that might help. I also hung your robe up in there."

"Thanks, did Wren take care of everything?"

"She made sure your dress, my dress and both of our shoes are here," I smile.

"Phew one less thing to worry about. You're the best. Let Wren know I said thanks."

After Tatum's shower I decide to help her blow-dry her hair to get her ready a little quicker. I section her hair, and begin round brushing it giving her hair a little bit of a pre-curl before the hairstylist gets ahold of it. I also grab some dry-shampoo to spray to dirty her hair up a little bit for them so the curls stay. I take my fingers and massage the spray into her roots, and just as I'm finishing up there's a knock on the door.

TALIA HENDRIX | SIXTY

✗✗✗✗

Once I hear the knock at the door I have the sudden urge to nervously pace the floor. I can't believe I'm going through with this. I have to do it for Tatum. The makeup artist and her assistant enter with both of their black rolling bags. Tatum has hired a woman by the name of Melissa Taylor, she is supposed to be some popular influencer and a professional makeup artist. She's a petite platinum dyed blonde and her hair is way past her shoulder blades. Today she has her hair in two cute french braids with a zig-zag part in the middle and her makeup is completely flawless. My immediate trust is won over, if she can do that to her own face I will gladly let her paint mine.

"What a gorgeous bride you will be!" Melissa gushes as she examines my face.

"We already went over how I'd like my makeup and hair to be done correct?" I question her.

"Of course honey! I got you! The groom's jaw will drop to the floor once he sees our finished work. So when we spoke on the phone you decided on a brown smokey eye, you did say that you wanted false lashes as well. As for your hair we are going to be doing a fishtail braid once we get your extensions put in. The braid will start from the left side and will travel down your shoulder to the cleavage. I'm also bringing in an assistant to help set up and do your hair and Aria's as well. Her name is Lana she's such a sweetheart you'll love her! So with all that said let's get started."

"Thank you so much, I want this day to be perfect," I smile at Melissa.

I sit in front of a bank of side by side mirrors in my white bride robe, just

237

staring at my reflection.

Melissa pulls my hair into a loose ponytail and bobby pins the hair completely away from my face. Lana her assistant opens both of their bags to begin the set up process. She lays down a towel just for all of her makeup brushes, she has A LOT of brushes.

Once the ladies have set up Melissa begins her work on my eyebrows. She takes the angled brush, dips it in the product and then takes the brush to one eyebrow following the natural arch and feathering strokes to make it look natural. Then she does the same to the next eyebrow.

Next she applies the concealer to prime my eyelids, then she takes out her fluffy blending brush and a huge palette with a rainbow of colors. She uses a darker brown color, and gives me the ultimate smokey eye. She then swipes her brush on a cloth cleaning off the residue of the brown.

She goes back in with a little concealer to clean up any lines and dabs a little on the inner corner of my eye and applies the last color. It's a shimmery color, not quite white but not beige either and then she uses the brush once again to blend the colors together eloquently.

"The next part is going to be putting your false lashes on. Just keep your eyes closed until I tell you to open them okay?" Melissa beams.

I've never had my lashes done, hell I hadn't ever had my makeup professionally done either. So far it wasn't a bad experience.

Once she had both lashes on I felt the air from her waving her hands on my face. Once they felt dry she told me to go ahead and open my eyes. I open them slowly afraid that my eyes may be stuck together. She takes the disposable mascara wand and dips it in the mascara and coats my new lashes. The lashes are very natural and long, I smile at myself in the mirror and immediately regret it.

I'm not supposed to be having a good time, my sister's suffering and it's my fault and here I am gushing over how great my makeup is going to look for *her* wedding. I sigh, louder than I thought obviously causing Melissa to worry.

"Is everything looking okay Tatum? I want you to be happy, it's your special day after all. Is it something I did or said?" Melissa says comforting me.

"It's not you. I just realized I forgot to get a manicure and pedicure done. It's probably too late now," I sigh.

"Aria you didn't tell her?" Melissa looks at Aria.

"Tatum, we are right by where you and Kendrick first met. I thought it would be fitting to bring some nail techs from the nail salon here to pamper us before the wedding...SURPRISE!" Aria squeals.

I can't help but smile, my sister has some amazing friends. I wish I had someone like Aria in my life. I guess maybe I should enjoy it while it lasts as soon as I get Tatum back, I'll be back to just Talia again. Will Tatum even want me in her life after this? After all I wasn't even apart of her wedding... How could I be so happy right now? She did tell me to take care of Kendrick for her, but none of this felt right. This was my sister's day not mine.

I look over at Aria, hoping she doesn't see the distress in my face and watch for a few seconds as she gets her makeup done by Lana. Her makeup is a little less smokey than mine, so lighter colors will be used.

"Close 'em again, gonna do the eyeliner now."

She dips her small angled brush into the black liquid liner and makes quick work of applying it. A swish of her wrist and I had wings.

"Part one complete! Now we gotta put a base on your face" she chatters.

She uses a flat yet fluffy brush to apply primer to my face.

Then out comes the beauty blender, it looks like a buttplug to me but if it works who am I to judge.

She swatches a few foundations on the inside of my wrist and finds the perfect match. She squirts the liquid foundation on the beauty blender, then dab, dab, dab on different parts of my face. She then grabs another brush and goes to work

239

blending it in. When she's satisfied it's blended enough, she takes out the contour and highlight palette and applies to my face.

To set everything she uses a white powder.

"Now we let you bake for a few," she smirks.

"You're going to bake me? What the hell?" I scrunch my face up.

"It's just a way of setting your face. Baking because it looks like flour. You are almost finished, you are sitting like a champ. Do you need to stretch your legs?" she asks.

"Yeah I gotta pee real quick, be right back" I hold my finger up to her.

"Don't touch your face, it's not set yet!" she yells after me.

I finish my business and head back out to where Melissa is waiting. I take my seat and let her continue to primp my face. I never knew so much work went into weddings.

She takes out a weird looking brush and she swipes it over the highlighting powder which is super shiney and holographic. She brushes it over the highest part of my cheek bones. She then moves on to my lips, she has a small lipstick palette of different colors of pinks, reds and darker colors. We choose the mauve looking color and she applies it. Once it's applied completely she then spritzes my face with a setting spray.

"It's time for the hair and then you will be all done!"

I watch her walk over to the end of the bed and pickup the platinum clip-in extensions for me. She sections my hair and clips a row of hair in then covers some with my natural hair. She continues in this pattern until all the clip-ins are installed in my hair.

Then she begins to do a fishtail braid from the left temple and and loosens it up as she reaches the bottom. There's about four inches of hair left out of the braid at the bottom that she takes the curling wand to and then sprays it with some strong hold hairspray.

She claps her hands excitedly, "My work here is done! You look absolutely gorgeous!"

She moves out of the way of the mirrors and reveals a woman I don't recognize, me.

"Wow I can't believe this, I look amazing! Thank you so much," I lean in and hug her.

"You are so welcome, I will be here the whole time in case you need touch-ups or anything."

"Aria is done as well! You both look wonderful" Lana coos.

Another knock at the door tells me the nail techs must be here. I'm keeping it simple. French tips, for both toes and fingers.

About 30 minutes later

Everything on the checklist is done for the wedding, now all I have to do is show up dressed and ready.

I shimmy my body into my dress and pull the straps up to where they need to be. Aria helps me zip the back of the dress up and gets my shoes ready. She's already in her flowey lavender colored dress, it fits her like a glove. She has her hair down, it's loosely curled but it looks like it could survive a hurricane. She opted the simple lavender polish on her toes and fingers, so we are both ready to go. Everyone has left for now and we are down to the wire. We have thirty minutes before the ceremony is supposed to begin, when yet another knock at the door.

Who knew our suite would be the most popular today. Aria opens the door and Prescott Sanders comes in.

"Hello Tatum" Prescott smiles.

"Hi Mr. Sanders, what's going on?" I ask him.

"I was just letting you know I was here, since I'm walking you down the aisle I figured I'd need to be here. I can wait outside and just let me know when you're ready."

"We'll be ready in a few minutes, thank you Prescott," I smile.

Old South Church

645 Boylston Street, Boston, MA

Friday, December 6th, 2019 at Noon

We've been at the church now for ten minutes and I'm pacing the floor. I could see why Tatum picked this place, it's beautiful. From the outside it looks like a giant gothic castle, lots of peaks and points. No description I could ever give would actually do it justice. The church was designed in the Gothic Revival style in 1873, it's also a National Historic Landmark. It's very Tatum of me to know these things. She loves all things books and no one can deny the history and beauty of this place. Now I would solidify my sister's union with her soon to be husband in the most gorgeous of places.

The song, *"Still Fallin" by Hunter Hayes* plays while the guests find seats that have been perfectly placed. In the first row of chairs on the left side belong to the bride's side. Tatum's parents Victoria and Danielle are sitting front and center holding hands. Behind them are the many other members of the Emerson Clan, aunts, uncles, cousins and friends from here and there.

On the groom's side the chairs to the right Kendrick's mother Pearl and a seat reserved for Prescott. Behind them are family members, and behind them I'm assuming business associates and their dates.

Kendrick is standing up by the officiant waiting to catch a glimpse of his bride, only it isn't *her*. I feel a pang of guilt for all of this, it is eating me up inside. I watch as I see Marcello and Aria waiting for their musical cue. That's when *"All of Me" by John Legend* starts playing. They lock arms like lovers do and hold each other close as they begin their long walk past all the guests and family members together. They part ways and Marcello stands next to Kendrick, while Aria is waiting on my bridal music to cue.

That's when *"I Was Made For Loving You" by Tori Kelly & Ed Sheeran* starts to play. Prescott locks his arm with mine and we begin our walk. I catch a glimpse of Kendrick's reaction when he sees me for the first time. He's choked up and it's not even over the right woman. I sniffle as I walk down the aisle and it's not the groom I expect. In this moment, I can only think of one man: Grant Thomas. The song ends just as we reach Kendrick. Prescott makes his way to his seat with Pearl and I lock hands with Kendrick. We both face towards the officiant and wait for him to begin.

"We are gathered here today in the sight of God, and the presence of family and friends, to celebrate one of life's greatest moments. Love, which in itself is full of beauty and life. We are also here to add our best wishes and blessings to these two wonderful people. The words today will unite Kendrick and Tatum in holy matrimony."

"Kendrick and Tatum, marriage is the most important of all relationships. It should be entered into thoughtfully and with full understanding of its sacred nature. Your marriage must stand by the strength of your love and the power of faith in each other and in God. Just as the sand and the sea meet so do your two lives when merged together to make one."

"1st Corinthians 13:4-8

Love is very patient and kind, never jealous or envious, never boastful or proud. Love is never haughty or selfish or rude. Love does not demand its own way. Love is not irritable or touchy. Love does not hold grudges and will hardly notice when others do it wrong. Love is never glad about injustice, but rejoices whenever truth wins out. If you love someone, you will be loyal to them no matter what the costs. You will always believe in them, always expect the best in them, and will always stand your ground in defending them."

"Please face each other and hold hands," he says with a smile.

"Please repeat after me. I, Kendrick take you Tatum to be my wife. I will cherish you, and love you today, tomorrow, and forever.

I will trust and honor you. I will love you faithfully.

Through it all, I will trust that you will be beside me, loving me.

Whatever may come our way I will always be there. As I have given you my hand to hold, I now give you my life to keep," Kendrick hums.

"I, Tatum take you Kendrick to be my husband, my partner in life and my one true love. I will cherish our friendship and love you today, tomorrow, and forever.I will trust and honor you. I will laugh with you and be a shoulder to cry on. I will love you faithfully from this day forward. Through the best and the worst, we are in this together. Whatever may come our way I will always be there. As I have given you my hand to hold, I now give you my life to keep," I say with a tear falling down my face.

"Kendrick, do you take Tatum to be your wife?"

"I do," he replies

"Do you promise to love, honor, cherish and protect her, forsaking all others and holding her only forevermore?"

"I do."

"Tatum, do you take Kendrick to be your husband?"

"I..I.. uhm.." I stutter.

The church doors swing open with a bang.

"She DOESN'T but I DO!" a voice yells from behind us all.

Everyone's attention is on the woman who just stormed in at the last minute saving my ass. My sister, my twin: Tatum.

"What is going on here?" the officiant asks.

"I'm really confused right now... who are you then?" Kendrick looks at me.

I make my way quickly to the door towards Tatum and trip over my dress. I shouldn't have worn four inch heels, I fall on my face and all I can hear is the gasps of the guests , everyone is in shock. The judgement is there, from these people I don't even know.

"I knew something was wrong!" Aria yells.

Amongst the chaos the church doors swing open for a second time. My eyes are drawn to the door for the second time now. I can't believe my eyes, and neither can he. Grant Thomas as I live and breath, he's looking at me and then looking at Tatum.

"I'm over here Grant..." I whimper.

He walks toward me, he can't get to me fast enough. I've been dying slowly inside since we last spoke, I need him.

"Grant I'm so sorry..." I begin to sob.

"I have something to say, it's important. I just need you, I know you didn't tell me the truth. I can't live without you, those days without you destroyed me. That's how I know I never want to let you go again."

Grant falls to one knee, "Talia Hendrix will you marry me?"

"I thought you would be furious with me right now, never did I think you would show up here and propose to me. How did you find me anyways?"

"Damnit Talia, I just asked you to marry me and all you can think about is how I found you and if I'm mad at you. Will you please answer my question," he begs holding the open ring box in front of me.

"Yes, a thousand times yes. I can explain everything I promise.."

He slides the ring on my finger. The ring has a ruby in the middle and it's surrounded by small diamonds that continue along the white gold band.

"It's beautiful.. I love you," I blurt out.

"Excuse me, can I please have everyone's attention? We need to take a short recess to figure things out, meet us all back here at four o'clock. Thank you for your understanding!" Kendrick announces.

"Let me go change Grant and then we can go, I'm not sure if I'm welcome here or not anymore…" I hear my own voice crack as tears fall down my face yet again.

"Talia, will you please come with me? We can explain everything to the men later, we have a wedding to attend to!" Tatum exclaims.

"You want me to stay?" I ask.

"Grant you can stay as well. Kendrick will take care of everything go with him," Tatum smiles and nods in Grant's direction.

"Of course, you are my twin sister. The other part of me, I don't just want you just to stay, I'd like it if you would be my bridesmaid, and Grant be a groomsmen."

"Let's do it then" I smile the first actual smile of the day.

Grant leans in to kiss me and then departs with Marcello and Kendrick.

Tatum, Aria and I retreat to the hotel room to press the reset button.

TATUM EMERSON | SIXTY-ONE

XOXO

Drama aside, today was my wedding day and I needed to get ready. I almost didn't make it in time, I wouldn't know how it would've worked if Talia really married Kendrick. I needed to focus, we only had so much time before we had to be back at the church for the ceremony, I'm sure a lot of people were pissed off and confused about us needing more time.

Aria went and called Lana and Melissa back so they could do my hair and makeup, because everyone else was already ready.

"Talia I had everything pre-planned before I was kidnapped, I had a dress made for you. I had plans on asking you that day in Salem but it all went to shit," I frown.

"You did?" Talia blushes.

"Yes when they brought you the dresses, my wedding dress was in there but so was your bridesmaid dress. Kendrick has a tux for Grant too. I had it all planned."

"Thank you for accepting me and wanting me to be a part of this after all I've put you through," Talia says apologetically.

"I had Melissa bring more of the clip-in extensions, are you still wanting your hair done like you planned?" Aria asks me.

"Talia can keep the braid, I had a backup plan just in case."

"Melissa and Lana are here to get you ready Tatum," Wren says.

"Let's get this going, I only get married once...well except for today," I laugh out loud.

"Too soon bitch, toooo soon." Aria smirks.

"Oh my, what happened Tatum?" Melissa questions me.

"I'd like to introduce you ladies to my twin sister, Talia," I smile at them.

"Holy shit, I mean excuse my language...This is crazy, but we have a wedding to get you ready for.. How are we doing your makeup and hair?" She smiles but is clearly a little confused and uncomfortable.

"I want my makeup really natural, but I still want to have somewhat of a smokey eye as well. For my hair I want it half up and half down," I show her the picture of the hairstyle.

"So we will put your extensions in and curl your entire head. Then I'll braid a crown like braid and pin it partially up in the back. We'll keep most of the hair away from your face but a few strands that will be curled towards your face. Does that sound about right?" Melissa states.

"Let's do it. I'm ready to get married already!" I exclaim.

Lana works on my makeup while Melissa meticulously works on my bridal hair. It takes them about an hour and then I'm done.

"Oh my gosh, I look so beautiful. Thank you both, I'm sorry you had to work extra today," I smile through the tears.

"Aw don't cry sweetheart it's our pleasure. We will send the nail tech up to do your toes and fingers. Good luck Tatum, may you have a love that defies all odds." Lana pats me on the shoulder.

It was time now to reveal my wedding dress. I had gone wedding dress shopping by myself and picked out the perfect dress.

"I need to change out of your wedding dress Tatum, where did you have my bridesmaid dress?" Talia asks me.

I can't help but chuckle.

"That's not my wedding dress. I already had mine picked, Kendrick didn't know so I guess you will just have to keep it for your wedding whenever you set a date."

"Your dress is over there behind the door, it's hanging up go check it out," Aria smiles.

I go into the bathroom with my dress bag that is keeping my secret for a few more minutes anyway. I unzip the bag and reveal the most gorgeous, elegant wedding gown I've seen.

The dress is made mostly of tulle, the interlayer is made of organza and the lining is made of satin. The design of exquisite lace appliqués, an honest neckline, sheer 3/4 length lace sleeves and the A-line skirt with a stunning chapel train create an elegant and vintage look. I felt like a princess. Slid into my dress, and stared long and hard in the mirror, I did the one thing I never thought I'd do. I did a spin, this was the dress that I would marry my soulmate in.

"Ladies can you come in here for a second? I need a zip!" I call out to them.

"Oh my .... Tatum you look fucking beautiful, amazing, spectacular...Kendrick is going to be so surprised!" Aria gushes over my bridal beauty.

"You do look beautiful Tatum," Talia adds.

Once they have my dress zipped up, I realize that I forgot to have them bring my shoes here.

"Talia now you can go change, I left shoes in there that match your dress. I may have to steal your fuck me heels," I laugh.

She hands them over and heads into the bathroom to change. Her dress is lavender and resembles Aphrodite's dress. It's almost a spaghetti strap dress but it knots where the straps connect to the fabric. It has a sash that fits under her ribs and umbrellas out soft and loosely flowing to the floor. The back is a criss cross that ties around the neck. It's beautiful. I knew it would look great on her, I tried it on for her, we are almost the same size so hopefully it works out perfect.

Talia walks out of the bathroom, and I see that it fits her like a glove.

"Am I supposed to look like Aphrodite?" Talia smirks.

"You are beautiful, let's get the right twin married this time," I smile back.

Prescott was waiting outside for me, and we all headed back to the church.

Back at the Old South Church Take 2.

The song *"Still Fallin" by Hunter Hayes* plays for a second time while everyone gets back into their seats. The crowd whispers, and speculates while Kendrick is standing at the front with the officiant. His nerves may have gotten the better of him. I've never seen him actually nervous. It was refreshing, he's usually a take charge type of man, today he was nervous and waiting for me this time.

I can see my mother and Danielle in the front row again, this time Pearl is seated next to them with a seat for Prescott saved. It's nice to see them getting along so well, I guess the shock of everything brought everything together.

I smile as I hear the next song begin, *"I Do" by Jessie James Decker.* Aria and Marcello lock arms and share a kiss before they begin their long walk to the front of the church. I could see the happiness in my best friend's eyes as she clung to him. This was better than I could've imagined. Then they went their separate ways, Marcello stood tall next to Kendrick and Aria anxiously awaits for me. Next up was Talia and Grant they hooked their arms and clutched each other's hands. As I suspected the guests were staring hard as they see the woman who was just an almost bride not even a few hours ago. Once they reached the front Grant and Talia share a quick kiss before parting, Grant stands to the left of Marcello and Talia to the right of Aria.

I could feel my body tremble a little bit, this was happening. I wasn't going to be a single lady anymore. I love him. My musical cue begins, the song, *"Tenerife Sea" by Ed Sheeran* plays, I pull my veil down and Prescott walks slowly with me

250

down the aisle to give me away to his only son. I make direct eye contact with Kendrick and he smiles through very obvious tears. I wipe my under eye as I tear up seeing him cry, he's my weakness. Both my mother, Pearl and even Dani are now bawling their eyes out. The emotion in this place was strong, but it was pure happiness.

There's something about knowing when your heart has found its counterpart, it's magical. An important face catches my eye, Melora was here as well smiling at me, sheer happiness radiates from her violet eyes.

I get to Kendrick and my first instinct is to reach for him. He takes my hands and intertwined them with his own.

"It's really you this time right?" he whispers to me with a smile.

"Of course it's me, promise," I smile back.

The officiant begins, "We are gathered here today again in the sight of God, and the presence of family and friends, to celebrate the finding of one's counterpart in another. Today Kendrick and Tatum will be united in holy matrimony. They will declare their love to each other and bound their souls together as one. We are here to celebrate this love."

"Kendrick and Tatum, marriage is not to be entered into lightly. Marriage joins two people until the end of time. It must be should be entered into thoughtfully and with full understanding of its sacred nature. Your marriage must stand by the strength of your love and the power of faith in each other and in God. Just as the sand and the sea meet so do your two lives when merged together to make one."

"I will now read from Ecclesiastes 4:9 as we've covered the Corinthians earlier," he beamed.

"Two are better than one, because they have a good return for their labor:If either of them falls down, one can help the other up. But pity anyone who falls and has no one to help them up. Also, if two lie down together, they will keep warm. But how can one keep warm alone?"

"Please face one another, hold hands and repeat after me:

--- -

I, Kendrick take you Tatum to be my wife. I will cherish you, and love you today, tomorrow, and forever. I will trust and honor you. I will love you faithfully. Through it all, I will trust that you will be beside me, loving me.

Whatever may come our way I will always be there. As I have given you my hand to hold, I now give you my life to keep." Kendrick repeats word for word.

"I Tatum, take you Kendrick to be my husband, my partner in life and my one true love. I will cherish our friendship and love you today, tomorrow, and forever. I will trust and honor you. I will laugh with you and be a shoulder to cry on. I will love you faithfully from this day forward. I also promise to never switch places with my twin sister under any condition. Through the best and the worst, we are in this together. Whatever may come our way I will always be there. As I have given you my hand to hold, I now give you my life to keep," I say with a smile.

"Kendrick, do you take Tatum to be your wife?"

"I will," he replies

"Do you promise to love, honor, cherish and protect her, forsaking all others and holding her only forevermore?"

"I will."

"Tatum, do you take Kendrick to be your husband?"

"I do," I blush.

"Do you promise to love, honor, cherish and protect him, forsaking all others and holding him only forevermore?"

"I do."

We all instinctively look at the door making sure that no one is interrupting again. Once we realize no one is there we stare at each other again.

"Who has the rings?" the officiant asks.

Marcello hands Kendrick the band for me and Aria hands me Kendrick's. Then she hands me my engagement ring from Talia.

"Repeat after me," he instructs.

"I Kendrick, take, Tatum to be my Wife to have and to hold, in sickness and in health, for richer or for poorer, in joy and sorrow, and I promise my love always to you. And with this ring, I take you as my wife, for as long as we both shall live," he vows to me as he slips the gorgeous white gold band that was designed in a criss cross as the two parts met as one. Very symbolic. Then he slips my engagement ring on after to complete my wedding band set.

"Tatum please repeat after me."

"I Tatum, take Kendrick, to be my husband. To have and to hold, in sickness and in health, for richer or for poorer, in joy and sorrow, and I promise always my love to you. And with this ring, I take you as my husband, for as long as we both shall live," I smile and slide his white gold band on his ring finger.

"I now pronounce you husband and wife. You may now kiss the bride."

Kendrick and I press our lips together sealing our marriage in front of everyone watching. I missed his kiss so much.

"I love you so much Mr. Sanders," I look deeply into his eyes.

"I love you too Mrs. Sanders," he smirks.

"Let's go we have a reception to go to!" I squeal as I swat his ass with my bouquet of purple and white roses.

"Thank you all for coming! We hope to see you at the reception at the *Boston Park Plaza*!" Kendrick announces.

Our exit song begins to play, *"I Do" by Colbie Caillat*. I couldn't help it my body hears the music and I start dancing with Kendrick down the aisle until we reach the outside doors. That's when I see it, he must've arranged for a very special ride. It's a black 1967 Rolls Royce! He really outdid himself, but it's beautiful.

"Come on you two love birds, we need to get you to the Plaza," Wren says as she opens the door for us.

"Thank you Wren! " I smile a big smile at her.

Our first stop was going to get our wedding photos done. I chose Alcorn Street here in Boston because of the beautiful stone walkways surrounded by red bricked buildings. We were there for about hour, the pictures from what I saw on the Nikon looked amazing. Now we have to head to the Boston Park Plaza for our reception. Everyone should be there by now.

"It's only about a six minute drive," she says as she fires up the Rolls Royce.

We make ourselves comfortable in the backseat. We can't keep our hands off of each other. He runs his hand down my neck tracing it down the lace on my dress

"Sweetface control yourself, we can have fun once the reception is over with," I giggle.

"Yes wife, we may even have to leave early, because I'm not feeling very patient today," he says assertively.

"Good I don't wanna share you for too long either," I lick my lips.

"We're here," Wren looks at us and smiles.

We make our way into the tall beige brick building that has 15 floors of window banks. The first floor is larger windows then as you go up they are smaller. The floor is a beautiful marble, that almost looked like wood. The large room is white with 14k gold trim it also has balconies all over the room. There were many tables all over the room leaving just enough room in the middle for dancing.

At the front of the room was a long white table, which is for the my husband and the wedding party. Wow I have a husband now that's so crazy.

"Attention everyone! Please give it up for Mr. & Mrs. Kendrick Sanders!" The DJ yelled into the microphone.

We are welcomed by an entire room of people clapping for us. Tingling their glasses to request a kiss from the bride and groom. We don't hesitate and we lock our lips in a passionate kiss,

We then take our rightful place at the table and waited as Aria, Talia and the guys joined us. The waiter brings us all glasses of champagne

"It's that time now, for the bride and groom to share their first dance as a married couple," the DJ announces.

Kendrick and I make our way to the dance floor as the lights dim. The song, *"At Last" by Etta James* plays and Kendrick pulls me close into his arms. I place my left hand on his shoulder and clasp my hand in his.

I can't take my eyes off this man, as if he knows what I'm thinking he grins. He spins me around slowly and then pulls me back to him and I can't help but grin. We continue to dance, as the wedding party is now invited to join.

I look over to see my sister and her fiancé and I feel a sense of renewal. She's come so far in the little time I've known her, I look forward to being there for her wedding. Now that she's in my life I never plan on letting her go again. Then I look at Aria and Marcello, the couple who never really wanted to be. It wasn't until they both opened their hearts to each other that they started to feel the connection between them. I look back at the man in front of me. My husband, we have been through a lot in the short time we've been together. I never knew I could love another person as much as I love you. The first day we met was fate, a game of chance. Today we made a choice, and we chose each other. I wouldn't have it any other way. I can't wait for the adventures that life has in store for us. For all of us.

THE END.

Note from the Author | xoxo

First I want to thank you for taking a chance on me and reading my first novel. I appreciate everyone who is reading these words. I would have never thought I would be writing, it just goes to show that even though it may seem impossible, never give up on your dreams.

Please consider leaving a review

Accidentally Identical is now on Goodreads!

Acknowledgements | xoxo

Patricia Ide Wedertz

Thank you for being the kind woman you are. You've spent hours helping me sort everything out, I just want you to know that I appreciate every second we've worked together. From the bottom of my heart thank you!

Kimberly Capozzi

To the only girl that could make Aria come to life. Thank you for being my best friend. You've always stuck by me through hell and high water. I will always be there for you through anything. I love you! I couldn't imagine my life without you in it. I promise you, there will be a happy ending for you.

My Love

Thank you for supporting me in everything I do, including in the hard times. I wouldn't have believed in true love if you never came and saved me. You're my love, forever and always. I love you. Here's to many more years together.

Bebe Bishop

I can't wait for your formal introduction to the world. You believed in me when I couldn't, thank you for helping whenever I needed and making me smile. You are an amazing soul and thank you for finding a friend in me. I'm so proud of how far we both have come.

257

Vanessa Foxford

You are a machine, woman! Thank you for being a big part of my book, you are the most reliable, trustworthy Beta reader I've ever met. I appreciate your skills but mostly I appreciate your friendship. Thank you for loving this story, and rooting for it to succeed!

Love always, Layla.

About the Author | xoxo

Layla McFadden is a new author following her passion of writing and her love of all things romantic. She writes about unsuspecting contemporary romance with room for a twist.

Layla has a degree in Cosmetology and she resides in a small midwest town in Indiana with her husband and four dogs who are more like children. When she's not writing, she's spending time with her family, reading some of her favorite author's books and binge watching some of her favorite shows: Pretty Little Liars, Dynasty, Charmed and Law & Order SVU, and more.

She also enjoys making people smile and laugh. She has a love for all animals and is a sucker for dogs.

Where you can contact Layla McFadden:

Email: mcfaddenlayla@gmail.com
Goodreads: https://www.goodreads.com/laylamcfaddenauthor
Bookbub: https://www.bookbub.com/profile/2117755498
Facebook: https://www.facebook.com/AuthorLaylaMcFadden
Reader Group: https://www.facebook.com/groups/LMReaderLockbox/

WHAT'S NEXT | xoxo

Accidentally Anzalone: Book 2 of the Accidentally Series
Coming Soon.

Aria Morretti and her best friend Tatum Emerson have an amazing bond. In fact it's the only real relationship that Aria has ever had. She's met them all: cheaters, liars and thieves, but when it comes down to it they never stuck around. She's shut herself off from anything and everyone that may make her trip and fall. That all changes the day she meets Marcello Anazlone.

Marcello Anazlone is the perfect gentleman. He's charming, sexy, stable and everything Aria is not used to having. He's good for her, but maybe it's all too good to be true. Will they end up with their own happily ever after or crash and burn?

CPSIA information can be obtained
at www.ICGtesting.com
Printed in the USA
LVHW090503020719
622965LV00001B/109/P